ALSO BY KAY SALTER

Twelfth Summer

Thirteenth Summer

Fourteenth Summer

For additional information contact: jsaltert8@hotmail.com

Fifteenth Summer

The Sarah Bowers Series

Kay Salter

authorHOUSE®

AuthorHouse™
1663 Liberty Drive
Bloomington, IN 47403
www.authorhouse.com
Phone: 1-800-839-8640

First published by AuthorHouse   5/23/2011

ISBN: 978-1-4567-6379-4 (e)
ISBN: 978-1-4567-6380-0 (dj)
ISBN: 978-1-4567-6381-7 (sc)

Library of Congress Control Number: 2011907399

Printed in the United States of America

Cover photo by Scott Taylor

This book is printed on acid-free paper.

To
My Biscuit Buddies
You know who you are

Contents

Chapter 1

"Joshua quit pushing against the back of the car seat!" Sarah Bowers turned around and gave her little brother a terrible frown. "I asked you once nicely, and if you do it again, I'm going to give you a swat."

"I have to do it, Sarah."

"What?" Sarah glared at her brother from the front seat. "What are you talking about?"

"Sarah," her nine year old brother patiently explained. "I have to help Mama make the car go faster."

"Just how can you do that, son?" asked their mother.

"I figure if I push on the back of the seat, the car will go faster, and we'll be in Beaufort sooner."

"That's the dumbest thing I have ever heard," mumbled his teenage sister, turning around and facing front. Sarah Bowers, fifteen year old daughter of James and Peggy Bowers, was running out of patience with her little brother.

"That's very thoughtful of you, Joshua," said their mother patiently, "but I don't think it works that way. We're going to have to let the engine do the work. I'll steer, and you take care of Amy and Frisky. If you stay busy, we'll be there before you know it."

Joshua looked over at his two year old sister, and Frisky, the family pet. Both were curled in a tight ball on the back seat. The loud voices awakened Amy, who immediately sat up. Her hair was matted with perspiration, even though every window in the car was rolled down. "Now you've done it, Sarah," announced Joshua. "You went and woke Amy up. So, you'll have to play with her."

"Potty," said Amy. Sarah scrambled for the white enamel potty that

1

was kept under the front seat of the car. She quickly retrieved it and helped her little sister. When Amy was finished, all clapped and cheered for the toddler. Every use of the training potty was a step closer to the end of diapers.

"Soon, Mama, diapers will be a thing of the past," said Sarah. "No more washer loads to be hung on the line every day, brought in, folded and stacked."

"It will surely be a relief, honey," said their mother. On a sadder note, she remarked, "That means we won't have a baby anymore. I can't believe my children are growing up so fast."

"The school year didn't seem to go by fast – especially algebra class."

Peggy Bowers and her three children were on their way to the small town of Beaufort, on the coast of North Carolina where they would spend the summer with Sarah's grandparents, Jewel and Tom Mitchell.

"I'm sorry daddy couldn't take time off from work to come with us," spoke Sarah. "He does love Clara's cooking, and she'll be upset when we arrive and daddy is home in Raleigh."

"Clara knows we're coming without him. This is the first summer we could drive the family car, because he needed it to get to work during past summers. Now that he has a truck, he's happy for any excuse to drive it. With the war over, gasoline and tires no longer rationed, he promised me he would join us several weekends this summer. Speaking of gasoline, I'd better stop at a filling station in New Bern and gas up. I'm not sure we have enough to get all the way to Beaufort."

Peggy Bowers stopped the 1940 Plymouth at a gas station a short time later. "Everyone get out and stretch your legs. Now is a good time to use the rest room and get a cold drink. This is our last stop until we roll into your grandparents' drive."

A short time later, the car was once again on the highway. "Phew, the price of gas has gone through the roof. Twenty-five cents a gallon! I hope it will come down soon," declared their mother shaking her head. The motion, along with wind pouring through the open windows, caused her blonde curls to dance.

Sarah was in no mood to mull over the high cost of gasoline. Instead, she began to think about the upcoming June wedding. "Mama, do you think Miriam is the right girl for Uncle Herb?"

"Honey, Miriam seems to be a wonderful person. She taught English this year at Beaufort High School, and Mama writes that all her students love her, and want to be in her class again next year. I expect they will be

2

coming to the wedding, plus most of the town. Our beautiful old church is going to be crowded."

Joshua's head popped up between the seats. "Tell me about the ring, Mama. You were going to tell me the other day, but you got too busy."

"Climb up here between your sister and me, and we'll tell you." Joshua quickly scrambled into the front seat and nestled down between his mother and big sister. Sarah held Amy in her lap and let her look out of the window.

"You remember we met Miriam last summer just before we returned home to Raleigh. She and your Uncle Herb kept seeing each other, and soon fell in love. They went to Binghamton, N.Y. for Christmas, so her family could meet Herb. He bought a diamond ring for her, making them formally engaged. As it turned out, there was a snow storm the day before Christmas. Late that afternoon, when it stopped snowing, the family went outside and built a snowman. They mostly did it because Herb had never seen so much snow. Well, that silly brother of mine slipped her ring on the end of the snowman's carrot nose. When Miriam looked up, there was a diamond ring, sparkling in the afternoon sun. She was so surprised!"

"Suppose the snowman had sneezed. That ring would have been blown away," decided Joshua.

"He was lucky it ended up on her finger. If it had gotten lost in a foot of snow, they might not have found it until spring," added Sarah.

"Did he get her ring out of a Cracker Jacks box?"

"No, son. He bought it at Bell's Jewelry store right in Beaufort. He had to swear Miss Mattie to secrecy, or the whole town would have known about the engagement before he ever had a chance to ask Miriam."

"Did he have to pay a lot of money for it?" questioned the boy.

"Miriam will wear the ring every day the rest of her life. I'm sure it was expensive because it is made of precious metals and valuable stones."

"How about if they get in a fight, can he get the ring back?"

"Stop asking silly questions," demanded his big sister. "Crawl in the back seat with that dog. You smell just like him."

"Sarah! His name is not 'that dog'. His name is Frisky."

Upon hearing his name, the family pet thumped his tail against the seat.

"Oh, all right. I don't want to hear anymore of this sissy stuff, anyway. Frisky and I are going to talk about going fishing with Papa Tom."

"Now maybe we can carry on an adult conversation, Mama."

With both hands on the steering wheel, Peggy Bowers glanced at her fifteen year old daughter. *She almost looks like an adult*, concluded their mother. Sarah's thick, chestnut hair was blowing in the breeze from the window. The figure Sarah had despaired of ever having, was well on the way to being perfect.

Sarah's voice interrupted the mother's thoughts. "Has Miriam decided on a color for the bridesmaids' dresses? Do you know what style they will be?"

"Mama said over the phone Miriam is leaning toward a very pale yellow. The dresses will have ruffled skirts and a small ruffle around the neckline. They will either be sleeveless, or have puffed sleeves. Only two of her three sisters will be able to come. The oldest one is going to have a baby in July, so she can't travel."

"I'm so excited about being a bridesmaid. I've never been one before." Sarah looked over at her mother. "Did I ever tell you that Uncle Herb asked me to be in their wedding? He asked me last summer, when we were leaving to come back home."

"You did tell me, after they were formally engaged. Honey, you really know how to keep a secret!"

"It was painful at times. I wanted to tell you so badly, but I promised not to say a word." Sarah put a finger up to her lips and smiled.

"That's good. If you give your word, people should be able to trust you to keep it confidential," said Peggy Bowers.

Sarah gazed from the car window. The fields were green with tall corn and leafy tobacco, but Sarah wasn't seeing them. Her mind went back to the summer before, when she was fourteen. One day, while she was trying to help her grandmother's friend find her glasses, she had accidently come upon the dear lady's stash of High Society sweet snuff. *I have never told a single soul what I found that day,* Sarah remembered, *because I know Miss Nettie would die of mortification.*

One hour later, Joshua hit his grandparents' front porch running. He pulled open the screen door and yelled, "Granny Jewel, Papa Tom we're here!"

Immediately, footsteps were heard coming from the kitchen. "Whose voice is that? Jewel, do you think a stranger is in our home? Do you think we should call the …"

Before Tom Mitchell could say another word, his grandson was hugging him around the waist. "I've missed you, Papa. Did you miss me?"

Granny Jewel flew from the house, letting the screen door slam behind her. "Where are all my girls?" she called. Sarah walked around the side of the car, hugged her grandmother, and gladly handed her little sister to the anxious woman.

"Down, Ganny Jewel, down."

The grandmother laughed, and placed her granddaughter on the green lawn, letting her walk to the house. Peggy Bowers hugged her mother while Sarah awaited her turn. "We are so *glad* you're here! We have been waiting and watching all day. Clara is in the kitchen making shrimp salad for lunch. She's disappointed your father didn't come, since she loves to fix his favorite dishes."

"Does that mean we won't be having clam fritters and clam chowder until he comes for a visit?" asked Sarah.

"I think if you request some of Clara's famous dishes, she'll gladly fix them for you." Arm in arm, they followed Amy into the house.

"There better be some hugs left for me," rang a voice from the kitchen. All moved toward the sound of Clara's voice, Joshua and Sarah in the lead. Granny Jewel swung Amy up in her arms before the child could attack the items on the coffee table in the living room. After greeting the two older children, she said, "Is my baby being bashful?" Amy kept her head buried in her grandmother's neck. "I know a little girl that's going to have some of Clara's fried potatoes for lunch."

Amy turned her head, and slowly grinned at Clara. "Oh, boy, oh boy," she exclaimed, clapping her hands.

While everyone was still talking, Sarah eased past them until she stood in front of a door in the corner of the room. Turning the smooth, porcelain knob, she gave the door a gentle push, and stepped inside the room. With shades drawn and curtains closed, it took a few minutes for her eyes to become accustomed to the dim gray light. Sarah walked over to the window, slowly raised the shade and drew back the ruffled pink curtains. Turning, she saw the small bed with the ruffled pink spread, her vanity table with mirror, a small dresser and a chair covered in rose pink fabric. *My little room is just the way I left it last summer, and the way I remembered it all winter.* Sarah slowly closed her eyes, remembering the delicate odor of rose petals which still lingered in the tiny room. On the foot of the bed lay one of her great grandmother's hand made quilts. She ran her hand over the old quilt, smoothing an imaginary wrinkle. *I love this quilt Granny Jewel gave me almost three summers ago. Whenever I look at it or run my hand over it, I feel closer to my great-grandmother Frances.*

Sarah's thoughts were interrupted by a voice from the direction of the door. "Have you missed your little room honey?"

The girl smiled, "Yes, Clara. My bedroom in Raleigh is much bigger, but it's not as cozy. Everything in this room was rescued from the attic, and has a family history. My furniture at home came from a furniture store, and all the pieces look alike." Sarah stood to follow Clara from the room, stopping to open the windows and let the ocean breeze fill the room.

"Oh, Lord, we have gathered around this table tonight as a family grateful to You for the many blessings You have bestowed upon us. We are especially grateful for our three grandchildren and their mother, and their safe trip to our home. We pray for Your protection as they enjoy the days ahead," prayed her grandfather before dinner that evening.

Sarah, with head bowed, whispered 'Amen,' when Papa Tom finished. As she unfolded her napkin and placed it in her lap, she looked around the room remembering the ornate mantle and high ceilings. *We're here at last,* she thought. *There will be swimming, boating, and above all, a glamorous wedding to prepare for.* A voice interrupted Sarah's thoughts. "Well, well, if it isn't the city folks, come to join us. Welcome all!"

Peggy Bowers jumped to her feet to give her brother a hug. "You look different, Herb," she declared.

"I am a man in love, Sis," he replied, taking Amy on his knee as he sat beside his mother. "There's going to be a lot of excitement around here this month. Sarah, are you still willing to get all gussied up in a fancy dress and help Miriam and me tie the knot?"

"Uncle Herb," Sarah answered quickly, "I have been dreaming of being in your wedding all winter. I thought summer would never get here!"

"Uncle Herb, do I have to get all dressed up just to go to a wedding? Can't you get married down on the shore, and then we could all go swimming afterward."

"Joshua," said his uncle, looking at his nephew, "This is something the ladies plan, and us menfolk have to do as we are told. There's no room for argument. With your mama and big sister here, your grandmamma has reinforcements. You, Papa Tom, and I have to show up when we're told, all dressed up and looking serious. Most of the time, we're supposed to stay out of the way, keep out of sight, and let the womenfolk make it happen."

Not knowing what advice her son would tell next, Granny Jewel interrupted. "Where is Miriam? I thought maybe she'd be with you."

"She's finishing up paperwork at school. Tomorrow is her last day before summer vacation." Herb Mitchell looked around the table. "Hmmm, supper looks mighty good. Clara outdid herself tonight for the folks from Raleigh."

"Clara has a delicious meal every night," added Tom Mitchell. "She loves to prepare dishes she knows I like best."

"Dream on," came a voice from the kitchen, followed by a loud snort.

In the gray dawn of early morning, before the breeze off the ocean began to stir, Sarah awakened to the lusty sound of the neighborhood rooster. "Mr. Peavey, you belong in a cook pot," declared Sarah, trying in vain to muffle his insistent crowing by covering her head with a pillow. *He sounds like he's under my window instead of over on Broad Street*, decided Sarah sitting up on the side of her bed. "I may as well get up," she told the girl in her mirror.

Sarah made her bed and put on a shirt and a pair of shorts. Familiar sounds and smells were coming from the next room. She quickly combed her hair and opened the bedroom door. "Good morning, Clara," she said. "Is there anything I can do to help?"

"Wash your hands and stick some more bread in the toaster. We have a hungry crowd this morning and they need filling up. An extra pair of hands will sure come in handy."

Sarah hurried to the bathroom at the end of the hall, greeting the family as she walked through the dining room.

"Good morning my fair princess," said her grandfather, reaching up for a hug.

"Good morning, everybody," Sarah answered, looking around the table. "Where is Joshua? He isn't still in bed, is he?"

"Do you remember his friend Billy from over on Broad Street?" asked her mother. Without waiting for a reply, she continued, "He was banging on the door first thing this morning. When Joshua saw him, he finished his breakfast in two gulps, and flew out the back door."

"How did Billy know we were here?"

"He has checked our driveway every day since school closed for the summer. This morning he saw your car and came right over," explained Granny Jewel.

When breakfast was over, Sarah cleared the table and was scrapping dishes when the back door flew open. "Sarah," exclaimed her younger brother, out of breath. "Mr. Owens has a chicken setting on a nest of eggs and they're hatching right now! You gotta' see them while they're breaking out of the shell. They look all wet and yucky at first. Some of them are already dry, and boy, are they cute! Let's take Amy over to see them. Come on!"

"Go on, honey," said Clara. "I can finish up here."

"I planned to call my friend, Nancy Russert this morning, but I guess that can wait." Sarah stepped out on the back porch.

"Hello, Billy. It's good to see you again," said Sarah, smiling at Billy's upturned face. "You're a lot taller than you were last summer. School must agree with you," Sarah said, smiling.

Billy vigorously shook his head. "Oh, no, I'm allergic to school. Some mornings the thought of it makes me feel bad all over." The boy took a deep breath and stood straight. "My mama says I'm getting taller from breathing the salty air off the ocean."

"Wait right here while I go find Amy," she instructed. Sarah hurried upstairs to find her little sister. "Mama," she called from the top of the steps, "Is Amy with you?"

"We're up here, Sarah," answered her mother.

Peggy Bowers was making her bed while Amy played on the floor. "Amy," asked Sarah, "would you like to see some baby chicks?"

"Has Mr. Peavy's wife presented him with another batch of babies?" their mother asked.

"Joshua and Billy said they are hatching now." Sarah felt a tiny hand slip into hers.

"Now, Sawah, see chicks now." Sarah swung her sister up in her arms and hurried out to join the boys.

Chapter 2

"Come on, Sarah. You can squeeze through the fence, can't you?" pleaded Joshua.

"It's not exactly easy with Amy in my arms, little brother," said Sarah, eyeing the small hole made by a missing paling. "Maybe we should get Papa Tom to repair this fence."

"No, Sarah. He promised two summers ago to leave a place where Joshua and I could get through," said Billy.

"Joshua, I'm going to send Amy through and you hold on to her. Then I'll try to squeeze through."

Sarah gently pushed her sister through the hole in the fence and watched to see that Joshua held her before attempting to join them. *I never had any trouble last summer. The hole has gotten smaller,* she decided. Sarah crouched on her hands and knees and pushed her head through the opening. After several tries, she realized she wouldn't fit through the narrow gap. The boys watched silently as she tried to back out. "I just don't fit anymore. There's no way I'm going to get through. I'll have to walk around." With this, the girl began backing out. In doing so, her shirt became firmly snagged on a nail. "I'm stuck, boys! I can't go forward or backward."

The three children on the opposite side of the fence stared open-mouthed at Sarah's plight. "Maybe we ought to call the fire department. They can get kittens out of trees, so maybe they can get your sister unstuck," suggested Billy.

"I heard that, Billy! Don't you dare do any such thing! I would die of embarrassment ten times over."

"Can you do that?" Billy asked.

"I don't know, Billy, but I can't take any chances of losing my sister. Hold Amy," he ordered. Joshua stepped over to the fence and studied the palings on each side of his sister. One was cracked and there was evidence of rot where the paint had peeled.

"Sarah, close your eyes for a minute."

Desperate, Sarah did as her brother said. Aiming carefully, Joshua took a deep breath, drew back his leg and kicked the paling with all his strength. A loud cracking sound was heard as the paling gave way. Sarah fell through the opening, catching herself before she landed on the ground. "Well! That was some experience," she declared, brushing dirt from her hands and legs. "Thanks, little brother for getting me unstuck."

"Here, Joshua, you can have your sister back," said Billy, handing Amy over to her big brother, glad to release the struggling child.

"You're not supposed to hold her by the neck of her dress, Billy," instructed Joshua. "She's not a dog you have to hold by its collar."

"I'm sorry," mumbled Billy. "I still think it would have been a lot more exciting if we had called the fire department."

Mr. Owens was standing in his back yard when the four came over. He turned when he heard the children's voices.

"Joshua, I had forgotten what a pretty sister you have," he said smiling.

"Hello, Mr. Owens," greeted Sarah. "Joshua and Billy insisted we come over and see Mr. Peavy's latest batch of biddies."

"I'm right proud of old Peavy," said the rooster's owner. He rocked back on his heels, never taking his eyes off his strutting pet. Finally, he looked at Sarah, concern on his face. "I hope his crowing early morning's doesn't disturb your sleep."

Sarah started to tell how Mr. Peavy's lusty voice woke her *every* morning, but decided to say nothing. She knew Mr. Owens would never try to muzzle his prize rooster. "My grandaddy says hearing a rooster crow early mornings is a comfort, because he knows he doesn't have to get up and do farm chores."

"Well, I'm mighty glad to know my rooster is performing a good service to the neighborhood." The man grinned and stuck his chest out even farther.

"Oh, brother," mumbled Sarah, shifting Amy to her other hip.

Their conversation was interrupted by the two boys. "The mama hen is leaving the nest," they said excitedly. "There's a bunch of baby chicks following her. Come see them."

"Down, down," insisted Amy, squirming out of her sister's arms and following the boys.

"Joshua," his big sister instructed, "keep an eye on Amy. "Don't let her near the babies or the mother hen might try to hurt her."

While the children watched the mother hen teach her brood how to hunt for bugs, Sarah looked over at the house next door. "Is that the Fuller's new home," she asked.

"Yep," replied Mr. Owens, "they finally got moved in just before Easter. After their old house burned last summer, they were a long time getting the lot cleared. Finally some men from the Baptist church borrowed a bulldozer and a dump truck from the town and cleared the lot. Each Sunday school class took a room to furnish. The ladies made curtains and folks donated furniture they weren't using. Since Mr. Fuller works at the hardware store, he got a lot of things he needed at cost. Mr. Clawson let him have paint at cost, too. He paints people's houses when the store closes to make a little extra money. They said Mrs. Fuller walks from room the room like she's in a trance. One day when I was in the yard, she hollered over and told me it was like living in a dream. 'I never knew people could be so kind,' she said."

"How about their son, Mackie?" asked Sarah. "He was mighty tough."

"Mackie pitched in and helped when he wasn't in school. It kept him busy and out of trouble. It turns out that he's a pretty good carpenter. He can pound a nail in a piece of wood with the best of them."

"I don't doubt that, Mr.Owens," replied Sarah, remembering the bruises her brother bore from Mackie's fist last summer. "Is he still as tough as ever?"

"I haven't heard any tales on Mackie lately. It could be he's settled down a little." The man hurried on. "Now don't get me wrong – I don't think Mackie has changed too much. A few days ago he grinned and said he'd be glad when his sissy friend from Raleigh got here."

"We'll have to hold our breath and hope for the best, Mr. Owens."

"That's what the whole neighborhood is doing, Sarah."

Again their conversation was interrupted. Joshua hurried over, an anxious expression on his face. "Mr. Owens, the mama hen left the nest too soon. I looked in the hen house, and there's still one egg left. It's cracked open and I think there's a biddy trying to get out."

Unhurried, Mr. Owens walked over to the hen house and stepped inside. Sarah held Amy while the boys followed. After several moments of looking down in the nest, Mr. Owens turned to the boys, a sad look on his face. "That baby chick isn't going to make it. There's something the matter with him, because he doesn't have the strength to peck his way out of the shell."

Joshua and Billy moved closer to the man. In a low, pleading voice, Joshua asked, "Can we help him? Wouldn't it be easy to peel him out of the shell? My mama lets me peel hard boiled eggs."

Mark Owens looked down into the young, earnest faces. He watched as a stray feather, borne on a puff of south breeze, slowly came to light on Joshua's tousled curls. Billy wiped sweat from his eyes, shifted his weight from one foot to another, and repeated Joshua's question. "How about it, Mr. Owens? Can't we help the chick get out?" After a moment he added, "It seems like he's getting awful tired."

The man studied a spider web woven between two rafters in the top of the coop. With a sigh he replied, "No, boys, we can't help the baby chick."

Now there were four sets of eyes all waiting for an explanation.

"It's mother nature's way, kids."

"I don't understand," whispered Joshua, never taking his eyes from the man's face.

Without looking at the nest, Mr. Owens continued. "Pecking your way out of an egg is a hard job. Only the strongest and healthiest are able to succeed. That weeds out the weak or deformed chicks, and keeps the species strong."

Joshua lowered his eyes, lingering on the almost empty nest. He saw a tiny yellow bill struggling in vain to peck away the hard shell. "I don't care about the other chicks. I want to help this one. What's the harm in trying? If he dies, at least we did all we could to help him," pleaded Joshua. "Can I have him, please, Mr. Owens?"

"Sure, but you're going to be sorry," he warned. "Don't expect any miracles."

Joshua reached a dusty hand into the abandoned nest and gently lifted out the imprisoned chick before the man could change his mind. He brought the hem of his shirt up, creating a sling for the egg. "Thanks, sir. I think we'd better be going now." Joshua brushed past his sisters, Billy following. They headed for the hole in the fence. Billy paused and looked back, to see if Sarah and Amy were coming.

"Are you going to crawl through the fence Sarah?" he asked hopefully.

"If you get stuck we can still call the fire department. The fire house is right down the street. They wouldn't mind getting you unstuck."

"No, Billy," answered Sarah. She put Amy down to rest her arm and continued, "I hate to disappoint you, but Amy and I and going to walk around the block." Billy made no attempt to hide the disappointment written on his face.

The walk home took longer than usual since Amy had to inspect dandelions along the way, blowing the seeds from each stalk. When they stepped into the cool hallway, Sarah was not surprised to hear Clara's raised voice.

"Get that poor 'critter' out of my clean kitchen, youngun'. It's fixin' to die, and I don't want it anywhere near me when it does."

"It's not going to die, Clara. Me and Billy are going to save it." Joshua's voice could be heard above Clara's.

Sarah could tell by her brother's voice that he was close to tears. She hurried toward the kitchen. "I think I heard Granny Jewel upstairs. Maybe she has a box you can put him in."

The boys gratefully pushed past Sarah before Clara could say anything else. They hurried upstairs, bare feet padding on each step. "Granny Jewel," called Joshua, still clutching the egg in the corner of his shirt. "Granny Jewel," Joshua called again, "Me and Billy have an emergency."

His grandmother came to the door of her bedroom. "Billy and I, Joshua," she corrected. "Now, what is this emergency? You're not hurt are you? Is there any blood?" Joshua could hear alarm in his grandmother's voice.

"No, Ma'am. We're not hurt, but this baby chick is." Joshua carefully unfolded his shirt, revealing the egg. "We're going to help him get out of his egg because he's not strong enough to get out by himself."

Granny Jewel bent down and cupped her hands under those of her grandson. She looked closely, took a deep breath, and started to speak. Joshua, his eyes searching his grandmother's face, whispered, "Everybody says he's going to die, but he's not dead yet. Won't you help us, please?"

From several inches away, Joshua watched his grandmother's eyes narrow, and her lips compress in a thin line. "Come on, boys," she ordered. "We need a bassinette, a light, a soft blanket and some tweezers." The grandmother spun around and retraced her steps. Both boys scurried behind her into the lovely, sun-bathed bedroom the grandparents shared. Joshua and Billy stood in the middle of the floor and watched as his grandmother emptied a shoe box, tossing the shoes on the closet floor.

Next, she rummaged in her sewing box, and found a large scrap of cotton flannel. Taking a pair of tweezers from a drawer in her vanity dresser, she turned and said, "Bring the egg over here in the sunlight, and let's find out what has to be done."

The boys hurried over, Joshua carefully transferring the egg from his small, sweaty hands to his grandmother's cool, capable ones. "Joshua, Billy, I think we should talk to God before we start," she whispered.

"Yes, Ma'am," they replied, and bowed their heads.

"Almighty and most merciful God, You are the creator of the earth and all that is in it. We pray that You will have compassion on this tiny creature of Yours. If it is Your will, preserve and protect its life. We pray in Your holy name. Amen."

Now, the grandmother's eyes flew open, and she began turning the egg slowly. At one point the beak was visible and a faint peeping sound could be heard. "We haven't a moment to lose. The chick is getting weaker."

The sound of distant voices and an occasional car horn, both borne on the south breeze, gently wafted through the second floor bay window. Sheer lace curtains moved slowly, dragged across the window sills by the soft breeze. There was no sound in that stately room as the grandmother slowly peeled and chipped away the shell encasing the exhausted chick. When the last piece of shell had been removed, Joshua looked at his grandmother and whispered, "Granny Jewel, why are they born wet? Isn't he supposed to be fluffy?"

"They're always wet when they first come out of the egg," she explained. "When he dries we can tell more about him. Now, we must keep him warm. I'm going to prop my bedside lamp over the box and the bulb should provide enough heat."

"His eyes are closed and he can't hold up his head." observed Joshua, disappointed.

"This has been a tough day for the little fellow," said Granny Jewel, who now picked up her dust cloth and continued polishing the furniture. "Why don't you move him to your room? That way you can check on him during the night."

"That's a great idea, Granny Jewel! I'll stay up with him all night in case he needs me. Maybe Billy can stay over 'cause it may take both of us to tend to him."

"That is something you'll have to clear with both mothers."

As the boys left the room, carrying the box and lamp, Joshua stopped. "Thanks, Granny Jewel for saving the baby chick."

"You're welcome, Joshua. Let's hope and pray that he'll survive."

"I will. I'll even pray all night," answered her grandson.

Papa Tom sat quietly through dinner, listening to every detail of the day's adventures. While Clara served thick slices of hot apple pie, with ice cream for dessert, she said, "That poor little baby chick ain't gonna' make it. You all are filling this child's head with false hope. It's hard enough to raise healthy biddies, much less one with two strikes against him."

"No, Clara," spoke Joshua quickly. "The chick is going to be fine. Granny Jewel prayed a real pretty prayer, and I'm going to pray all night. You'll see! He's going to be fine!"

During this exchange, Papa Tom looked knowingly at his wife. When all were finished, he stayed at the table and waited while the women cleared the dishes. "Jewel," he whispered, when they were alone in the dining room, "I hope you haven't given Joshua false hope. He's going to be crushed tomorrow morning when he finds the chick didn't survive."

Jewel Mitchell slid a chair over close to her husband. In a low voice, she said, "How do you know the chick will be dead? He'll live if it's God's will."

"When we go to bed, I'm going over to Mr. Owens' house and buy a healthy chick and put it in the box," stubbornly declared Papa Tom.

"You may not have to, dear," stated his wife.

Before bedtime, Billy stepped in the kitchen door. "My mama says I can't spend the night, but I'll be over first thing in the morning."

Tom Mitchell deliberately stayed up late that night, waiting for the family to settle down. When the house was dark and silent, he quietly made his way up the stairs. He looked in Joshua's room, smiling at the sight of his grandson curled up on the floor beside the box. He was fast asleep and never knew when his grandfather gathered him in his arms and laid him gently on the bed. As Papa Tom tucked in the sheet, he heard a slight peeping sound. Stepping over to the box he was surprised to see a fluffy, yellow chick lying in the folds of the soft cotton flannel. "Well, just look at you," he whispered to the chick. "It looks like you're going to make it after all."

As he prepared for bed in the darkened room, Granny Jewel asked, "Are you still planning to go over to Mr. Owens' house?"

"No, dear," whispered Papa Tom, "I don't think it's going to be necessary."

By morning, the peeping of the baby chick was stronger and more insistent. The sound awakened Joshua before anyone else in the house was up. Joshua hurried over to the box, and peered inside.

"Oh, gosh," he breathed, looking inside. "You made it! You're alive!" Before he could lift the chick out of the box, he noticed it was having trouble standing. "Maybe it's because of the blanket," he whispered. He cupped his hands around the tiny animal and lifted it from the box. When he put it on the bare floor, the chick struggled to stand, but kept falling over.

"What's the matter, little fellow," whispered Joshua. "Why can't you stand up?" Once again he picked up the chick and examined his legs. It appeared as if one leg was deformed. Where one leg was straight and the foot normal, the other leg was crooked, the foot slightly twisted. As he stared at the chick, his eyes welled up in tears. He continued staring, although he could no longer see clearly. "You're crippled, aren't you, little chick? You can't walk, can you?" The more the tiny animal struggled, the more Joshua's tears flowed.

"How are things going in here?" A voice from the doorway startled the boy. He looked up and cried, "Papa Tom, the chick is crippled! He looks OK, but he can't walk straight. I'm going to have to take him to the doctor."

"Why don't you put him back in the box and let him rest. We'll talk about it at breakfast. Go wash your face and hands and we'll see what needs to be done."

Breakfast was eaten in near silence as the baby chick peeped loudly in his box in the living room. "He wants his mama, and his brothers and sisters," declared Sarah. "He's lonesome in that box all by himself."

"He can't survive in the chicken pen, Sarah. He couldn't keep up with the rest of the biddies," replied her brother.

Clara set a plate of steaming scrambled eggs and crisp bacon in front of Joshua. "I'm not hungry, Clara. I don't want any breakfast."

"Oh, yes you do!" Clara insisted, hands on her hips. "You're not going to get weak and stumble around here like that chicken, because you won't eat Clara's good cooking. I'll pinch that biddie's head off before I let something like that happen."

"No, Clara!" the boy said, stuffing scrambled egg in his mouth.

The rest of the meal was eaten in troubled silence. When he had finished, Joshua announced, "I'm going to take the little chick to Dr. Maxwell. He'll know what to do."

"Son," spoke his mother, "Dr. Maxwell treats people, not animals."

"I don't care. He'll know what to do." Joshua slid from his chair and walked into the living room. "I'll be home soon," he announced. Picking up the box, he walked toward the front door.

Peggy Bowers made a move to stop him. Before she could get up, Granny Jewel grabbed her arm. "Wait, Peggy. There's something very important going on here."

"What do you mean, Mama?"

"Let's stop a minute and think. Our country and our world have just come through years of cruelty, fighting, and death in another world war. We saw instances where human life had no value. Fortunately, we live in a country where a small boy is free to grow up fearless, and have the opportunity to love and respect life, even if it's a tiny animal. We should applaud Joshua's effort."

No one spoke for several minutes. Finally, Sarah said. "I think I'll walk down to Dr. Maxwell's office and wait for Joshua."

"I think I'll go outside and see if I can find something we can use as a chicken house," added Papa Tom.

"There's some grits left in the bottom of the pot. I'll scrape it out and save it for the biddy," said Clara in a gruff voice.

"Little chick, little chick," chanted Amy. "I want little chick."

"That's a good name for him," declared Granny Jewel. "Let's call him Little Chick."

By eleven o'clock Sarah and Joshua returned. Joshua was carefully holding the shoe box with both hands and wearing a grin as he stepped in the front hall. "Is anybody home? We have some good news!"

From all parts of the house the family came. "What did the doctor say?" asked Granny Jewel.

"He checked the biddy over very carefully. You should have seen him listening to his heart with a stethoscope! It was bigger than the chick. Dr. Maxwell said he sounded hale and hearty." Joshua's grin faded. "The only trouble was that one leg and foot. He cut a straw open and made a splint. Then he showed me how to do it. He said when the chick is grown he will be able to balance with his wings."

"Joshua, I'm surprised the doctor let you in his office with an animal," said Papa Tom.

Joshua looked up at his grandfather. "He started not to, but I reminded him of how he fixed your leg three summers ago, and that now you're good as new."

Clara stepped up. "Well, it looks like we have a new member of the family. Take good care of him, fatten him up, and we'll have fried chicken one Sunday before the summer's over."

"Clara!" exclaimed the whole family.

While Papa Tom and Joshua went outside to build a chicken coop, Sarah saw this time as her first real chance to phone her friend, Nancy Russert.

"Hi, Nancy," she said over the phone. "I'm sorry I didn't get to call you yesterday, but there has been so much going on around here."

"I want to hear all about it, Sarah. Why don't you come over and have lunch with Mama and me. We're having sandwiches and deviled eggs."

Sarah paused for only a second. "Did you say deviled eggs? Thanks, Nancy. I'll come over **after** lunch."

Chapter 3

Sarah hurried along the tree-lined street. She had not seen her friend in nine months, since Nancy had not come to Raleigh for a visit during the school year. As she turned the corner onto Marsh Street, Sarah waved to Nancy's neighbor sweeping her porch. "Good morning, Miss Loftin," called Sarah. "How are you?"

Miss Sadie Loftin shaded her eyes with one hand. "Is that you, Sarah? Your grandmother told me you'd be coming soon. I'm glad you're finally here. Your grandparents miss you something terrible during the school year."

"We miss them, too. I tried to talk my grandfather into moving to Raleigh. He said he wouldn't leave the coast for a king's ransom."

"I know just how he feels, honey. I wouldn't be happy living away from the ocean."

Sarah waved again, and continued walking toward Nancy's house. *I almost feel the same way,* Sarah thought. *When I'm in Raleigh, I can't see the shore birds, or watch the tide come in. You can't grab a pole and go fishing in the city, and you can't go in the stores barefooted.* Sarah stopped suddenly and stood under the shade of an ancient elm. She closed her eyes and breathed in the salty ocean breeze. The smell of the salt marsh was wonderful. It reminded Sarah of her other summers in Beaufort and the fun she had. With her eyes still closed, she listened to the distant sound of the shore birds across the channel, and the occasional whinny of a banker pony. *When I'm grown, I'm going to live in Beaufort all year long,* she decided.

"My gosh! Look at you! Sarah, how much taller are you going to get?" questioned her friend when she opened the front screen door.

Sarah laughed, and hugged her friend. "You look wonderful, Nancy!"

Sarah exclaimed, "And I don't know how much taller I'm going to get. I can almost see over my mama's head now."

"Come in the kitchen and speak to Mama." Nancy, dressed in a shirt and shorts, led the way through the small, old-fashioned house. Following Nancy, Sarah once more admired the ornate furniture and delicate porcelain decorations. "Mama," she announced, "Look who's here."

Mrs. Russell turned from the bowl of potatoes she was peeling, "Hello, Sarah." Mrs. Cora peered at Sarah over the rim of her glasses. "It's good to see you again. How was your first year of high school? Are you going to be here the whole summer? How's the rest of your family?"

Sarah knew Mrs. Cora could fire questions faster than bullets from a gun. Sitting down at the kitchen table, she answered each question as carefully as she could. Nancy sat across from her, arms folded, elbows on the table. She would grin at Sarah, and roll her eyes as her guest endured the mother's interrogation.

Finally, Nancy interrupted, "Mama, I declare, Sarah is going to be worn out if you keep asking questions."

"Sarah," she said, looking at her friend, "would you like a glass of lemonade? We could sit on the front porch and sip it just like we did last summer."

Sarah shot her friend a grateful look. "Sure Nancy. Lemonade would be great."

The girls slowly rocked a few minutes before either spoke. After taking a sip of lemonade, Nancy turned to her friend. "I'm sorry Mama asks so many questions. When she does, it embarrasses me. I wish she wouldn't do it. When I ask her not to, she says she won't know things if she doesn't ask."

Sarah grinned and shook her head. "I don't mind, Nancy. I'm so glad to be sitting in this big rocking chair, sipping lemonade, that I don't believe anything could make me unhappy right now." The girls sat in companionable silence for a few moments, enjoying the cool breeze. "Nancy," said Sarah, "you wrote about meeting a cute boy in high school. Did you go out with him?"

"Oh, no," Nancy hurried to explain. "You remember I wrote you about being on the girl's basketball team? I joined the booster's club, and since Clifton plays sports, he was at the meetings, always surrounded by the pretty, popular girls."

Her friend interrupted. "You're pretty, Nancy."

Nancy threw back her head and laughed. "You sound like my parents. They think I'm the prettiest girl in Beaufort High School. The trouble is; they are the only ones."

"Well, now there are three people who think you're the prettiest."

Nancy reached over and patted her friend on the arm. "You are a true friend, Sarah. Thank you for the compliment."

Nancy continued. "At one of the meetings I had a chance to talk to him. We were on the same committee and when we were making posters, he asked what color I thought the letters should be. I started to answer, but when he turned those blue eyes on me, I couldn't think. All I could see was a lock of hair that had fallen across his forehead. At that moment I couldn't have told you the name of a single color in the rainbow."

"What did you do?"

"In an instant, one of the other girls caught his attention and had a million suggestions. He never looked in my direction again." Quietly she added, "He doesn't know I'm alive." Nancy slumped in her chair, and sipped the last of her lemonade. Sarah was surprised to see such an unhappy expression on her friend's face.

"I'll bet he watched you play basketball for the Beaufort Seadogs. Maybe he cheered for you when you made a basket."

"Thanks, Sarah, but no, I spent most of my freshman year warming the bench."

"Are you going to join the team next year?"

"At the last game of the season, Coach McGraw patted me on the back and told me if I practice during the summer, I'll probably be in the starting line up next year."

"Congratulations, Nancy."

"We'll see." After a moment, Nancy asked, "How about you, Sarah. Have you been out on a date?"

Sarah sat up, sighed deeply, and said, "No I haven't had a real date. Sometimes there are socials at church for teenagers, and I go to them, but we're all just friends. Broughton is such a big school, and I was a lowly freshman, so, I didn't get a chance to meet many boys. My friend Lindsey and I were in the same classes, so we stuck together." Sarah looked over at her friend. "At the rate I'm going, my grandmother won't have to worry about making my wedding dress for a **long** time!"

"Why don't we walk downtown and look in the store windows?"

suggested Nancy. "If we sit here much longer, Mama might think of some more questions to ask you."

Sarah stood, wiping the condensation from her glass off the arm of the rocking chair. "Good idea," she agreed. Nancy hurried into the house with the empty glasses and was back in a few moments. Sarah looked closely at her friend. "Nancy, are you wearing lipstick?" she asked in a shocked voice.

"Yes, Mama said it would be all right if I don't cake it on, and if it is a light shade." She gave Sarah a doubtful look. "Do you think it looks good?"

"It looks so good, I want to put some on, too," declared Sarah.

When the girls turned onto Front Street, the breeze caught in their hair, tossing it about. Sarah looked across Taylor's Creek, trying to see the Outer Banks ponies feeding along the shore.

"Where do you suppose the ponies are, Nancy? Usually you can see them from here. I heard one whinny before I got to your house."

"I don't know, Sarah. I hardly ever pay any attention to them."

"You would, if you lived in a hot, crowded city all the time. You'd appreciate living on the coast with the cool breeze."

"Sarah, I'd trade a lifetime of living on the coast for one symphony concert in Memorial Auditorium in Raleigh."

"Maybe we should get our parents to trade daughters," suggested Sarah.

"That sounds good, but I'm not ready for a brother and sister."

Their conversation was interrupted by the high-pitched whine of the drawbridge siren. Sarah crossed the street, stood on the breakwall and watched as a shrimp BOAT plowed toward the open span. When it was once more in the open channel, the crew spread the outriggers so nets would dry. Overhead, seagulls followed, hoping someone would toss a fish over the side of the boat.

After looking through the shop windows, the girls wandered out on a nearby dock and sat down, cooling their feet in the clear, blue-green water.

"Nancy, did you have Miriam for freshman English?"

"Oh, you mean Miss Thompson!" Nancy clasped her hands under her chin and looked up. Sarah smiled, having seen her friend strike this pose many times before. "She is just wonderful! Everyone in the freshman class loves her. She would come sweeping into the classroom every morning in a dress or sweater and skirt wearing a flowing silk scarf around her neck or in her hair. The boys in my class couldn't keep their eyes off her, and all us girls tried to dress like her and wear our hair shoulder length, like hers. Of course, with my curls, I couldn't let my hair get that long. I would look like the dirigibles that used to fly over town during the war."

"I hope Uncle Herb brings her over tonight for supper. There is still a lot of planning to be done for the wedding, and it's not too far off." Sarah turned to her friend, "Say, Nancy, why not come home with me. We can ask Clara to fix us a snack and find out if Miriam is coming tonight - oh, I mean, Almost Aunt Miriam." The girls laughed and turned toward her grandparents' home.

Before they reached the front porch, Sarah grabbed Nancy's arm. "I'd better warn you. Joshua has a new pet."

"What's so terrible about that?"

"It's a baby chick; a crippled baby chick."

"I'll bet there's a story behind that," reflected Nancy.

"If I told you, you'd think I was making it up." All thoughts of pets were forgotten when the girls stepped into the front hall. "Sarah, I'm so glad you're here," said her grandmother in a worried voice.

Sarah could feel herself growing tense. "What's the matter, Granny Jewel? Is someone sick?"

"No, girls, Miriam's father has had a heart attack and is in the hospital in Binghamton, New York. Miriam has to go home right away."

"How is she going to get there?" Sarah, feeling weak, leaned on the hall table.

Papa Tom joined them. "Herb is going to drive her. Airplane connections are so bad since the war, he thinks he can have her home as quickly if they go by car."

Sarah turned once more to her grandmother. "What about the wedding, Granny Jewel?"

"All wedding plans have been put on hold."

"For how long?" whispered Sarah.

"Indefinitely, honey."

"Who will fill in for Uncle Herb at the store?"

"We will," answered her grandfather, giving her a wink.

"*We?*"

"That's right, you and me, Sis."

Sarah plopped down on the bottom step to try and absorb this new information. She felt someone tap her on the knee. Looking up she saw

Nancy. "Sarah, I'm going to run on home. You have things to talk about, and I need to practice my scales."

Sarah nodded numbly. "OK, Nancy. I'll call you."

Sarah followed her grandfather back to the kitchen. "Papa Tom," she asked, speaking to his back. He stopped, turned and gave her an inquiring look. "What will I be doing at the grocery store and what do I have to wear?"

"You can wear the same thing you wore to school. You sure don't have to dress up. Besides, you can wear a long white apron over your dress to keep it clean."

"When do you think Uncle Herb will be back?"

Papa Tom tapped his chin with his forefinger. "Hmmm, they left this morning, and will drive all day. They'll be staying with relatives in Washington tonight and will get into Binghamton some time tomorrow. If Miriam needs to stay longer than a week, Herb will drive home. Nothing is definite until the doctors run tests." Her grandfather looked at the worried expression on the face of his beautiful granddaughter. "This won't be for long, Sis. We're short-handed at the store and we need you."

"I don't mind working, Papa Tom. Families help each other wherever they are needed. Granny Jewel told me it is called, "filling in the gap.""

"That's true, and there are many ways of doing it," reminded her grandfather. "This will be one of them."

"Wouldn't mama like to work in the store, instead of me?" inquired Sarah.

"I'm sure she would love to get away for a few hours every day. She could greet people she hasn't seen in years, dust the merchandise, polish fruit and sweep the floor. But, if she helps out, you're going to have to watch Amy, entertain Joshua and Billy, and keep Frisky from eating the baby chick."

"I'll be ready in the morning."

Sarah wasn't ready the next morning. Mr. Peavy was tuning up for his first announcement of the new day when Sarah felt a hand on her shoulder. In the pearl-gray light, Sarah could see the outline of her mother standing beside the bed. "Rise and shine, my girl," she said, "you have a job to do, and it's time you were up and getting ready."

Sarah stumbled from her bed and headed toward the closet. "Mama, it's a good thing I brought my school clothes. Papa said last year that the summer I was fifteen, I'd be old enough to help out at the store."

Peggy Bowers sat on the foot of her daughter's bed, staring. "I can't believe how fast my children are growing up. It seems you were running around in braids such a short time ago, and now you're going to work!" Her mother shook her head in wonder.

Later, Sarah stared at her plate of fluffy scrambled eggs and crisp bacon. "You better eat up, girl," said a voice behind her. "You're gonna' be mighty hungry before lunch time if you don't eat everything on your plate."

"It looks good, Clara, but it's so *early*! I really don't have much appetite this time of day."

"Cheer up, sweetheart, we'll be so busy, time will fly, and we'll be home for lunch before you know it," said her grandfather.

Clara glared at her employer, pointing her wooden stirring spoon in his direction. "You take care of this baby," she ordered. "Don't you work her too hard, and see that she gets a snack in the middle of the morning."

"Clara," explained Papa Tom, with exaggerated patience, "I promise I'll take good care of my granddaughter, and make sure she doesn't faint from hunger. After all, she'll be working in a grocery store!"

Sarah was amazed at how still it was as they walked toward Front Street. "I didn't know it could be so quiet in the middle of town. This is better than all the noise you hear when people are up."

Tom Mitchell took his granddaughter's hand as they walked. "This is my favorite time of day, Sarah. It is cool and quiet, and you have time to think about things you have on your mind. It's the best time to have family devotional, which gets your day started off right. Every morning I say, "God, please guide me through this day.""

"That's a short devotional," said Sarah smiling at her grandfather.

"Well, Sis, prayers don't have to be long and complicated. God already knows what's in your heart. However, He still loves to hear from you."

Turning the corner, they walked toward the store. "Papa Tom," asked Sarah, "why is your grocery store on the opposite side of the street from the other two grocery stores?"

Papa Tom paused, looking across the street at the line of stores on the water side of Front Street. "Many years ago, when my father bought land and built our store, he decided he would rather have it on this side of the street, so trucks could back up to the rear entrance and unload produce and merchandise. The others have docks behind the store, so people from down east communities can come to town in their boats, tie up behind the stores, buy their groceries, and load them right in the boat."

"Do we have any customers from the islands down east?"

"We sure do. When the highway department connected all the islands with roads and bridges, it was no longer necessary to come to town by boat. Most folks come to town by car, although a few old-timers still enjoy coming to town and tying their boat behind the grocery store."

Papa Tom unlocked the front door of Mitchell's Grocery Store and stood holding the door for Sarah. "Enter your kingdom, my princess," he said, smiling. Sarah watched as he pushed back the wooden door and turned on the fan overhead.

"Why is there a fan over the door?" Sarah inquired.

"That, my dear, is to discourage flies and other insects from coming in the store when a customer opens the screen door. The smell of fruit and candy is mighty attractive to six-legged pests."

While her grandfather walked to the back of the store to unlock the service entrance, Sarah let her eyes roam around the large room. Behind the wooden counters were shelves of canned goods reaching almost to the ceiling. One shelf held coffee products. Sarah loved the smell of ground coffee but wasn't fond of drinking it. *If I'm going to start getting up so early every day, I'd better learn to love coffee,* Sarah thought. Fresh fruit and vegetables were kept in bins near the front door, while the butcher shop was in the far back. Sarah didn't enjoy looking at the uncooked meat on display. By far the worst was the tray of raw liver. Sarah shuddered as she thought of the nights her mother served it. Not even onions and gravy could disguise the strong, bitter taste. While she tried to eat her portion, she listened to Joshua plead his case against eating his serving. No amount of whining, begging or pleading could change their mother's determination that her family needed the rich iron in the meat. *When I grow up,* Sarah resolved, *I shall never make my family eat liver, never, never.*

"Here, Sarah," said Papa Tom, holding out a clean, white apron. "Put this on and tie it in the back. It will protect your dress, and you'll look like an official grocery store clerk."

After Sarah put on the apron, her grandfather handed her a feather duster. "To begin, give everything a good dusting. After you finish, I'll show you how to work the cash register and you can check out groceries for customers. Mr. Case just came in the back door, and we'll be unpacking boxes that came in late yesterday."

Before Sarah finished dusting one shelf, the door opened. Sarah looked up and recognized Morgan Stewart. Before she could ask, "May I help you?" Morgan gave a low whistle.

"Boy, it's about time Tom Mitchell hired a movie star," said their first customer of the day. "That'll really hurt his competition. All the men in Beaufort will come here to shop even if they don't need anything."

"Mr. Stewart, it's me, Sarah! I'm not a movie star. I'm just helping out while we're a little short handed."

"Somebody sick?" he asked, replacing his smile with a serious frown.

"No one in our family." Sarah proceeded to explain that her uncle's fiancé was called away suddenly, and her uncle accompanied her. When Mr. Stewart was satisfied he knew all the details of this turn of events, he selected several grocery items and was ready to check out.

"I'll have to get my grandfather or Mr. Case to check you out." While they waited for Papa Tom to come to the front of the store, Sarah inquired about Mary Stewart.

"She's about as excited as a body can be," said Mr. Stewart. We got a letter from the adoption agency. It seems our little war orphan is being processed in England right now, and will be coming to America in a few days. We'll drive to Raleigh and be at the airport when the plane arrives." Morgan shook his head. "I hope it's soon. Mary has swept the floor and polished the furniture so many times in his bedroom, that she has almost worn the finish off the dresser." Morgan Stewart looked at Sarah and grinned. "Thanks to your little brother's idea, we're finally going to be parents. We may be a little old for a young'un, but I always say, 'better late than never." As he started out, he turned. "I hope you get some good news soon. Everybody in town is looking forward to the big wedding."

"Thanks. Please tell Mrs. Stewart hello for me."

While they were waiting for other customers, Sarah's grandfather explained how to use the ornate, silver cash register. "How about if I make a mistake, Papa, what happens then?"

"We'll make a note of it and put it in the cash drawer. At the end of the day, we'll make any corrections."

Before Sarah could resume her dusting, the bell over the front screen door jingled merrily. Sarah looked up and smiled graciously at the new customer. "May I help you?" she asked.

"Uh, no," stuttered the young man, "I don't want anything. I just passed Morgan and he told me there was a pretty girl working at the grocery store, and I wanted to see for myself." The tall, young man suddenly appeared embarrassed. "Maybe I will get a pack of smokes, since I'm here." He took a pack of cigarettes from the display rack in front of the counter and handed Sarah a quarter. She pressed a key marked twenty and one marked five and depressed them both at the same time. A cheerful ring came from inside the cash register as the change drawer flew open. *Wow,* thought Sarah, *I just made my first sale!* She smiled at the gentleman as he turned to leave.

"Morgan was right," he said smiling at Sarah.

"I beg your pardon?"

"There is a pretty girl working at the grocery store."

"Thank you," she replied, and returned his smile. The rest of the morning passed quickly as Sarah continued dusting and checking out customers. At noon, Papa Tom came to the front of the store.

"Is the hired help getting hungry? I'd better get you home for some lunch, or the whole family will come trooping in here to find you."

"I'm not real hungry, Papa. I've been nibbling on a box of animal crackers all morning. I started a 'tab' with my name at the top, just like some of the customers. You can subtract five cents from my pay check at the end of the week."

Papa Tom held the door for her as they stepped out in the warm sunshine. "Please tell Clara that you have had a snack. She's afraid you'll be hungry and I won't let you stop and have something to eat."

"I won't starve in my papa's grocery store,"

"Tell her that. Maybe she'll believe you."

Chapter 4

By Friday, Sarah had learned her way around the store so well Papa Tom seldom had to help her. "Uncle Herb will be back to work on Monday. He and Miriam will return over the weekend," her grandfather said, popping open a Coca-Cola and handing it to Sarah.

Sarah gratefully took the cold drink and sat on the cover of a wooden barrel containing sour pickles. "I'm glad Miriam's father is doing well enough for them to come home."

"This probably means we'll be out of a job, Sis," said Papa Tom, smiling at his granddaughter. "Now you'll be forced to sleep late and hang around with your buddy, Nancy." He paused for a moment. "Seriously, I think your mother could use some help at home. Amy seems to be quite a handful."

"It's been a lot of fun working in the store this week, Papa Tom." Sarah leaned her head to one side. "You know, the thing that most sticks out in my mind is how fast news travels in Beaufort. On Monday morning, I told Mr. Stewart about Miriam's father. Before lunch, I'll bet a dozen people came in the store to find out if we had heard any more, and if there was anything they could do to help."

"Morgan went home and told Mary. Mary got on the phone and told her friends. They told other friends. Soon the whole town knew Miriam's father was in the hospital. That's the way people are in small towns, Sarah. It's true you can't keep a secret, but on the other hand, people rush to help any way they can. Neighbors can be a great comfort in a time of trouble."

"Some people stopped by, and didn't even buy anything. They just wanted to know if there was anything they could do to help. It's like a whole town 'filling in the gap.'"

Their conversation was soon interrupted by the familiar tinkling of the bell over the screen door. "That's the signal we both better get back to work," said Papa Tom. "We can talk more tonight at dinner." Her grandfather returned to the small office, while Sarah went out to the front of the store.

"Hi, Sarah," called a familiar voice. "We came by to see you."

Standing just inside the store was Joshua, Billy, and Mackie, dressed in play clothes, their feet bare. Sarah noticed Joshua seemed nervous as he moved about the store, Billy close behind. Mackie, the oldest boy, seemed perfectly at ease as he hovered about the candy counter. Sarah followed her brother down the aisle of canned goods. "Is there something I can help you with, gentlemen?" she asked smiling.

"Oh, no, Sarah. We're just looking," said her brother vaguely.

Sarah was mildly curious about the boys' behavior, but thought perhaps they were self conscious about being waited on by a big sister. Both kept glancing over their shoulder to check on Mackie's whereabouts.

"Does Mama know you are downtown with Billy and Mackie?"

Joshua was instantly defensive. "Sure she does, Sarah," a scowl crossing his face. "I'm not a baby who has to have his mama along every time he leaves the house!"

"Excuse me, little brother. I just thought I'd ask."

"Come on, you two," ordered Mackie from the front of the store. "We gotta' go." Both boys hurried after their friend. Joshua hurriedly waved goodbye and let the door slam behind him. *Hmmm*, thought Sarah. *They acted mighty strange. Maybe that's how boys behave when they're away from home.* Sarah had no time to wonder any more about the boys' behavior, as customers came in during the afternoon and picked up groceries for the evening meal.

At four o'clock, Papa Tom came out of the office, stretched, and smiled at Sarah. "Why don't you run along and see if you can help your mother with Amy. She probably needs a break."

"Thanks, Papa Tom," said Sarah, relief in her voice. "It's been a busy day, and my feet are ready to go home."

The phone rang as Sarah hung up her long white apron. "Oh, no," she groaned. "I hope that isn't a fish boat with an order that needs to be filled. It takes me half a morning to 'grub up' a fishing boat that plans to be out at sea for a week."

"Sarah," came a familiar voice on the other end of the line. "I'm glad I caught you before you left."

"Hi, Mama. Do you want me to bring something home for supper? I'm just leaving and I'll be home in a few minutes."

"I'm not worried about supper, honey. Joshua is sick. Please bring home a bottle of Pepto-Bismol. I think it'll sooth his aching stomach."

Sarah hung up and hurriedly put a bottle of the pink medicine in her skirt pocket and made a notation on her tab in the cash register. "Papa Tom, I'm going home now," she called as she headed for the back entrance to the store. "Joshua has a stomach ache and I'm taking mama some medicine."

"Go ahead, honey. Tell him I hope he'll feel better."

When Sarah eased open the front door, she could hear her brother upstairs groaning and whining. She hurried up the steps, stopping at the doorway of his room. The shades were drawn against the fierce, late afternoon sun, still the room was stifling hot, and there was a strange odor Sarah could not identify. Their mother was sitting on the side of the bed, holding her son's hand and crooning softly to him. *My gosh,* thought Sarah, *his face and lips are the same color as the white pillow case.* At that moment, a deep groan emitted from the pitiful form on the bed. "Mama," came a weak voice, "am I going to die?"

"No, Joshua! Don't even think such a thing." Sarah could hear the worry in her mother's voice. "You ate something that didn't agree with you and this bad feeling will soon pass. If it doesn't, we'll call Dr. Maxwell and have him come over and take a look at you."

One eye cracked open, and in a weak voice from the bed asked, "He won't give me a shot will he?"

"I don't know, son. He'll do whatever he thinks is necessary to make you well." The closing of the front screen door interrupted their mother. "Sarah," she said, "look over the banister and see if that's Granny Jewel. If it is, ask her to come up right away. I'd feel better if she took a look at Joshua."

Sarah hurried out into the hall and leaned over the railing. "Granny Jewel, is that you?" When Sarah saw the face of her grandmother come in view, she whispered, "Can you come up right away? Joshua is real sick and Mama needs you."

Bundles and packages went crashing onto the hall table as Jewel Mitchell took her stair steps two at a time. Peggy met her mother at the bedroom door, a finger on her lips. "Mama," she whispered, "Joshua came home about three o'clock, doubled over and clutching his stomach. He was the color of that old gray cat next door. I put him to bed and put a cold cloth on his forehead. Nothing I have done has been any help. Sarah brought some medicine, and I'm going to try to get a little bit in him; although I doubt if it will stay down."

"Do you have a deep pan handy?" asked Granny Jewel in a hushed voice. Her daughter nodded. "You may want to keep it close by the bed." She stepped into the bedroom, worry etched on her face. "I want to take a look at him. It could be appendicitis, you know. You must prepare yourself for the worst," said her mother, holding Peggy's hands.

"I know Mama." Before they could continue, there was a loud groan from the bed. All three hurried to the child's bedside. Granny Jewel, taking her grandson's limp hand in hers, eased down onto the bed where she could observe her stricken grandson. She stared at him for a few moments, then leaned over and brought her face within two inches of his. Sarah heard her sniff loudly. *Is my grandmother crying*, she wondered, *beginning to feel a sense of panic*. Once more she heard a loud sniff, but before she could ask what was happening, she saw her grandmother suddenly sit up, her back straight.

"Joshua Mitchell Bowers, have you been smoking cigarettes? Before you answer, you'd better weigh your words and tell me the real truth!" Sarah saw her mother's hands fly up and cover her mouth.

"Mother! How could you think such a thing? This poor child is suffering, and you're asking him such a horrible question. Joshua has **never** smoked a cigarette. He wouldn't know how!"

Instead of answering, Joshua gave a loud groan, rolled his eyes back in his head, and lay still. "Sarah," commanded her grandmother, "I know how we can settle this. Go ask Clara to turn off the fire under supper, and please come up here."

Sarah flew down the steps, grabbed the newel post, spun around and headed for the kitchen. "Clara, oh, Clara, Granny Jewel needs you upstairs right now." Clara, peeling potatoes, threw down her knife, spun around and headed from the room. "She said to turn out the light under supper," added Sarah.

"You can do that, honey. When your granny needs me, a few boiling pots won't stop old Clara." Sarah turned off the oven and burners on top of the stove and followed. By the time the older woman got to the top step, Sarah was behind her.

"Clara," asked Granny Jewel, standing up, "would you please get a real good whiff of this child's breath. I want to know what you think is causing his suffering."

Clara sat gently on the side of the bed and looked at the sick child. She smoothed his hair back from his forehead and rubbed his tummy with her other hand. Joshua cracked one eyelid and looked at his beloved Clara. "Clara, am I going to die?" he asked, his voice weak. "Will you cry at my funeral, and miss me when I'm gone?"

"Boy," Clara said in a loud voice. "You're the one who's gonna be crying if you don't tell me right this minute what you been smoking. Don't deny it, cause you smell just like a smoke stack. Now start talking!"

"I'm going to die anyway, so I might as well tell the truth," Joshua answered in a weak voice.

"Go ahead, we're all waiting," spoke his grandmother.

"Me and Billy and Mackie,"

"Billy, Mackie and I," corrected his mother.

"Peggy, this is no time for a lesson in proper grammar," stated Granny Jewel.

"Anyway," came a tiny voice from the bed, "Mackie said he wanted some candy, and that we could steal it from Papa's store. I told him Papa would give us some candy, if we asked him. Mackie said it would be more fun if we stole it." Joshua rolled his eyes at his grandmother.

"Why did you go along with something you knew was wrong?" asked his mother. Tears welled in his eyes and spilled over, wetting the pillow case.

"Because," he continued, "Mackie would think I'm a sissy. He calls me 'Sissy Pants' if I don't do what he says."

"How about Billy? Why did he go along with such a thing?"

"Billy is scared of Mackie, and does anything he says." Joshua took a deep breath and wiped his eyes with the cold cloth. While he was doing this, Sarah hurried into her mother's bedroom and took Amy from her playpen. She returned quickly to her brother's room with her sister on her hip. Granny Jewel was asking, "Where did you all get cigarettes? Did you take a pack of Mr. Fuller's?"

Joshua looked sadly at his big sister. "Mackie stole them from the store this morning while Billy and I talked to Sarah." From the look of betrayal on his sister's face, Joshua hurried to explain, "He was only going to steal candy bars, but he took a pack of cigarettes, too." He covered his face with the cloth. "I don't feel like talking any more. I think I'm about to die for good."

His grandmother grabbed the cold cloth. "You're not through talking, and you're sure not about to die. Continue!"

After taking another deep breath, the boy whispered, "We hid in Billy's daddy's shed. We ate all the candy bars and Mackie told us to bury the wrappers. That was when Mackie reached in his pocket and showed us the pack of cigarettes. He started bragging about how it had been so easy to steal the candy, he stole cigarettes, too."

"Tell me, Joshua," interrupted his mother, "didn't you feel that you were doing something wrong?"

"Yes, Mama, I knew it was wrong, but what could I do?" whined Joshua. "If I left and told on them, they wouldn't ever speak to me again, and I wouldn't have anybody to play with."

"Tell about the cigarettes," demanded his mother.

"Mackie said we'd have to smoke all the cigarettes so nobody would know what we'd done."

"How many did you smoke, little brother?"

"I lost count after about five or six. Mackie smoked more than Billy or me. After while I started feeling real bad. Billy didn't look too good, either. I told them I had to go home and help out around the house. By then I knew I was dying, and I didn't want you all to find my body in that old shed full of spiders and mice. Mama didn't know what the matter was, so I didn't tell her because I didn't want her mad with me at my funeral." Joshua turned his head to the wall and began to wail, "I'm sorry! I'm sorry for everything I did. I promise if I live, I ain't never going to smoke another cigarette ever again!"

Peggy opened her mouth. Before she could speak, their grandmother turned to her daughter and said, "Please, Peggy, don't tell him not to say ain't. This **ain't** the right time!"

Joshua turned back and propped up on one elbow, an agonizing expression on his face. "He looked up at his loving family and said, "You're not going to tell Papa Tom are you?"

"No, Joshua," replied his mother, "you're going to tell him."

The boy fell back on his bed, placing one arm over his eyes. "I'm dying now. I'm going to heaven and sleep in the sweet bosom of Jesus."

Clara, getting up from the side of the bed, answered, "Oh, no, boy. You're not getting off that easy. Besides, when you do go to heaven I hope there's no cigarette smoke on your breath."

Once more the front door closed loudly. All heads turned toward the sound. "Where is everybody? How is my number one grandson?" Papa

Tom appeared in the doorway, paused a moment, then went directly to Joshua's bed.

"I'm going downstairs and stir supper," declared Clara, hurrying from the room.

"I'll help," stated Granny Jewel, following Clara.

"Me, too," agreed Sarah.

"Me, too," echoed a tiny voice.

Papa Tom looked at his daughter with a bewildered expression. "Honey, what is wrong? Is it anything serious? You women are scaring me."

"Joshua," said his mother, "turn over and face your grandfather, and tell him all that has happened today. Do not lie, or stretch the truth. Daddy, when you are ready, come down to supper. Joshua will remain in bed. I doubt if he's very hungry anyway."

Bowls and platters of steaming hot food cooled and grew cold as each family member sat around the table. Everyone remained silent except Amy, who was cheerfully eating bites of pork chop, apple sauce, and creating strange designs in her creamed potatoes. Occasionally she would look at each face, wondering what was different. "Eat!" she would command. "Keen your pate!" When no one responded, she continued with her meal. Sarah looked enviously at her happy, carefree sister. *Two year olds are lucky,* she decided. *They don't have a worry in the world. The older I get, the more problems I have to face,* she realized, sighing deeply.

Footsteps on the stairs let them know that Papa Tom was on the way down. Granny Jewel began quickly serving the plates. Clara appeared at the kitchen door. "Do you want me to heat up the supper?" she asked.

"No, Clara, this will be fine. No one will know what they are eating tonight, so it won't matter," stated Granny Jewel. "Thanks for staying late. We'll clean up after supper so you can get on home to William."

"Good night," Clara called in a sad voice.

"Good night," the family echoed.

All eyes were on the grandfather as he took his place at the head of the table. No one spoke as he slowly unfolded his napkin and placed it in his lap. He turned to Granny Jewel and asked in a whisper, "Has anyone asked the blessing?"

"No, dear," she answered. "We were waiting for you." All bowed their heads as Papa Tom prayed. Sarah, eyes closed, listened as her grandfather blessed the food, then petitioned God for wisdom in dealing with unpleasant situations and asked that God would bless each of them with a forgiving heart.

The meal was eaten in silence. When Peggy got up to get the dessert, she asked her father, "Daddy, what must I do? James is not here and I think he should know what our son has done. When he comes in two weeks, I want this whole unpleasant business behind us."

"Peggy," said her father, "after supper call James on the telephone and tell him what happened. Your mother and I will abide by whatever you decide to do."

Peggy looked relieved. "Thanks, Daddy. I'll call James before the evening news on the radio."

"Talk as long as you want. The news can wait until you have talked to James. That's more important."

Mother and daughter exchanged glances. Seldom had anything taken precedence over the evening news.

"Peggy," said Papa Tom slowly, "Most kids are going to try something forbidden at one time or another. I remember the summer I was twelve, a friend and I hid behind our shed and smoked corn silk rolled in paper. When daddy looked out the back door and saw smoke, he thought the shed was on fire, and came running with a bucket of water. We thought for a minute he was going to pour it on us, but instead he poured the water out, turned the bucket over, sat down and watched us. He didn't say a word, and pretty soon we were feeling mighty uncomfortable. It would have been a lot better if he had fussed at us. When we started to stomp out our smokes, he insisted we keep right on puffing on that old corn silk. "Don't mind me," he said with a strange smile on his face. "Just pretend I'm not here."

"I'm telling you, the more we puffed, the greener everything looked. Pretty soon I was lying on the ground, moaning and groaning. That was when daddy told my friend he'd better get on home. After he left, daddy asked me if I would like another cigarette. I shook my head, because I was so sick, I couldn't speak. He had to help me in the house and up to my bed. Mama was upset, but he told her I only needed to rest, and that I'd be better in the morning." Papa Tom paused a few minutes and continued, "You know, he never did tell Mama."

"What about the stealing, Tom," asked Granny Jewel, wearing a pained expression. "That was very serious."

"We talked about it. He knows what they did was wrong. He feels especially bad about lying to his sister, and asked if there was some way he could make it up to her. I suggested he talk it over with his mother, apologize to Sarah and never do anything like that again."

Sarah turned to her grandfather. "What was it like to go to bed with no supper? Did you get real hungry in the night?"

Papa Tom smiled, remembering, "I didn't want anything to eat at first, but later on, I got really hungry. When he came upstairs to bed, daddy slipped in my room and handed me a biscuit with a slice of country ham inside. Boy, that was the best food I ever ate! I told him I was sorry, and started crying. He patted me on the top of my head, which made me cry even harder. The worst punishment was knowing I had disappointed my father."

"Did you ever want to smoke again?" asked Sarah."

"No, I never had any desire to smoke after that day."

"What about Joshua's punishment?" Sarah asked her mother.

"Honey, I think his tummy has punished him enough for tonight. Tomorrow, he'll have to apologize to you and his sister."

Papa Tom took a large helping of creamed potato. "He is going to pay for the stolen items from his allowance. Mackie and Billy have parents who need to know about this. They can handle it any way they want. Personally, I think the boys should come down to the store and work off the cost of their merchandise. I'd like to have a talk with them about the importance of being an honest person."

Papa Tom took a deep breath. "If you steal, your reputation is ruined. There are people who come in the store and we keep an eye on them because they have a reputation for taking items and not paying. I don't want that to ever happen to anyone in our family."

Sarah was awakened before day by a cool hand pressing on her shoulder. She heard a whispered voice call her name. "Sarah, are you awake?" Before she could answer, the small hand shook her insistently, and repeated, "Are you awake, Sister?"

Sarah stretched and turned toward the voice. The light on the kitchen stove was bright enough for Sarah to see that a small intruder had entered her room and left her bedroom door open. He was now standing beside her bed. "Yes, Joshua, I think I'm awake," she mumbled.

"I want to talk about what I did, but my feet are getting cold."

Sarah sighed deeply. "Do you want to crawl in with me?" she asked half-heartedly. Almost before she finished speaking, Joshua lifted the corner of the sheet and slid in beside his sister before she could change her mind. The warmth of the sheets was cozy and comforting to the boy.

"You can stay if you don't put your cold feet on me."

"I promise I'll keep my feet to myself."

"What's the matter? Did you have a bad dream?" asked Sarah, sharing her pillow.

Joshua thought for a moment. "No," he whispered, staring at the ceiling, "a nightmare didn't scare me. I was afraid you wouldn't love me anymore."

Sarah put her arm across her brother's chest and pulled him to her. "You know better than that, Joshua. Love is not something you can turn off and on like a light bulb." In the early morning gloom, Joshua could see his sister's face close to his. He turned toward her, needing to believe her words. "I'll always love you, no matter what," she whispered. "But," Sarah's voice grew louder, "I don't always have to love the things you do. Besides, someday I'll probably do something that disappoints you, but I expect you to keep right on loving me – no matter what!" Sarah reached over and tweaked her brother on the nose.

Joshua suddenly sat up. "Someday," he declared, "I'll be bigger than you and Amy. Then I'll be the BIG brother, and I'll protect both of you."

"That sounds good to me, brother. I feel safer already. Now, lie down and let's try to get a few winks before the sun comes up." Sarah leaned up on one elbow and looked at her brother's dark curls on her pillow. "Joshua, just one more thing, aren't you hungry? You didn't eat any supper, so you should be starving."

"I was hungry when I woke up a little while ago, but when I started downstairs, I looked on the bedside table, and there was a ham biscuit! So, I ate it. It was the best biscuit I ever ate." Joshua thought for a moment. "Sarah, do you think an angel left it there so I wouldn't starve?"

"Yes, brother, I'm sure it was an angel, disguised as a grandfather."

"Huh?"

"Shhhh. Let's get some more sleep before you-know-who tunes up to make his morning announcements."

Chapter 5

"Here, Frisky! Here, Frisky!" Joshua's voice rang out as he circled his grandparent's home for the third time.

"Boy, you could wake up the dead with all that yelling," called Clara, sticking her head out the back door.

"Frisky's gone, Clara. I can't find him anywhere." The sight of the small boy standing at the foot of the steps softened Clara's voice. Her irritation melted when she observed the worried look on the child's face.

"Now don't you worry one little bit," she replied sympathically. "It's for sure nobody gonna' steal a dog that looks like him – unless they want the world's ugliest mutt." A tear escaped from Joshua's eye. He quickly wiped it away, leaving a streak of dirt across one cheek. "He's probably off visiting and will be back before you know it."

Clara let the screen door slam, having no more time to concern herself with Frisky. A pot of steaming clam chowder simmered on the stove, and needed her attention. She picked up her wooden stirring spoon and gently lowered it into the pot of thick, bubbling chowder. As she stirred the creamy white potatoes, slivers of onion, and thick meaty chunks of fresh clams, she muttered to herself. "That sorry old dog better not be gone. That child's heart never will mend back right if something has happened to him." A delicious odor rose from the savory chowder, driving all thoughts of Frisky from Clara's mind. She tasted a spoonful of the delicious-looking mixture and rolled her eyes toward the ceiling. "Hum – hum," she murmured, a smile playing at the corner of her lips, "Old, Clara has done it again." All thoughts of Frisky's disappearance were erased from her mind.

When the family was seated for lunch, a bowl of steaming chowder and moist corn bread at each place, Joshua spoke, "Papa Tom, I can't find

Frisky anywhere. Before you finish saying the blessing, will you ask God to tell him to come home? He won't mind if you add it to the blessing, will He?"

Papa Tom looked down at his grandson. "Frisky has disappeared? When did you last see him?"

Joshua put down his spoon and replied, "He's been missing all day. When I went to bed last night, he was on the back porch where he always sleeps. This morning he was gone, and I can't find him anywhere."

"To answer your question, Joshua, no, God doesn't mind if we ask for more than the food being blessed. God loves for us to call on Him anytime."

"If Frisky still hasn't returned after lunch, why don't you put some notices in the stores and on telephone poles? Put his name, his description and your address and phone number on the paper. I'm sure someone will call," added his mother, looking sympathetic.

"Frisky gone," piped a small voice. Before anyone could think of a suitable answer, Amy's face puckered and a pitiful wail escaped from her lips. Everyone at the table rushed to comfort her, but it was no use. With all talking at once, Amy cried louder, determined not to be quieted by mere words. Now tears were streaming down her tiny face. "I want Frisky," she managed to say between bouts of crying. Joshua went to his little sister and patted her on the hand. "Don't worry, Amy. We'll find him soon. Maybe he'll come home tonight. If he doesn't, we'll pray for him and then I'm sure he'll come back."

While Clara cleared the dining room table, Joshua hunted for paper. "I have the very thing, honey," his grandmother told him. "It is paper I use for writing letters to my friends."

With paper and a pencil, Joshua began:
MY DOG FRISKY IS LOST. HE IS NOT REAL LITTLE OR REAL BIG. HE IS JUST RIGHT. HE DOESN'T HAVE MUCH HAIR BUT WHAT HE HAS IS SOFT AND CURLY. HE IS SORT OF YELLOW. PLEASE CALL 3-4-9-6 IF YOU KNOW WHERE MY DOG IS. THANKS. JOSHUA BOWERS

He took the finished paper to his grandmother. "Is this OK, Granny Jewel?" The grandmother looked it over and handed it back.

"Make several more copies and put them up in the stores. Someone is bound to call if they have seen your dog."

Joshua slumped in a near by chair. "All this writing is as bad as being in school." He looked hopefully at his grandmother. "It would be fun if we wrote the notices together, wouldn't it? I could say the words and you could write them down."

Granny Jewel looked at her grandson, her eyes narrowing. "Joshua, how badly do you want your dog?"

"More than anything I can think of right now," he answered.

"Then get busy. If he means a lot to you, you should be willing to work to get him back."

"Yes, ma'am."

Joshua finished several notices when Sarah stuck her head in the dining room. "What are you doing? You've been mighty quiet in here." She picked up a notice and read the message. "This ought to help get him back. Why don't we take them downtown now and post them in the stores."

Joshua brightened. "That's a good idea, Sarah. If we get them up fast enough, somebody might call tonight."

"Don't get your hopes up too much. Let's put one on the bulletin board at the store and see what happens. Papa Tom can suggest where we should put the others."

"Can we take Amy with us? If she cries for our lost dog, maybe people will feel sorry for us and help look for Frisky."

"Amy is taking her nap, and besides if she looked as pitiful as she did at lunch, everyone in town will be bringing stray dogs here."

Uncle Herb was stacking boxes of Rice Krispies when his niece and nephew came in. "Hi, kids. What brings you out on this hot afternoon?"

Joshua was telling his uncle of Frisky's disappearance when Kevin came from behind the meat counter, wiping his hands on his white apron. "You say your dog just up and disappeared? Do you think somebody stole him?"

Joshua, looking discouraged, said, "No, Kevin. Clara says he's too ugly for anybody to steal."

Kevin smiled. "It just might be that he's off somewhere courtin'."

Joshua looked up, hope written on his face. "He's off courtin'? What does that mean?"

"You know, he might be in love." Kevin looked over at Sarah and winked.

"Frisky don't love nobody but me," Joshua declared. By now Uncle Herb had moved down the aisle, so Sarah followed.

"I'm glad you stopped in, Sarah," he said. "Miriam wants to talk to you and Nancy about the wedding plans. The date has been changed to early

August. We'd like some time to go on a honeymoon and get settled in the apartment before she has to go back to school." Sarah glanced over and noted that Kevin and Joshua were posting the notice. Kevin had cleared all outdated ads from the bulletin board and had placed Joshua's in the middle where everyone coming in the store could not fail to see it.

Sarah started to ask her uncle how Miriam's father was getting along when she was interrupted by loud voices and shouting out on the street.

"What's going on, Uncle Herb?"

Herb Mitchell hurried to the door, with Sara close behind. "I don't know Sarah. I hope it's nothing too serious." They stood in the doorway and were soon joined by Kevin and Joshua.

"People are running by, but I can't tell……" Before Kevin could finish speaking, Papa Tom hurried in, letting the screen door slam behind him.

"Daddy, what's happening? Where's everyone going?"

Tom Mitchell was out of breath. All waited patiently while he mopped perspiration from his face. Finally, he took a deep breath and began, "There is an outer banks pony stranded in the mud across Taylor's Creek. It's the same place the dredge boat threw the sand when it deepened the channel last winter. It must have created several sink holes."

"Can you see him from Front Street?" asked Uncle Herb.

"No, not really," his father replied. "The word is, Miss Mildred Jones spotted him from her upstairs front porch. The mare was acting strange, so Miss Mildred got a pair of binoculars and looked more closely. She could see the foal trying to free himself. The more he struggled, the deeper he sank."

"What's going to happen now, Papa?" asked Sarah.

"Can we go see?" asked Joshua. "Everybody in town will be down there but us." Joshua's voice had risen to almost a shout.

"You and the kids go ahead, Daddy," said Herb. "Kevin and I will stay here and mind the store."

By now Joshua was pulling his grandfather along by the arm. "Hurry, Papa, hurry," he kept repeating.

Out on the sidewalk, they joined other people going in the same direction. As they hurried along, they noticed crowds of people standing in front of the post office. Some were standing on the porch and front steps, trying to get a better look. Sarah glanced at the large two-story houses along the street. Friends had gathered on all the upstairs porches, trying to see the foal. Tom Mitchell, his grandchildren in tow, made his way through the crowd and out on the Inlet Inn dock. There, tied to the pilings, was a large row boat with several men inside. They were rushing to get oarlocks in place, position oars and untangle lengths of rope.

"Hi, fellows," called Papa Tom, looking down into the boat. "Do you all need some help? What can I do?"

One of the men paused, "Well, Captain, we're waiting for Fred. He lives the closest, so he went home for more rope. How about if we shove off, and you bring him along in your boat when he gets here."

"You can count on me, John. I'll wait right here and row across as soon as he comes back."

The men looked relieved, since they were anxious to cast off. When they pushed off from the dock and began rowing with powerful strokes, a cheer was heard from the townspeople. Turning around, Sarah saw a tall man with broad shoulders push through the crowd.

"Wait," he yelled to the men in the boat. "Come back! I got the rope!"

Papa Tom grabbed his arm. "It's all right, Fred. You're going across with me. Let's get down to my boat and we'll catch up with them." He turned to his grandchildren, but before he could speak, Joshua yelled, "I'm coming, too. I won't take up much room, and you may need me."

"You're not going without me," declared Sarah, not sure they had even heard her.

The men had already broken free of the crowd, and were hurrying along the sidewalk. Sarah grabbed her brother by the hand and hurried behind them. She caught a glimpse of her friend Nancy in the crowd. "Hi, Nancy," she called. "I can't stop now. Call me later!" Sarah noticed Nancy had on a spotless white dress with starched ruffles. *Of course,* she thought, *this is the day Nancy's sewing circle meets.* She offered a prayer of thankfulness that she was not entangled in the group, *or* their thread.

When the children reached the dock where their grandfather's boat was tied, the men were already on board placing oarlocks in their holders, and pulling oars from under the seats. Just in time they scurried aboard and huddled in the bow of the boat. "Shove us off from the dock," barked their grandfather. Both children hurried to do as he ordered.

Fred sat in the stern seat, facing Papa Tom as he rowed the boat. After a few moments, Fred offered to help row the boat. "Most all the young men in town are at work," he said, "so, I guess it's up to us old fellers to do the job."

"And we can," replied Papa Tom, giving an extra strong pull on the oars.

Sarah and Joshua sat quietly, their eyes trained on the men ahead of them. They were already pulling their boat up on the shore and hurrying toward the mud flats where the foal was trapped. The mare was circling the area, knowing the danger of getting too close to a sink hole.

Sarah slowly became aware of how rapidly they were moving through the water. She glanced at her grandfather's back. His white shirt was plastered against his skin, soaked with perspiration. The oars were in perfect time. She watched in fascination as they were plunged into the water, drawn quickly along the boat, then up in the air, water dripping off the tips in a fine stream, then shoved forward and back into the water. It was a contrast to the many times she had been in the boat with her grandfather, when he playfully rowed along, laughing and talking.

A scraping sound on the bottom of the boat let all know they had reached the far shore. "Joshua, Sarah," barked Papa Tom, "the tide's going out. Anchor the boat out a-ways so we won't be aground when we start home."

"Aye, aye, sir," called Joshua, giving a salute.

"Oh, brother," muttered Sarah.

Following Fred, Papa Tom looked back once and yelled, "Watch where you step so you won't get cut on oyster shells, and *stay out of the way!*"

Sarah waited while Joshua waded out in water to his knees and secured the anchor in the sand. Overhead she could hear the cry of gulls and the gentle lapping of waves on the shore. As they walked toward the men she once more smelled the strong, pungent odor of the marshes. *It'll get a lot worse as the tide goes out,* she realized. From a short distance, Sarah and Joshua watched the men try in vain to rescue the foal from the gooey, sucking mud. One of the men from the other boat had successfully gotten a noose over its head and was pulling with all his might. "Hold up, men," shouted Fred. "You're going to pull his head off."

The mare, frantic with worry, was a hindrance. While they were working on a plan, she continually circled them and the foal, at times pawing the air in frustration. "Watch out for those hooves," cautioned Fred. "She doesn't know if we're friend or foe."

Sarah's attention was drawn to the foal. He now seemed exhausted, struggling less and less. At times he would lay his little head down in the mud and close his eyes. Tears filled her eyes and blurred her vision. "Hold on, little fellow," she whispered, "I know my grandfather will get you out somehow. I just know he will."

"Tom," one of the men said, waving his arms, "there is no other way except to pull him out. He's a tough little critter and it won't hurt him too much, maybe." The man looked doubtful.

"What if he breaks a leg as we are pulling him out?" argued Papa Tom.

"So, what are you going to do, wade in that sink hole and bring him out in your arms?" asked one of the men.

The man's question was met with silence. Papa Tom put his hands on his hips and looked at each man. "Yes," he said quietly, "that's exactly what I'm going to do."

He turned and walked toward the circle of dark oozing mud. Wading in slowly, his feet and legs were out of sight in a second. He spread his arms wide and eased over to the small animal, talking in a low, soothing voice. The mare had settled down and was not moving, but watching every move the human made. Occasionally, she would snort and show the whites of her eyes. When the foal looked up, he began struggling feebly, then once more lay still. Papa Tom, struggling through the ooze, reached him, plunged one arm under the soft mud and brought it around the foal's rump. The other arm he shoved under the baby's chest. With a mighty push, the foal's legs broke free. Another push, and he was able to get his legs on firm sand. The men surrounding the mud hole pulled him gently toward them so they could take the rope from around his neck.

"Oh, Joshua, isn't he cute? His mane and forelock are soft fuzz. I wish we could keep him!"

"Yeah, Sarah. We can drag him home, mud and all. What do you think Clara would say when we tell her he has to be fed from a bottle every few hours? Clara, you won't mind mixing up a batch of formula for the baby will you?" Joshua asked in a sweet voice.

"It was just a thought, brother."

Without warning, the foal lunged forward, circled the men and ran for his mother. Together they galloped across the sand, mud flying in all directions and soon disappeared in a group of low trees. From across the channel there rose a sound all could hear. Looking toward town, they heard cheers and saw people waving. The men waved back and started coiling up the rope.

"Uh, aren't you forgetting something, guys?" came a voice from the gooey mud.

The men looked at each. "Fred, did you hear something?" asked one.

Without smiling, Fred answered "No, it must have been the wind you heard. Now that the foal is safe, I'll get these kids across the channel and then help you secure your boat."

Without warning, Joshua flew at the three men. He pounded them with his fists and screamed, "You get my granddaddy out of the mud. You're not going to leave him over here!"

Not realizing how upset the boy was, the men continued teasing. "It's all right son, we'll come back tomorrow or the next day and get him. He'll be fine."

Joshua yanked the rope from Fred's huge hands and ran back to his grandfather who was struggling to free himself from the soft, black mud. He threw one end to his grandfather but it didn't reach. "Don't give up Papa! I'm going to rescue you! I just need a little more practice."

Before he could throw the rope again, large capable hands gently took the rope from Joshua. "Oh, all right, boy, if you insist! We'll get the old man out of the mud."

With little effort, the rope sailed through the air once more. Papa Tom grabbed it, and tied it around his chest. With the men pulling, he was able finally to step on firmer ground. When he was free of the rope, the men shook hands.

"That's some young'un you got there, Tom. I believe he was about to dive head first in the mud to save you." The men were smiling, and suddenly Joshua felt self conscious.

"Can we go home now, Papa Tom? I'll bet it's almost supper time."

All looked once more at the place where they had last seen the mare and foal. Both had disappeared from view. As they turned toward the boats, Fred commented, "That was a real brave thing you did, Tom. I hope you saved some of that bravery for when the missus sees what you've done to your nice clothes."

For the first time Papa Tom looked down. He was covered in soft, black mud which was rapidly drying, forming a crust on all his clothing. "Oh, boy, I'm liable to be in a lot of trouble," he said, smiling.

When they reached the rowboats, Fred decided to return with the other men. "I don't want to be on the shore if your wife is there to greet you," he laughed.

"I'm not scared," returned Papa Tom.

"Oh, sure," called one of the men.

All three waded out to the little row boat. With the outgoing tide, it was almost against the shore. "Hey, kids, what do you say we take a swim? I can get some of this mud off my clothes, and we can cool off in the water."

"All right!" agreed Joshua. He plunged in, followed by his grandfather. "Come on, Sarah. The water feels so good."

"Hmmm, no thanks. I'm not going to walk through town with my clothes dripping wet, my new sneakers going, 'squish-squash'. That would be the very time I'd see somebody important."

"I guess we're not very important, Joshua," whispered his grandfather.

"It's not that, Papa. Sarah isn't very much fun anymore. She's real serious about everything. Can't we do something to help her?"

"It's only going to get worse, lad. Wait until the boys start coming around."

"What boys?"

"You'll soon find out. Let's go home."

Papa Tom pulled in the anchor while Joshua climbed into the boat. "Why don't you take the middle seat, Son. It's time you had your first rowing lesson."

Joshua joyfully sat in the rowing seat, while his grandfather sat in the stern.

"I know how to row, I think. I've been watching other people do it and it doesn't look hard." He took an oar in each hand and waved them wildly in the air. With some instruction, he began to get the rhythm of rowing even though the boat mysteriously turned in lazy circles as they neared home.

"It's not as easy as it looks," admitted Joshua, still struggling with the oars. Sweat was running down his face, his tongue almost touching his nose.

"We'll never get home at this rate," observed Sarah.

"I'm not in any hurry to get home, honey."

Sarah laughed, "I know why! Your brand new sneakers from Upton's Department store are ruined! So are your clothes! What is Granny Jewel going to say?" Sarah's hands flew to her mouth. "What is *Clara* going to say?"

"Joshua, see if you can row a little slower," the grandfather instructed.

"I don't care what they say, Papa Tom!" said Sarah indignantly. "You were a hero today! Nobody else would have scooped that baby out of the mud and set him free. You're the best and bravest grandfather in the whole world!"

"Thanks, Sis." He settled back in the stern seat, his arms draped across the back of the boat. "You know I always did want to be a cowboy and work with wild horses."

"You mean like in the movies?" asked Joshua.

"Well, sort of. You can say the foal was wild, and someday he'll grow up and be a horse."

Joshua paused, oars in the air, "Gosh, Papa. You sure are good at bending the truth." Joshua's eyes shone with admiration.

"It's a special talent, son. One I have perfected over the years. Now, row us up to the dock, and let's go face the music."

Chapter Six

Sarah heard Nancy's voice on the other end of the telephone line. "Hi, Nancy. It's me."

"Hello, Sarah. What are you doing today?"

"Nancy, I wanted to tell you what happened yesterday." Sarah gently placed the heavy, black telephone on the hall floor and sat down beside it.

"Do you know if the baby horse is all right?"

"I think so. Someone called my grandfather early this morning and said they were seen at first light grazing along the edge of the marsh. Nancy, it was an exciting time, and I wish you could have been there."

"Oh, Sarah, I can't imagine anything more horrifying than crossing Taylor's Creek and getting all muddy."

I can imagine at least one thing more horrible, Sarah thought. A vision of girls in starched dresses, sitting in a parlor, embroidering dresser scarves and pillow cases swam before her eyes.

"It was strange," Sarah continued. "My grandfather was sure Granny Jewel would be angry for ruining his clothes, *and* a brand new pair of sneakers. He was so afraid she was going to fuss at him. Instead, when we got home she rushed out, gave him a big hug, and said, 'My hero!'"

"Oh, my," sighed Nancy, "That is so romantic."

"Nancy, do you think our husbands will be afraid of us?"

"Sarah, I've told you before, I'm never going to get married. I am dedicated to my music. It is my whole life." Sarah heard a loud sniff from the other end of the line. "I have no time for boys, or dating."

For a moment Sarah thought about Porter Mason, the red-haired boy from Ohio. "How about Porter Mason, the boy we met three summers ago?"

"Hummm, I might change my mind if he were here. He was *so* cute!"

For some unexplained reason, Sarah felt a rush of jealousy. As quickly as the feeling came, it disappeared. *Why should I care about some old boy who lives a million miles away and is too lazy to write?*

"Nancy, what I really called about is this. Last night my 'Almost Aunt Miriam' called. She wants us to come over to her apartment after lunch so we can talk about wedding plans."

"Oh, Sarah, that would be lovely!" breathed Nancy.

Two hours later the girls were walking down Craven Street. A cool breeze from the ocean, and giant elm trees overhead, kept the heat from being too unbearable.

"Sarah, don't you think it would be wonderful to have a cozy apartment all your own?" asked Nancy. "You could have darling ruffled curtains at every window, and soft, rag rugs on the floor. The sofa could be covered in flowered chintz and lots of soft pillows. You could have a kitten that would sit in your lap and purr while you listened to the radio."

"It does sound wonderful, Nancy. Maybe someday after college, we'll have a place just like that."

The girls walked along in silence for a few minutes. Sarah became aware of the tapping of her friend's shoes against the sidewalk. "Nancy," said Sarah, turning to her friend, "why did you wear a dress and Sunday shoes?"

Nancy looked horrified. "I wouldn't want Miss Thompson to think less of me by showing up in shorts and sneakers. I want to make a good impression."

"You've already done that in school this past year. She knows we're friends, so she asked especially for you to come today." Sarah was rewarded with a smile.

They reached the bottom of the outside stairway which led to the entrance of Miriam Thompson's apartment. An older couple living in the large old house had turned their upstairs into an apartment to supplement their retirement income.

"You go first, Sarah," whispered Nancy, who suddenly became self conscious.

"Why?"

"Well, because you're practically *family!*"

Quietly the girls mounted the stairs and tapped lightly on the outside door. Nancy moved closer to her friend. "Sarah," she whispered, "Straighten your collar and smooth your hair."

Sarah rolled her eyes, murmuring, "Oh, brother," but did as she was told.

The door opened and Miriam Thompson stood in the doorway smiling. She was wearing slacks and a shirt, her dark hair covered in a bright silk bandana. Nancy noted she was wearing scuffs and no make-up. All these things Nancy determined to remember so she might emulate her favorite teacher.

"Hi, Sarah. Hi, Nancy. Won't you come in?" With one hand on the doorknob, the teacher made a sweeping gesture with the other. "Welcome to my home. Please sit down." When all were seated, Miriam started the conversation. "What have you girls been doing since school closed?"

"I have been practicing at the piano, Miss Thompson. It requires several hours every day. Also, I try to do needlework each day," answered Nancy.

"Oh, what kind of needlework do you like?"

Nancy sat a little straighter, her feet crossed at the ankles. "I mostly embroider dresser scarves, napkins and pillow cases."

"Hmmm, that's very interesting, Nancy."

The teacher was rewarded with one of Nancy's spectacular smiles.

Oh, please don't ask me, prayed Sarah. *What would I tell her, that I spend a lot of time chasing my two-year old sister,* or, *I am helping my brother look for his dog,* or, *maybe I could tell about being a clerk in my grandpa's store? I could mention I feed my brother's crippled chicken on days when he forgets.*

"Girls, I'm going to fix each of us a glass of lemonade. I baked cookies this morning, and we can see how they taste. I need a lot of practice in the kitchen because I don't want Herb to starve after we get married."

At the mention of Sarah's uncle, Miriam's face glowed, color coming to her cheeks.. *Wow,* thought Sarah, *she really loves my uncle a lot. I guess that's a good thing since they're getting married.*

She looked at her friend to see if she had noticed, but Nancy was too busy taking in every detail of the room. The landlady, 'Miss Dee' had furnished the tiny apartment with lovely old pieces of furniture. There were marble-topped tables and dressers, a sofa and two chairs covered in gay, floral chintz fabric. The walls, a soft green, were covered with oil paintings in wide, gilt frames. The shiny, dark floors had an occasional scatter rug.

Miriam Thompson stuck her head around the kitchen door. "Would it be better if we sat in the kitchen? That way we can discuss wedding plans, and I can take notes." The girls moved to the kitchen, where Nancy was impressed with the cheerful appearance of the little room.

"Hmmm, this room smells delicious," offered Sarah.

"It's from the cookies I baked. The recipe was one my mother always used when we were growing up."

"You'll have to talk to Clara," suggested Sarah. "She has a lot of good recipes she *might* share. Don't be surprised if there are some she keeps a deep, dark secret. Granny Jewel is a pretty good cook, but I don't think Clara wants her messing up the kitchen and getting in her way."

"That's something I'm going to have to get used to. Up north, a hired servant takes orders from the lady of the house."

Sarah looked confused. "I guess you could say Clara takes orders.... No, that's not right. Clara and Granny Jewel work things out together. If my grandmother is having a party, or a luncheon, she is the commander-in-chief, and everybody rushes to obey her. I guess you'd say Clara is like family. We all love her dearly, and she loves us with the fierceness of a mountain lion."

"This is very interesting, Sarah. Tell me more."

Sarah grinned and bit into a sugar cookie. "Clara and Papa Tom keep a feud going all the time. He loves to tease her, and when she's had enough, she threatens him with her wooden stirring spoon. My granddaddy might be getting old, but he sure moves fast when Clara waves her spoon around and comes after him."

"Maybe he doesn't really like her."

"Oh, Miss Thompson, Papa Tom loves Clara almost as much as he loves Granny Jewel! And, she loves him, too, but she'll never admit it — except maybe on her death bed. Now, don't ever let on that I told you this, but Papa Tom sent her twin boys to college. They're about Uncle Herb's age, so he had three in college at one time. He would have had four, but my mama met my daddy, and she lost all interest in getting an education."

"Sarah, you can't keep on calling me Miss Thompson. We have to decide what you can call me before the wedding." Miriam tapped her fingernail on the side of her now empty lemonade glass. "Why don't you call me Miriam, because 'Miss Thompson' sounds so formal."

Sarah looked uncomfortable. "Would it be all right if I called you 'Miss Miriam,' until after the wedding? Most grown ups are called by their first names, especially in a small town."

"That's fine with me," replied Miriam. "You know, girls, I'm going to love living in the South."

"Miss Miriam," began Nancy, "perhaps we should discuss wedding plans."

"You're absolutely right, Nancy, but you'll have to call me Miss Thompson. After all, I can't have my star pupil calling me by my first name."

"Yes, Ma'am."

Miriam removed the glasses and plate of cookies from the table, wiping it dry from condensation circles and cookie crumbs. Armed with pencil and a writing tablet, she returned to her chair. "While Dad was in the hospital Mom and I had a brief opportunity to do some shopping. We ordered dresses for the bridesmaids and the maid of honor. The bridesmaids' dresses are made of the most beautiful rayon and satin fabric. They are lavender with tiny pink rosebuds. The maid of honor will wear a dress that is pink, with lavender rosebuds." Sarah was faintly disappointed that her dress would not be pink. *Oh well,* she thought, *lavender is first cousin to pink.*

"What do the dresses look like, Miss Thompson?"

Miriam smiled and began sketching the dresses on paper. "The neckline will be round with a deep ruffle. There are tiny cap sleeves, and a three-tiered skirt of wide ruffles." She looked at the girls, her eyes shining. "They are very beautiful, something a princess might wear."

"Who are the bridesmaids?" asked Nancy.

"Only two of my sisters and Sarah. My oldest sister is going to have a baby in August, so she can't travel. My sisters' dresses will be picked up at the store in Binghamton, but Sarah's will be mailed to Beaufort so she can try it on before the wedding and see if it needs to be altered."

"If the dress needs anything, Granny Jewel can fix it. She can make dresses or alter them," added Sarah.

"I must have a new dress, too, if I am to preside over the punch bowl," added Nancy.

"You have a new white dress, Nancy. Can't you wear it?"

"Only the bride is supposed to wear white at a wedding. After all, it's her special day."

Sarah leaned toward her friend, "Nancy," she asked, "how do you know so much stuff about what to do, and what not to do?"

"Well," sniffed Nancy, "I read books on etiquette I check out from the library."

"Oh."

"Uh, girls," asked Miriam, looking from one to the other, "Can you keep a secret?" Both stared mutely, nodding their heads in unison. "I brought the wedding dress back with me."

"Oh," exclaimed Nancy.

"Oh," exclaimed Sarah.

"May we see it?" both asked in unison.

"Yes, you may, but no one else! I want it to be a surprise to everyone on my wedding day. Herb didn't ask what was in the box when we packed the car to come back, and I'm so glad he didn't." Miriam stood. "If you're finished, we can go into the bedroom and I'll lay the dress out on the bed." She turned around and smiled. "Remember, this is our deep, dark secret."

The girls nodded solemnly, each vowing silently that not the tiniest detail of the gown would be disclosed. Miriam Thompson had earned the girls' unfailing loyalty and adoration.

"I know it's all wrinkled, but you can tell what it will look like once it is pressed." From under the bed, Miriam slid a large, flat cardboard box and carefully placed it on the bed. Nancy forgot to see how the bedroom was decorated, so intent was her concentration.

Without speaking, Miriam slowly removed the lid. There were layers upon layers of soft tissue which she carefully folded back. Both girls sighed when they saw the shimmering, white satin gown inside. Miriam lifted the dress from the box and spread it across the bed. The bodice was encrusted in lace and seed pearls with long tapered sleeves. The rest of the gown and the chapel train were plain white satin.

"What do you think, girls?" asked Miriam, smiling.

"It's the most beautiful gown I have ever seen," breathed Nancy.

"It's the most beautiful *bridal* gown I've ever seen," added Sarah, remembering the pink dress her grandmother had made. It had been three years ago, but Sara knew every detail of the dress, and where it still hung in her closet. It would always be the most beautiful gown ever.

"Why don't I slip it on while you're here? It's the gown my sister wore, and when dad saw the bill, he announced all his daughters would have to wear it. Mom said it would be the first wedding gown in history that was thread-bare from so many wearings."

"Do you need any help getting it over your head?" asked Sarah.

"My hair is in curlers under this bandana, but I don't think I will have any trouble."

Minutes later, an anguished cry could be heard from the bedroom. Sarah and Nancy, sitting in the living room, jumped to their feet.

"Girls, can you come here a minute?" Both were in the doorway before Miriam finished speaking.

Sarah's first impression was that her 'almost aunt' was wearing a shapeless, white bathrobe. Looking more closely, she saw that the lovely gown she wore was several sizes too big for the dainty woman.

"I knew Sis was bigger than I, but not that much bigger! I suppose I have lost weight this year since I've had to eat my own cooking." Miriam's attempt at humor made Sarah feel heartbroken for the lovely woman. "What am I going to do?" asked Miriam, almost in tears "I can't fit it to myself, and Mom isn't coming until a week before the wedding. I don't want to wait that long to be fitted."

"Miriam," said Sarah, forgetting to put the 'miss' in front of her name, "I know just the person who can fit the dress, and do anything else it might need."

"Who, Sarah?"

"Granny Jewel."

"I wanted the dress to be a surprise to everyone, especially Herb's family," replied Miriam.

"The way it looks now will be a surprise to the whole town. Sarah's granny can keep a secret better than anyone. Not even her cousins the Baylor ladies will be able to pry a single detail of the dress from her," said Nancy.

"Sarah," Miriam whispered to her niece-to-be, "call Mrs. Mitchell and tell her what has happened. Ask if she has time to come over and see what needs to be done."

Sarah rushed to the phone on the little table next to the sofa. "Mitchell residence," came Clara's familiar voice.

"Clara, it's me."

"I know it's you, Child. I know your voice."

"Thanks, Clara. Is Granny Jewel there?"

"You sound upset. Are you all right?"

"Yes, Clara, I'm fine, but I need to talk to Granny Jewel."

"She's in the backyard watering the garden. We haven't had any rain, you know." Clara paused and then asked, "Do you want me to give her a message?"

"Thanks, Clara, but I need to talk to her."

"Are you in trouble, Child?"

"No, I'm fine."

"She's coming in the back door now," stated Clara, seeming reluctant to pass the telephone to her employer.

"Hello?"

"Granny Jewel," whispered Sarah. "Can you come over to Miriam's apartment? She tried on her wedding gown, and there is an emergency. Oh, and this is a deep, dark secret. She doesn't want anyone to see her dress until the wedding."

"I understand. I'll be right there."

"Oh, and bring plenty of straight pins."

Jewel Mitchell hung up and turned to go upstairs. She noticed Clara standing in the hall doorway, arms across her chest, lips pushed out. "I don't know what's going on, Clara. I'll tell you when I can."

"Humph," said Clara.

Granny Jewel stepped quickly inside the tiny apartment, saw the problem, and declared, "Miriam, take the dress off, box it up and bring it over to the house. I'll be upstairs in my bedroom getting things ready. A few pins won't take care of this problem."

All three hurried along the sidewalk, Miriam clutching the box holding the gown. "Now don't worry, Miss Miriam, like I said before, my granny can fix anything with a needle and thread."

"I hope you're right, Sarah. From the looks of the dress, there's a lot of fixing to be done."

Clara held the screen door for them as they came up the steps. "I guess you ladies got something mighty mysterious going on. I'll bet it has to do with that box you're carrying, hmmm?"

"Yes, Clara," answered Sarah in an abstract way. "Is Granny Jewel upstairs?"

"Yes, your granny is upstairs, with her bedroom door closed."

"I don't have to go in the kitchen just yet, if you need me," called Clara as the girls disappeared around the steps leading to the upstairs hall. Sarah tapped lightly on her grandmother's bedroom door.

"Come in," Granny Jewel called from inside. Sarah slowly opened the door, revealing her grandmother in bare feet, standing in the middle of a large white sheet.

"Mrs. Mitchell, I know this is a terrible imposition, but it looks like we have an emergency," said Miriam, looking apologetic.

The older woman glided across the white cloth and took her soon-to-be daughter-in-law in her arms. "Now, don't you be upset. Between the four of us, we can take care of this problem. Did you bring a petticoat and high heel shoes?"

"No, I never thought of that."

"No worry. You can use one of my slips, and a pair of my shoes. We need to make sure the hem is the right length while you have the dress on." Quickly Miriam slipped on high-heeled shoes and a petticoat. All helped lower the dress over Miriam's head. "Girls, you can help by buttoning the dress."

Sarah and Nancy were eager to help, and began fastening the many tiny satin buttons that reached from the neckline to below the waist. When they finished, they stepped aside, while Granny Jewel, hands on hips, slowly surveyed the scene. Before her stood the lovely girl who would soon be her son's wife. Her delicate figure lost in the heavy folds of a dress many sizes too large. "Girls, please call Clara. I want her opinion on how to go about reconstructing the bodice."

Sarah opened the bedroom door and called over the banister. From the bottom of the stairs, Clara looking up, said, "I am *very* busy, but I'll try to find a few minutes."

Clara was up the stairs in a flash. "Phew, child," she remarked from the doorway, "whose dress do you have on?"

"Oh, Clara, that's a long story..."

"We don't have time for any stories now. It looks like there's work to be done," declared Clara. Both women were now barefoot as they circled the edge of the sheet. Not speaking to anyone in particular, the older women began talking. Sarah and Nancy were forgotten.

"It has to be nipped in a knuckle's width in every seam," Granny Jewel said to Clara, while Miriam held out her arms.

"The shoulders need to be raised at least one inch," stated Clara, holding the dress up at the shoulders. "We can't touch the back seam, there are too many buttons."

"Oh, oh, Clara, look at the length of the sleeves! They're at least two inches too long." The beautifully tapered sleeves with a myriad of tiny satin buttons were made for a person with much longer arms.

"Oh, lordy, what can we do?"

Sarah watched as her grandmother stood back, eyes half closed, lips in a thin line. With one hand on her hip, she tapped her chin with a finger from the other hand. *Oh, brother,* thought Sarah. *My granny's coming up with a plan. Everybody better hold on to their hat!*

They were interrupted by a voice from downstairs. "Where is everybody?

Mama, are you upstairs?" Sarah hurried out in the hall and leaned over the banister rail.

"Hi, Mama. We're up here." Peggy's feet could be heard hurrying up the steps and in the hall.

"Hi, everybody...." Her voice trailed off as she surveyed the scene. The bride-to-be was standing in the middle of a sheet, the heavy satin dress hanging in folds from her shoulders. The brightly colored bandana Miriam had placed around her head hours ago had loosened and drooped on one side. Peggy noticed her large, dark eyes were filled with tears. Quickly she placed Amy in a chair, tiptoed across the sheet and hugged the weary girl.

"Now don't you worry, my soon-to-be sister. Whatever is wrong, Mama and Clara can fix it better than new."

Miriam gave her a grateful look. "Everyone is being so helpful. I never realized the gown was too big until today."

Peggy stood back. "It'll look great as soon as it is taken up on the sides, on the shoulders, the sleeves are shortened, and the front is hemmed."

"Darling Daughter," said Granny Jewel, "I think you're right. Now, I imagine our bride-to-be is growing weary and needs to get the dress off. Why don't we all enjoy a glass of lemonade and some of Clara's sugar cookies. We can plan how to attack the dress over refreshments."

When all were seated on the front porch, Clara appeared with tall glasses of iced lemonade and a large platter of cookies. "Now don't you go and spoil your appetite for supper. I'm fixin' to go in the kitchen and fry up some chicken, stew a pot of squash, boil some potatoes and slice some tomatoes and cucumbers I got from the garden."

"Thank you, Clara, for all your help today," said Miriam.

"Law, Child. That wasn't anything. Wait till it gets closer to time for the wedding, then you'll see old Clara get in high gear."

"Clara, do we have enough for Herb and Miriam to join us?"

"You know I always fix enough for two families."

"Good," declared Granny Jewel. "Then it's settled. Sarah, go call the store and tell Herb to be here promptly at six o'clock."

Miriam' eyes widened. "Oh, no!" Her hands flew to her head. "He can't see me with my hair in bobby pins!" I have to run back to the apartment and get ready."

"Finish your lemonade, Miriam, honey. It won't take you many minutes to look beautiful."

When Sarah went inside to call her uncle, Miriam added, "Sarah, ask him to stop by the apartment and we'll walk over together."

From the porch, Granny Jewel and Peggy watched Miriam's retreating figure. For a few minutes neither spoke. Finally, Peggy asked, "What do you think, Mama? Will she make Herb a good wife?"

"I can't answer that, honey. Only time will tell. She seems to love Herb, and he seems devoted to her. They go to church together every Sunday and she talks of joining the Episcopal Church. I just hope she'll be happy living in the south. It's a different lifestyle from what she's used to."

"Do you think they'll want children someday?"

"I hope they'll wait awhile and enjoy being together. They could travel and someday build a home...."

"What's this? Is my wife planning her son's life? Be sure and let them know what you've decided."

Both looked up and saw Papa Tom sticking his head around the screen door. "Oh, Tom, be serious! It doesn't hurt a bit to help guide your children along the path of life."

Tom Mitchell joined his wife and daughter. "Honey, we didn't want any interference when we were starting out. They won't want any either."

"Mama, a few years ago I guess James and I messed up your well-laid plans for my future."

"Things worked out for the best. We love James like a son, and you have given us three lovely grandchildren."

"Speaking of grandchildren, where is Joshua?" asked Papa Tom.

"He's playing with Billy. I'd better call him home since supper is almost ready," said his mother.

"I hope I get a drumstick," announced Joshua, watching the platter of crisp, fried chicken being passed around the table. He had hurried home and washed up after his mother called knowing Clara's fried chicken was on the menu that evening.

"Me, too!" agreed Amy. "I want a drumstick."

"Humph," snorted Clara, "somebody's gonna' have to invent a chicken with four legs." Room had been made at the table for two guests. This was not a hardship, because the family was accustomed to sitting closer if someone appeared unexpectedly.

"Thank you for having me over," spoke Miriam. "I feel I'm practically one of the family already." She smiled at the others, her eyes lingering on Herb.

"You'll be our newest daughter, Miriam," said Papa Tom. "We love you already and gladly welcome you into the family," declared Papa Tom. "However, you'll have to gain Clara's approval. She has the last word on who is accepted and who is rejected."

"If Clara had anything to do with who goes and who stays, old man, your suitcase would have been packed long ago," rang a voice from the kitchen.

Sarah looked quickly at Miriam. She wore an alarmed expression. "Remember what I told you, Miss Miriam," whispered Sarah. "Don't be shocked at anything those two say."

"It's because of my sweet disposition and forgiving nature, that I let you stay," said Clara from the doorway. "Now, you better stop your teasing, or I'm gonna call the Inlet Inn and see if they have a spare room for rent."

Papa Tom looked at his wife, wearing an expression of fear. "Honey, she can't do that, can she? You wouldn't let Clara put me out on the cold, dark street, would you?"

"Hmmm, I'm thinking," murmured Granny Jewel. "It's neither cold nor dark, so..."

Amy stopped gnawing on her drumstick and let out a wail. "I don't want Papa to go away." Tears mingled with grease spots on her cheeks.

The grandmother reached over and patted Amy on the hand. "Don't worry, darling. Your Papa isn't going anywhere." She cut her eye at her husband and said, "Not tonight, anyway."

Chapter 7

"I need to speak to Joshua Bowers," a tiny voice spoke over the telephone. The soft child-like voice brought a smile to Sarah's lips.

"Who may I say is calling, please," answered Sarah, trying to sound like her father's secretary at Bower's Chemical Company in Raleigh.

"My name is Marie, Marie Wallace," she replied nervously.

Still in a playful mood, Sarah inquired , "May I ask the nature of your business with Mr. Bowers?"

"Yes, Ma'am. I think his dog is at my house."

"Oh, my gosh!" All pretense of being an executive secretary vanished. "Please hold on while I find him," she said quickly. "Joshua," she called, hurrying through the house. Again she called her brother's name when she stepped out on the back porch.

"Here I am, Sarah," he called. "I'm trying to teach Little Chick some tricks."

"You need to put him back in his pen and come answer the phone."

"Me?"

"Yeah. It's a girl who thinks she knows where Frisky is." Joshua thrust Little Chick in Sarah's hands and ran to the house, letting the screen door slam behind him.

"Hello," he said breathlessly. "Who is this and do you know where my dog is?"

"This is Marie Wallace. I think your dog is in my yard. He took up here about a week ago, and won't leave. If he's yours, I wish you'd come and get him. He wants to be with my dog, and we don't want her to have a mess of puppies, especially if they're going to look like him."

"There's nothing wrong with the way my dog looks," replied Joshua defensively.

"Oh, there's nothing wrong with him, he just isn't a cocker spaniel. Our dog is pure bred, and we don't want her to have puppies by any other kind of dog. Uh, what breed is your dog?"

"Frisky is a very rare dog. There isn't another one like him anywhere," explained Joshua. "He's sort of the best of lots of breeds."

"Oh," Marie replied.

"Tell me where you live, and I'll come see if it's my dog." Marie gave Joshua her address and hung up.

"Mama," yelled Joshua. His mother's head appeared over the banister.

"What's wrong, son?"

"I think Frisky's been found, but I have to go get him. Can you come with me? I'm not sure where Moore Street is."

"Amy and I are going visiting. Ask Sarah. She may not be too busy."

Joshua headed in the direction of his sister's room. He tapped on the door and whispered, "Sarah, are you in there?"

"Yes, Joshua."

"Can I come in?"

"I'm busy writing letters and don't need to be disturbed," came her muffled voice. Joshua cracked the door a tiny bit.

"Is your hand getting tired? Maybe you need a little rest. Everybody says fresh air is good for you and maybe we could go get some." He eased the door open another inch.

Sarah looked up from the desk Granny Jewel had found for her in the attic the summer before. "Joshua, what are you up to? I know you're not the least bit concerned about my health."

"Sarah," her brother said easing into the room, "would you walk with me over to Moore Street to find Frisky? Marie Wallace says she thinks the dog that's been staying in her yard is ours. He must be lost and can't find his way home."

"Sure, little brother. I'll go with you." Sarah looked at Joshua without smiling. "Don't get your hopes up. The dog might not be yours, and I don't want you to be disappointed."

The boy sat down in the chair covered in soft pink flowered material. A few minutes later Sarah had made no move to get up. "Sarah, do you know where Moore Street is?"

"Hmmm…. Yes, I know where Moore Street is," answered his sister, concentrating on her correspondence.

Several minutes passed, and the brother asked, "Do you think there's a chance you might forget if we don't hurry?"

"Not a chance," Sarah replied, not turning around.

"We'll need to be back before dark."

"Joshua, it's the middle of the day."

The boy emitted a deep sigh and slumped over. His forlorn appearance was a contrast to the perky, pink flowers blooming all around him in the chair's slipcover. When waiting one more minute would have been too much, his big sister mercifully stood, closed her box of stationary and turned around, hands on hips. "Ok, I'm ready to go. Let's go search for your lost dog."

Joshua leaped to his feet and reached the door before Sarah could run a comb through her hair. "Clara," she said, as they walked through the kitchen, "We're going to look for Frisky. Joshua thinks maybe he is over on Moore Street."

"I hope you find him," she replied, peeling potatoes. "I'm getting mighty tired of praying every night for that sorry excuse to come home."

Joshua took Clara's hand in his. "Did you really pray for Frisky, Clara? I thought you didn't like him."

"I'm praying for him to come home so someday you can be famous for having the world's sorriest old dog, fleas and all."

Joshua squeezed her hand. "Thanks, Clara. I knew you were beginning to love him."

"Miss Nettie Blackwell lives on Moore Street," Sarah told her brother as they walked along. "Maybe we'll get a chance to say hello." In the distance they could hear the wail of the drawbridge siren. "Boy, the bridge tender stays busy in the summer time with so many boats going through the draw," observed Sarah. Joshua didn't comment, being so intent on maybe seeing his dog again.

"You know how Daddy goes on business trips sometimes and we can't come along because there's no time for fun? Well, Sarah, this is a business trip. We have to get Frisky, so there's no time for talk."

"Hmmm, Miss Nettie always has a cold Coca-Cola and a batch of just-baked cookies for anyone who might stop in."

Joshua thought for a moment. "Maybe we could anchor Frisky to the porch and stop for a short visit."

"I thought you might see it that way, little brother."

When they reached 104 Moore Street, there was no dog in the yard. "Go knock on the front door and see if Marie is home."

"Why can't you do it, Sarah? You're older."

Sarah rolled her eyes. "It's your dog."

Joshua climbed the front steps and knocked. The wooden door was open, and Joshua peered through the screen door. He heard someone in the back of the house, and knocked louder. "Come in," a voice shouted. He heard footsteps in the hall, so he stood back from the door. A young girl near Joshua's size appeared in the doorway.

"Are you Joshua?" she asked, smiling.

"Yeah, I've come for my dog. Is he still here?"

Marie opened the door and stepped out on the porch. She was close to Joshua's height, her skin tanned from the summer sun. Marie's dark hair was pulled back in long, thin braids which matched big, dark brown eyes.

"I'm glad you're here. That little dog lies curled up by our gate day and night. I feel sorry for him because he looks so lost and lonely." Joshua nodded, remembering the summer he and Papa Tom found Frisky. They had gone clamming and returned home with a stray dog.

Sarah walked up. "Hi, I'm Sarah. Are you Marie?"

The girl smiled. "Yep, I'm Marie. Come around back and I'll show you the dog." Joshua hurried down the driveway, anxious to see if the dog was his. He was the first to see the familiar dark yellow coat curled in a tight knot.

"Frisky!" he called, clapping his hands. Immediately the ball of fur sprang up and leapt into the boy's out spread arms. Joshua lost his balance and sat down soundly on the ground, laughing while Frisky licked his face.

Sarah turned to Marie. "Maybe he didn't know the way home, and that's why he stayed here."

"Oh, no, honey," came a voice from behind. "Your dog is in love with Buff." Sarah turned to see a woman coming toward them.

"Mama, this is Sarah and that's Joshua. They've come for their dog."

The mother put her hands in the pockets of her apron. "Why don't you come in and have a glass of cold water? It's mighty hot out here today."

Sarah noted Mrs. Wallace was very thin, and spoke without enthusiasm. Her hair didn't look as if it had been combed since early morning. *Gosh,* she thought, *she must be about Mama's age, but looks ten years older..*

Joshua held tightly to Frisky's collar and answered, "Thanks, but we'd better get on home. I don't want to lose my dog again."

Mrs. Wallace smiled weakly, "Joshua, you don't need to worry about losing Frisky. I think he's glued to that spot." The four hurried through the gate, leaving the forlorn little dog sitting on the outside. A mournful howl followed them as they disappeared inside the house. Joshua looked back once and saw his dog's black nose squeezed through the fence palings.

"We can't stay long, Ma'am. It sounds like my dog is about to die of a broken heart."

Sitting down, Sarah looked about the kitchen. The walls and counter tops shone, but had a shabby, tired look. Linoleum on the floor was so worn in places you could no longer distinguish the flowered pattern. A hole had been worn in front of the sink and cook stove. Floor boards beneath could easily be seen. A curtain on the window over the sink reflected the weary droop of the mother's shoulders. Mrs. Wallace poured ice water from a pitcher in the refrigerator. Each was given a gaily decorated jelly glass painted with fruit patterns.

"My mama collects jelly glasses," offered Joshua, slowly sipping his drink.

Sarah smiled, "One company had a series of glasses with different cowboys. Joshua wanted the one that had Gene Autry, but the jelly was awful! Mama warned him, but he talked her into buying the apricot jam anyway. I thought he would choke trying to eat it, so he could have the glass. Mama wouldn't let him throw out the jam. She said that was wasteful."

Joshua put his hands around his neck and rolled his eyes. "Yuck! I thought I had been poisoned! My daddy took one sniff and said it smelled a lot like his shaving soap." He looked over at his big sister and smiled. "Sarah helped me. She ate some on toast. She always helps me when I need her." His big sister returned his smile.

Sarah heard a noise in the next room. She looked over her shoulder as a cream-colored cocker spaniel appeared in the doorway. Her long fur hung in a mass of curls. They even seemed to sprout from the top of her head. She studied the strangers with big brown eyes.

"Oh-h-h," crooned Sarah, sliding to her knees. "You must be Buff." At the sound of her name the dog came eagerly, her tiny stump of a tail wagging happily. "She's *so* soft!" Sarah ran her hands down the dog's back and patted her head. Buff immediately flopped down and waited for Sarah to scratch her stomach. "I don't blame Frisky for being in love with you. You remind me of a cream puff."

"She is pretty," agreed Joshua, helping Sarah pat the dog. "But, she's no prettier than Frisky. In fact," he decided, "they look alike in a lot of ways."

"Joshua, they both have four legs, and that's where the similarity ends."

"Buff will be your friend for life with that much attention," said Mrs. Wallace. "Do you live in Beaufort? I don't think I've ever seen you before."

"No Ma'am. We're staying with our grandparents and are only here during the summer. Our mother and little sister are here, too. Daddy always comes for a week around the Fourth of July."

"Who are your grandparents? Maybe I know them."

"Tom and Jewel Mitchell. They own Mitchell's Grocery."

"Oh," she replied without enthusiasm. "We've only been living in Beaufort since the war. My husband was in the Marine Corps and when he got out, we decided to move here. We didn't want to go back home – too many sad memories." The mother lit a cigarette, inhaled deeply, and stared at the table. It was as if she had forgotten the children were present. Joshua and Sarah watched fascinated, as the smoke was carried across the room on the gentle breeze coming in the kitchen window.

Feeling uncomfortable, Sarah gave Buff another pat on the head. "We should be leaving now. Thank you for the cold water, Mrs. Wallace." When there was no response, she turned to the girl. "Thank you for calling us, Marie. Finding Frisky is the answer to a prayer."

"A lot of prayers," added Joshua.

"I'm glad He answers somebody's prayers," mumbled Mrs. Wallace. She rose slowly, walked to the door and held it open. "Why don't you come back soon? Maybe Marie could go see you sometime. She needs to be around happy people and hear laughter."

"What was that all about, do you suppose?" asked Sarah once they were out on the sidewalk.

"I don't know. I just know I got my dog back and that makes me happy."

"What a treat!" rang a soft musical voice. Both looked up in time to see Miss Nettie Blackwell smiling at them from her front porch. "It's Sarah and Joshua Bowers if my memory serves me right. Come up on the porch and cool off for a minute. I declare it seems to get hotter every summer. And it appears you two are getting taller every summer." she added.

"It's nice to see you again, Miss Nettie," said Sarah, shaking hands.

"And who might this be?" the lady asked, looking down.

"This is my beloved dog, Frisky."

"Beloved dog," repeated Sarah, rolling her eyes. *Where did he come up with that?* she wondered.

"He looks to be a fine dog, Joshua," said Miss Nettie, watching her four-legged visitor scratch a flea. "Is he a special breed?"

"Well, yes Ma'am. He's the best of several special breeds. Or, maybe a *lot* of special breeds."

"He looks awfully thirsty to me. Why don't we bring Frisky a bowl of cool water, and while he is drinking, we can have a Coca-Cola. I just happen to have a batch of cookies fresh from the oven. Maybe you could help me eat a few." Miss Nettie gave Joshua a sly smile.

"Yes, Ma'am, Miss Nettie. We'd love to help you with those cookies," replied the boy. "I believe I can smell them all the way out here."

Miss Nettie stood. "You all sit right here and rest while I prepare a tray of refreshments."

When the woman disappeared, Sarah turned to her brother. "Where did you get that 'beloved' business?"

"I heard a man on the radio a few days ago. He was singing about his beloved, and how much he missed her. It made me think about how much I missed Frisky, and I got real sad."

"Well, cheer up, brother. Frisky is back."

"Here we are," stated Miss Nettie, pushing the screen door open with her arm. She was balancing a tray with three bottles of Coca-Cola, a plate heaped with warm cookies and a saucer of cool water.

When all were settled, she asked, "Have you been here long? During the summer I seldom get to see your grandmother and catch up on the news."

"We've been here almost three weeks. One week I worked in the store for Uncle Herb. He had to take Miriam to New York to see her father."

"How is he doing?"

"He seems to be getting along all right. He's saving his strength for the trip down here and the wedding." Sarah didn't mind answering Miss Nettie's questions. Somehow it was different from being interrogated by Nancy's mother, Miss Cora. She could fire questions faster than you could answer. Sarah studied the woman over her bottle of soda. "You look different, Miss Nettie."

"I'm a year older, for one thing, and I'm wearing my hair shorter. Emily at the Duchess insists I get a cold wave to give my hair more body. When I was young my hair was long and thick. I could put it up in a bun and forget it."

"How is Emily? She put a cold wave in my hair last summer, and I suppose she'll fix it for Uncle Herb's wedding. She looks like a movie star when she puts her hair up and all those blonde curls bounce around on the top of her head."

"Emily won't be fixing your hair for the wedding."

"Why, Miss Nettie?"

The older woman sighed. "Soon after Christmas Emily packed her suitcase, and hopped on the bus. Everybody at the beauty parlor says she met someone and fell in love. When he left town, so did Emily. I don't mean to gossip, but I understand her parents begged her not to go, but she wouldn't listen."

Miss Nettie took another sip from her bottle of soda and shook her head. "Everyone thinks she'll come home, sadder but wiser." Miss Nettie paused. "I hope she has found her true love and they have a happy life."

Not able to listen to another word about hair-dos and true love, Joshua spoke. "We best be going Sarah. Frisky is getting restless and wants to get home."

Frisky, stretched out fast asleep, seemed perfectly content. However, Sarah knew her brother wouldn't be physically able to sit still any longer. Thanking Miss Nettie for refreshments, and promising to visit again soon, the children took their leave.

When they reached their grandparents' home, Sarah stood as Joshua and Frisky plunged into the house. "He's back, everybody! Frisky's back!"

The family, having lunch, greeted the little dog with open arms, Frisky barking all the while. "Here Frisky! Here Frisky!" called Amy, clapping her hands.

"Put him on the back porch, Joshua, wash your hands and come eat your lunch," ordered Papa Tom.

Clara, bringing two glasses of iced tea remarked, "You would think it was a scene from the movie, "Lassie, Come Home.""

Joshua took a swallow of the cold liquid. "It was just like Kevin said down at the store. Frisky's in love and that's why he left home. You should see his girl- friend. She's the most beautiful girl dog I have ever seen."

Clara, clearing the lunch plates, added, "She might be pretty, but she's got poor taste in four-legged men."

Sarah and Joshua related the morning's events while the rest of the family enjoyed dessert. "Granny Jewel, do you know Mrs. Wallace?"

The grandmother was silent for a moment. "No, Sarah, I don't believe I've ever met her."

"I think she has been in the store, and now that you mention it, she did seem sad and distant," added her grandfather.

"Hmmm," murmured the Papa Tom. "I'll call Nettie, and we'll look into this. Perhaps there's something we can do to cheer her up."

After lunch, Amy followed Joshua out on the back porch to check on Frisky. He had finished his lunch and was stretched out, fast asleep. When he heard their voices, his tail began to thump against the wooden floor. Looking down, Joshua told his little sister, "He's so glad to be home. I know he'll never leave again."

The following morning Frisky was gone. Once more, Joshua walked the neighborhood, calling his dog. "Come and eat your breakfast," his mother ordered when he returned home. Joshua, close to tears, obeyed.

"He must not love me anymore, Mama," he said, eyes brimming with tears he was trying to hold back.

"Sure he loves you, son," declared Papa Tom. "It's just that Frisky's in love, and all he can think about right now is that pretty blonde down the street. Why, when your daddy met your mama, he hung around here with the most love- struck expression you ever saw. It seemed like every time I moved, I almost stepped on him. Between your beautiful blonde mama, and Clara's cooking, there was no way he'd leave."

Joshua turned to his mother, "Mama is that true? Did daddy have a 'love struck expression?' What did it look like?"

Before she could answer, her father continued, "His face was long like this." Papa Tom put his hands on his face and pulled down. He rolled his eyes and gave a loud moan. By this time, Joshua's tears had dried, and he was laughing.

"Your mama was just as bad. If he wasn't here your mama would droop around the house with a sad and sorrowful face," added Granny Jewel. "I couldn't trust her in the kitchen, because she'd burn the supper and let pots boil over."

Clara appeared in the doorway, her stirring spoon in hand. "It seems to me I remember a time before that, when my mama was working for your great grandmamma. I'd come to work with her lots of times to help out. You know," she said, warming to her subject, "your grandmamma was the most beautiful girl in Beaufort. She'd walk through town, head high, skirts swishing, and the boys would fall by her side." Clara walked around the table, chin up, shoulders swaying, pretending her spoon was a silk fan. "There was always one or two draped on the front porch, just hoping for a glimpse of the beautiful Jewel Harris." Clara moved closer to the table, her eyes on Joshua. "It seems there was one in particular that just wouldn't go away. Day and night, there was that skinny boy with a love-sick expression." Clara cut her eye toward the grandfather.

"Was that you, Papa Tom?" whispered Joshua, his eyes wide.

"Yes, my boy. It proves that persistence pays off. I won the hand of the beautiful Jewel Harris, much to the envy of every other eligible bachelor in Beaufort." Papa Tom's proud smile beamed across the table.

"I'm not ever going to act that way over some skinny old girl," declared Joshua, thinking of Katie Higgins on Piver's Island.

"Maybe not for awhile, son, but before you know it, boys will be hanging around your house in Raleigh, just trying to get a glimpse of your beautiful sister."

"Ugh! Yuck! That's never going to happen, is it Mama?"

The mother smiled. "I wouldn't be surprised."

"Joshua," said Granny Jewel, "that boy Clara told you about was the handsomest, most dashing man I had ever met."

"Humph," interrupted Clara, returning to the kitchen. "That proves only one thing. *Love is blind.*"

Chapter 8

"Sarah...."

"I know, Joshua. I know. You don't have to ask me to help you look for Frisky. We'll go right now. Why don't you get the stroller off the back porch, and I'll get Amy. We can take her with us and give Mama a few minutes peace."

Joshua rushed to the back porch. "Ramie!" he exclaimed opening the back door. "I didn't know you were out here." Joshua smiled at the tall, dark-skinned man sitting on the top step.

"I came by to say hello to Aunt Clara. I don't get to see her much since I got that good job at Machine and Supply Company over on the causeway. Now that the war's over, there's a lot more boats being built, and the big ones need diesel engines. I know how to repair and install them in the shrimp boats It's something I learned in the Army during the war." Joshua's eyes rested on Ramie's leg. "Hey, you want to knock on my wooden leg for good luck?" He gave the boy a lazy smile.

"Sure, Ramie. I need some good luck. My dog has disappeared."

"Again?"

"Yep."

"Aunt Clara told me he was gone. She was worried you might never find him." Ramie rolled up one pant leg, exposing an artificial limb.

"Does it matter where I knock on it?"

"Nope," the older man replied. "It's lucky all over."

With a determination born of need, Joshua rapped soundly on the wooden appendage. "Thanks, Ramie. I gotta' go now, and get my dog." The boy yanked the metal stroller off the porch, hurried down the driveway, and met his sisters on the sidewalk.

"Here, brother," said Sarah, handing Joshua the dog leash. "We may need this to get him home. Then you'll probably have to keep him tied until he forgets his girlfriend."

"Go get Frisky," demanded Amy, crawling in the stroller.

"There's no need to knock on the door this time," decided Sarah when they stood in front of Marie's house. "We might as well walk around back. I have a feeling that's where he is." Sure enough, the familiar-looking dog was sitting at his post, ever hopeful of a chance to see the object of his undying devotion. Joshua hurriedly fastened the leash to Frisky's collar. Looking up, he saw Marie in the backyard. She was sitting under a huge pecan tree, reading a book. Lying beside her was beautiful Buff.

"Hey, Marie," called Joshua. The girl raised her head, smiled and waved. She got up quickly and hurried toward the gate. "Hello, Joshua, hello Sarah." She looked in the stroller. "Who is this?"

"This is my little sister, Amy," replied Joshua.

"Would you like to come in?"

Joshua anchored the leash to a paling in the fence. Sarah lifted Amy from the stroller and they entered the yard. Sarah noticed the yard was a much more cheerful place than the interior of the home. There were two other pecan trees, with flowers blooming along the edge of the fence and around the back porch.

"Did your mother plant all those flowers?" asked Sarah.

"Heck no. She doesn't even notice they're there." All watched as Amy and Buff romped in the thick grass. Laughter bubbled up from Amy, while Buff pretended to growl at her new playmate.

"Marie, why didn't you let me know we had company? We've been expecting you ever since we saw Frisky's nose through the fence this morning." The children looked up to see Mrs. Wallace walking across the yard. She studied Amy and Buff for a few minutes. "And who might this be?" the mother asked in a voice barely audible.

"This is my little sister," answered Joshua. "Her name is Amy."

Mrs. Wallace knelt down, never taking her eyes from the child. "How old are you, Amy," she asked. Amy held up two chubby fingers, then promptly turned her attention to the waiting dog. The woman straightened suddenly and hurried toward the house.

Marie, sitting cross-legged on the grass watched her mother's receding figure. "Now Mama's going to have another one of her spells. Anytime she sees a little girl about the age of Amy, she comes home, curls up on her bed and cries for hours."

"Why, Marie?" Sarah was sure she had never seen a more sorrowful expression on a tiny face.

"I used to have a little sister, too. It was when we lived down in Georgia. Daddy had to go to war, and while he was gone, Jeanette got sick with polio."

Marie looked up from where she had been picking at blades of grass, and stared at Amy. "She was just about your sister's age when she died. She was in the hospital, and we thought she was getting better. Then early one morning she quit breathing." Amy's laughter was the only sound breaking the silence of the little group.

Sarah reached over and patted Marie's hand. "I can't imagine anything more horrible than losing your little sister." Sarah vowed silently to be more patient with Amy, and give her more hugs.

"Yeah, it was horrible. It still is." Marie drew her knees up to her chin and clasped her arms around her legs. "When Jeanette died, it was like a light went out in my mama's eyes. They're always filled with tears now. Daddy and I keep hoping someday she'll laugh and be happy again – like she used to be."

"Marie," said Sarah, looking at the small girl, "I heard a story once I'd like to share with you."

"I like stories. What's it about?" she asked, returning Sarah's gaze.

Sarah paused a moment. "It's a story about angels."

"Oh, good, I like angels. Jeanette's an angel now, you know."

Joshua sat down to listen, keeping his eyes on Amy and Buff.

Sarah gazed up into the limbs of the pecan tree. Sunlight filtered through the leaves, moved by the gentle south breeze.

"Once upon a time in Heaven," she began, "there was a group of little angels playing a game. They wore short, white robes and no shoes."

"There aren't any shoes in Heaven?" interrupted Joshua.

"That's right. They were all barefoot. Their tiny wings fluttered as they ran and played. Each angel held a small candle. The object of their game was to see who could run the farthest before their candle burned out.

Soon, a new angel joined them. She could barely take a step when her candle would go out. The others returned again and again to relight it.

'I don't know why my candle won't burn,' the little angel wailed to the others.

The tallest angel said, 'When you first get to Heaven your parents tears keep putting out the candle.'

'Don't worry,' another angel said, giving the newcomer a hug. 'Someday you'll be able to keep up with the rest of us."

When Sarah finished, all were quiet. The distant cries of shore birds across the channel, punctuated by the insistent wail of the bridge siren, were the only sounds heard.

Marie's hand crept into Sarah's. "Does that mean someday Mama won't cry anymore?"

"I think it means that time will dry your mother's tears, but the ache will always be in her heart. Parents and the rest of the family learn to live with the ache, but have to go on with their lives."

"I'm going in the house for a minute," declared Joshua. "I'll be right back."

Joshua walked up on the back porch and knocked on the screen door. "Mrs. Wallace, can I come in?" Not waiting for an answer, Joshua quietly entered the kitchen. "Yoo-hoo," he called, knowing that was the universal greeting when entering a house in Beaufort.

A muffled voice replied, "I'm in here, Joshua. What do you need?"

"I don't need anything, Ma'am. I just wanted to tell you something." The boy stepped closer, shocked by the appearance of the woman's face. Her eyes were red, tears streamed down her face. She sat holding an old worn towel.

"What's wrong, Mrs. Wallace?"

The woman didn't answer at first. Finally, she spoke. "I once had a little girl about the age of your sister. When I saw Amy, it made the heartache even worse."

Joshua took another step closer. "I had an Aunt Louise once. She died. Clara told me when people die, they're asleep in the sweet bosom of Jesus. That's where your little girl is, in the sweet bosom of Jesus, taking a nap." Joshua took another step closer to the heart-broken woman. "When you get to Heaven you can wake her up, and you can spend forever and forever together. In the meantime, Marie is still here, and I think she misses her mother."

For the first time, it was as if Marie' mother focused on Joshua and his words. "That's the most comforting thing anyone has ever said to me since we lost little Jeanette." Mrs. Wallace's voice grew stronger. "In the Bible it says our loved ones can't come to us, but we can go to them. So, someday I will hold my baby again." She held out her arms. "Come give me a hug, Joshua. You've made me feel better. Let me wash my face and we'll go out and see what the girls are doing." Soon, they joined the others under the tree.

"Joshua, Amy is getting restless. Maybe we'd better get Frisky and head on home," suggested Sarah.

"Yeah, I'm supposed to go over to Billy's this afternoon."

Mrs. Wallace turned to her daughter. "Marie, why don't we walk downtown and get an ice cream cone. We can look in the store windows, and who knows, we might see a pretty dress."

Marie's face shone. "That would be fun, Mama." She leapt from her place on the grass and slid her arms around her mother's waist.

"What happened back there, Joshua?" asked his older sister when they were on the sidewalk. "Mrs. Wallace looked different when she came out of the house. What did you two talk about?"

"I said I believed her little girl was sleeping in Heaven, and someday she can go up there and wake her up and hold her forever."

They walked along in silence a few steps. "Thanks for reminding me why I love you so much, little brother."

"You're welcome."

In the next block, the little group was walking past Ma Baylor's stately home. Sarah noticed a strange car in the driveway. There was something faintly familiar about it, but for the moment Sarah couldn't remember who it belonged to.

Suddenly the front door slammed open and out rushed a tall, gorgeous girl, blonde curls bouncing as she hurried down the steps. She was dressed in rose colored shorts and a flowered blouse. On her feet there were dainty white sandals. At the bottom of the steps she turned, put her hands on her hips and called, "Come on, Sylvia! I can't stand out here in this heat and wait for you all day!"

"Oh, no! Oh, no!" whispered Sarah. "Marnie's here!" Sarah increased her pace, pushing the stroller even faster along the bumpy sidewalk.

"Whee!" squealed Amy, enjoying the sudden burst of speed.

A second girl hurried from the house and down the steps. She stared at the little group passing on the opposite side of the street. Seeing her friend stare, Marnie slowly turned. She put her hand up to shade her eyes against the glare of the sun. "Sarah Bowers, is that you?"

Sarah stopped reluctantly and called back, "Hello, Marnie."

"Come over here this minute and speak to me. I haven't seen you since last summer."

When Sarah, with her brother and sister, crossed the street, Marnie was already wearing her predatory smile. "What's this? Out for a family stroll?"

"We went to get my dog. He was lost but a girl called and told us he was at her house," offered Joshua.

"Oh, my, how interesting," exclaimed Marnie, leaning toward Joshua, and giving him her most dazzling smile. At that moment Frisky stepped from behind the stroller. "Don't tell me! Is this handsome dog your pet?"

Joshua, encouraged by Marnie's attention, replied, "Yes, this is my dog Frisky." At the sound of his name, Frisky, wagging his tail furiously, barked and tried to get close enough for a pat on the head. Marnie stepped back quickly to avoid an enthusiastic kiss from the dog.

"Sarah, this is Sylvia Staton from Greenville. We go to the same high school. Sylvia, meet my cousin Sarah."

"Are you from Beaufort, Sarah?"

"No," Sarah replied, "I live in Raleigh, but we spend our summers here with our grandparents."

"Yeah, Sarah gets stuck in this little town every summer, just like me," complained Marnie.

"I like being in Beaufort, Marnie. It's not as boring as you think."

"Oh, yes. You can look for lost dogs, go fishing and sit around with your grandparents." Marnie's laughter was harsh and unfriendly.

"Go home! Go home!" demanded Amy, standing up in the stroller.

Sarah moved forward. "I have to go now."

Marnie turned to her friend, "Sylvia, get the rest of my things out of the car. I need to get back in the house and sit in front of the fan or my make-up will be ruined. I declare, I'm going to melt standing out here on this hot sidewalk!"

Sarah called, "It was nice meeting you, Sylvia. I hope I see you again."

"Oh, you will, Cousin," declared Marnie, following them. "Come back after lunch *by yourself,*" Marnie added, looking at Sarah's brother and sister. "I have a new copy of Vogue magazine and there is some information in an article I think you need."

Sarah, interested, "What's it about, Marnie?"

"It's about how to fix your hair, and how to apply make-up to make you look older. She studied Sarah's thick, straight chestnut hair. "That droopy look really doesn't do a thing for you."

Sarah felt a sense of excitement. "I will, Marnie. If Mama doesn't have something special for me to do, I'll be back."

"Sarah, don't start with the 'parent thing' again. Tell your mother what you're going to do, and then do it!"

Sarah walked away, not looking back. In the next block Joshua asked, "Are you really going to tell Mama what you're going to do, and then do it?"

"You know better than that."

"I just thought I'd ask, cause if you are, I want to be there to see Mama's face."

After lunch, Sarah found herself hurrying down the sidewalk toward Marnie's grandmother's home. She thought about her mother's words at lunch.

"Sarah," she had said, her expression troubled. "I know Marnie is your cousin, but she can be harsh and cruel to others. If she hurts your feelings just excuse yourself and come home."

Sarah wondered if you were supposed to put up with people's ugly ways just because they were kin to you. *There's a lot of people that I'm not related to, that I trust more*, she concluded.

"Yoo-hoo," Sarah called, stepping inside the long hall in Ma. Baylor's spacious home. Not getting a response, she called again, "Marnie, are you here?" Suddenly, a head appeared over the banister rail.

"Come up, Sarah," said Sylvia. "We're in Marnie's room." Sarah hurried up the stairs, eager to see what the others were doing. When she got to the door of Marnie's room, she took a deep breath. "Hmmm," she remarked, "It smells like a flower garden in here."

"It should! I brought all my lotions, perfumes and make-up with me. Sylvia and I are already made up, and now it's your turn! Come over here and sit on the vanity stool and let's get started," ordered Marnie.

Sarah sat down obediently. Somehow it was easier to do as Marnie directed, than to argue. Looking in the mirror, she saw that Marnie and Sylvia had been transformed into glamorous women. It was a contrast from the girls they had looked like earlier. Both had swept their hair up and had caught it in combs and hair clasps. Curls bounced on the top of their heads. "Oh," breathed Sarah, "that's the very hair style I have always wanted. Emily at the beauty parlor wears her hair like that."

"So does Betty Grable, and a hundred other movie stars," added Sylvia.

"Oh, Sylvia, what do you know? You don't even have a subscription to 'Photoplay' magazine! Hush up and hand me that card of bobby pins!"

Ouch, thought Sarah, her eyes darting to Sylvia to see her reaction to Marnie's ugly remark. To her surprise, the girl hardly seemed to notice.

When Sarah looked back at her reflection, she saw that Marnie had expertly swept her thick hair up and was securing it with bobby pins and combs.

"Since you don't have any natural curl, we'll take the straight ends, loop them over and secure them to the top of your head with bobby pins."

Sarah sat, fascinated, as Marnie's hands flew expertly gathering, twisting and securing Sarah's hair.

"I declare! I've never seen such a mane of thick hair, except on a horse," declared cousin Marnie. Sylvia, sitting in the middle of the double bed, giggled.

"You have no room to laugh, Sylvia. Your hair is so stringy, I could hardly do anything with it." The laughter quickly faded, replaced by an injured look.

"I think I hear somebody at the front door," Sylvia declared, changing the subject. All listened and sure enough, a faint, 'yoo-hoo' was heard below.

"Go and see who it is," commanded Marnie. Sylvia scurried off the bed and rushed once more out to the banister rail.

"Yes, she's here. Would you like to come up?"

Marnie stopped, comb in mid air. "Now who is she inviting up, without my permission? Honestly, I'm so popular, people can't leave me alone."

"Marnie, aren't you afraid you'll hurt Sylvia's feelings the way you talk to her?"

"Of course not! She's lucky I show her any attention. The other girls in our class all wanted to come down with me, but they already had other plans. Sylvia's parents will be coming down to their beach cottage next week, and she'll stay with them. She doesn't want to, but they'll insist."

A week of this kind of treatment, and she may be glad to go, thought Sarah.

"Your grandmother told me where you were," spoke Nancy Russert from the doorway.

"Oh, hi, Nancy," exclaimed Sarah. "Have you met Sylvia? I know you remember my cousin, Marnie."

"Sylvia and I have already met. Hi, Marnie." Nancy joined Sylvia, sitting on the edge of the bed. All watched in fascination as Sarah was transformed from a teenager into a young woman. When Marnie was finished with Sarah's hair, she began reading the labels on the myriad of bottles and tubes on the vanity top.

"The article in Vogue says to cover your face with smooth, creamy lotion. When it dries, apply rouge to the cheeks and powder to the face and neck." Marnie squirted lotion in her hands and applied it to Sarah's face. When finished, Marnie deftly applied rouge to each cheek. She was amazed at the difference in Sarah's appearance. "You must never have shiny skin, so always have your compact with you, ready to powder your nose. Marnie handed Sara a tube of lipstick. "Put this on, and be careful. It has to be straight, or you'll look like a clown."

Sarah leaned toward the mirror and carefully applied the lipstick. Leaning back, she felt she had been magically transformed from her former self, into a glamorous movie star. Her stunned expression was soon replaced by a wide smile. She was captivated by her reflection as she turned her head from side to side.

"Now, girls, each one paint the other's nails. That way there won't be any mistakes." Marnie produced a bottle of scarlet nail polish with a long tapering lid. When she finished Sarah's nails, the girl waved her hands in the air, flashing the bright red paint.

"Wow, Sarah! You look sensational!" exclaimed Nancy. "If you had a long slinky dress, and a gardenia in your hair, you could sing in a night club."

"That would be fine, until I opened my mouth."

"That's all right. I'll accompany you, and I'll play real loud."

"Stop being silly, you two," ordered Marnie. "Nancy, you're next."

"Oooo, not me!" my mother would never approve," said Nancy, her voice tinged with envy.

Sylvia remarked, "I'm hot and thirsty. Why don't we take a break and drink a soda?"

"Fine," replied Marnie. "I'll go down to the kitchen and get everyone a Coca-Cola."

Nancy stood, "I'll go with you, Marnie. You need a break from all the wonderful magic you have created."

Marnie thought for a moment. "Hmmm, you're right. I have put my exceptional talent to good use today. Come on Nancy, and I'll tell you about a lot of other wonderful things I have done while we're opening the drinks."

When they had disappeared down the stairs, Sarah dragged her eyes away from the mirror. "Sylvia," she said quietly, "why do you let her talk to you that way?"

"It's not so bad once you get used to it," mumbled Sylvia, picking at tufts of cotton on the chenille bedspread.

"Sure it is," hissed Sarah. "Nobody can get used to being talked to like a slave, *and* nobody should ever have to."

"Everybody at school tries to stay on Marnie's good side. If you make her mad, or hurt her feelings, she'll talk awful about you to everybody else. Pretty soon you won't have a friend in the whole school. Or, nobody will have anything to do with you, because they don't want Marnie talking bad about them."

"Sylvia, I go to a big high school in Raleigh. Broughton High is probably the biggest high school in the whole state. I don't know of anybody in my school who acts like that. Sure, there are cliques. Like, for instance, there are the real popular girls who are cheerleaders or majorettes. They are always the home- coming queen or prom queen. The girls who are good at sports hang around together and talk about ball games. There are real brainy girls who are quiet and keep to themselves. Nobody bothers with them unless they need help with their school work."

"Are you popular, Sarah?"

"Heavens, no! I have four friends and we go everywhere together. One of them is my best friend. Her name is Lindsey, and I can tell her all my secrets. She's coming down for my uncle's wedding this summer. I hope you get to meet her."

"You're lucky. I wish I could go to your school. I'd sure like to be one of your friends." Now they could hear the others returning.

"Sylvia," Sarah whispered, "don't settle for this treatment. Someone in your school needs a good friend, too. Start praying God will put this person in your path, or put you in their path. You know that old saying, "In order to have a friend, you have to be a friend." I know you'll make a wonderful friend for someone."

"Phew, it's hot in here!" announced Marnie a soda in each hand. She plopped down on the window seat, blocking any breeze from coming into the room. Occasionally a stray puff of wind would move the sheer curtain.

When the soda bottles were empty, Marnie announced, "I have convinced Nancy she has to be glamorous, too. So, now it's time to work on her."

"Hmmm, I'm not so sure, Marnie. I don't know what kind of reaction my mama might have if I come home looking like Bette Davis." Nancy gave a nervous laugh.

Marnie stood, hands on hips. "I can't understand why you two are so afraid of your mamas. I announce what I am going to do, and *my* mother doesn't try to stop me. Or, if she does, I raise such a fuss, she always says, "Well, all right dear, whatever you think is best." Marnie spoke in a voice that mocked her mother's words.

"Anyway, my hair is short, and you can't sweep it up on top of my head. It's naturally curly, like yours, and does whatever it wants."

Marnie grinned. "Do you think my hair is naturally curly? Ha! I sleep on bobby pins every night."

"Don't they hurt your head?"

"Of course, silly. But it's worth it to have gorgeous hair the next day." Marnie rolled her eyes and patted her curls with one hand. She turned her head to one side and stared at Nancy. "Come here and sit down." The girl pointed her finger at the vanity stool. Sarah had already joined Sylvia who was sitting on the side of the bed.

Marnie stood behind Nancy, and ran her fingers through the dark, silky curls. "Your hair will be a challenge, no doubt, but the magazine mentions a way to handle short hair." From a glass tray on the vanity, Marnie produced two curved ivory combs. She raked Nancy's curls away from her face and anchored them behind her ears with the combs. Immediately there was a change in Nancy's appearance. With her hair smooth around her face, she lost the appearance of a girl, and resembled a young adult. "Ah, ha!" she cried in triumph. "You look older already. Now, for make up." Skillfully, the girl applied the lotion to Nancy's face, after which she smoothed each cheek with rouge from the metal rouge pot. Face powder and bright red lipstick completed the make up. Nancy remained still, staring in the mirror.

"Wow," she finally whispered. "When I walk out on the concert stage someday, I hope I look just like this." She turned to Marnie, gratitude in her expression. "Thanks, Marnie. I really like the way I look. I'll bet you go to Hollywood after you graduate and make up the movie stars."

"Oh,no, ma'am! I'm going to *be* a movie star, not make up others. Someone will be doing my make up. Of course," Marnie took a deep breath, "I won't need much. *I* have natural beauty." Marnie clapped her hands smartly. "Now, girls, we can't sit here looking so beautiful. Everyone roll your shorts up one notch, and tie the front of your blouse in a knot. Hair styles like ours deserve a bare midriff."

The girls finished altering their clothes and looked expectantly at Marnie. With hands on her hips and chin held high, she announced, "Now we're ready to walk downtown and window shop. We'll turn this little town upside down."

Chapter 9

"Did you see that?" asked Nancy when the four glamorous girls stepped out on the sidewalk. She nudged Sarah with her elbow. "Those guys nearly fell out of their truck! They are waving and honking the horn at *us*!"

In a few minutes the same truck came around the block again, this time going a bit slower. The truck was old, with rust spots on the fenders. Two teen age boys rode in the cab, and two sat in the back. A faded sign on the door read, 'Gaskill's Feed and Seed.'

"Hi, ladies," called one of the boys in a musical tone.

"Don't look at them, Nancy. Maybe they'll go away," said Sarah hopefully.

"There's not much chance of that, friend. Your cousin is waving back and smiling to beat the band! Don't be such a stick in the mud, Sarah! They're just flirting with us. There can't be any harm in that!"

"I guess you're right. They're just being friendly." Sarah patted her friend on the shoulder. As they passed an althea bush in full bloom, Sarah reached up and picked one of the lavender flowers. "How do I look, Nancy?" she asked, poking the flower behind her ear.

"Oooo, that's the perfect touch. Now you really do look like a night club singer."

"We should know, since we've been to so many night clubs," added Sarah.

"What are you two giggling about," demanded her cousin. "If it's so funny, why don't you share?"

"We were just discussing our night life, and all the night clubs we have been to," replied Nancy.

Marnie broke off the conversation as the truck glided by once more.

"Can we give you ladies a ride? If you're new in town, we'd like to show you around."

"New in town, my eye," muttered Nancy. "Those guys go to Beaufort High. I saw them every day in the hall last year when we changed classes. They never even glanced my way or knew I was alive."

"See how the right make-up can change your life, girls," said Marnie proudly, still smiling at the eager boys in the truck. When the four girls turned the corner onto Front Street, the breeze threatened to rearrange their sophisticated hairdos.

"Now I understand why mama never wants the windows down in the car. She's afraid it will mess up her hair," offered Sylvia.

"Yeah," added Marnie. "Boys are so lucky. Their hair is two inches all over their head so they never have to worry."

"Have you all noticed the stares we're getting?" asked Sarah. Strangers on the sidewalk nodded and smiled. Customers in stores stopped and watched the girls out of sight. "We're going to be famous. Maybe people think movie stars have come to Beaufort to 'take the salty sea air."

"I'm hot," declared Marnie. "Why don't we stop in your grandfather's store and get a cool drink."

"Oh, I didn't bring any money," said Sylvia.

"We won't need any money," Sarah hurried to explain. "I can have all the sodas I want, and can treat my friends."

"Good!" declared Marnie, pushing the screen door open and stepping inside Mitchell's Grocery.

It was cooler inside. The hum of fans could be heard, and the distinct odor of fresh vegetables and fruit made Sarah think about her week of working at the store.

"May I help you, ladies?" came a booming voice from the back of the store. Sarah saw Mr. Case hurry from behind the meat counter.

She stepped forward. "Hi, Mr.Case. We stopped in to get a cold drink, if that's OK."

"Sarah, is that you?" The older gentleman looked genuinely surprised.

"Yes, sir. It's me."

"Goodness, gracious, you look enchanting. You all do," his eyebrows still raised. He looked at each of the girls, his eyes resting on Marnie. "Who are these lovely young ladies?"

Sarah introduced each of her friends. "Excuse me, but I think your Uncle Herb would like to meet everyone," Mr. Case said hurriedly. He walked quickly to the office in the back of the store. "Come out here, Herb. Your eyes are in for a treat." Curious, Herb Mitchell followed the gentleman.

"Well," he exclaimed. "To what do we owe the honor of a visit from such lovely maidens?"

Marnie, preening under the attention of a man, began to flirt. "Oh, kind sir, we are fainting from the heat, and wish for something cool to drink."

Herb Mitchell hurriedly dusted the small, round table and chairs near the front window. "I'll take the order, ladies. What will it be, Coca-Cola, orange crush or perhaps ginger ale?" His speech was light and playful but his gaze never left Sarah.

As they were sitting down, the back door opened and Kevin entered the store. "Boy, it's hot out there! That last delivery was murder. I had to carry the order….."

His words were interrupted by the sight of the four pretty girls enjoying a cool drink. "Kevin," began Uncle Herb, "I'd like to introduce you to these lovely ladies." Kevin hurried over, mopping his forehead with a handkerchief and raking his fingers through his hair. His eyes were the size of saucers, his grin wide.

"How do you do, ladies. Uh, welcome to Mitchell's Grocery store. Is there anything you need, a straw perhaps, or a napkin?" When his eyes rested on Sarah, he gave her a curious look. "Sarah, is that you? Boy you look so, uh… different!"

The way he looked at her was unlike any look he had given her when she was working. This type of attention was different. Kevin continued hovering over the girls like a moth to a flame. It was evident that Marnie's dazzling smile assured them of all the attention they would need or want.

While the others were enjoying their drink, Uncle Herb motioned to Sarah to follow him. "Ask Nancy to come, too." he said quietly. The girls followed him to the door of the tiny office. Uncle Herb sat down behind the desk and stared at the girls. He motioned to them to step inside.

"Sarah, maybe it's none of my business, but, what's going on here?"

Her back stiff, chin up, Sarah replied defensively, "I don't know what you mean, Uncle Herb."

"I think you do, Sarah."

Nancy moved from behind her friend. "Marnie styled our hair and shared her make-up." Under her uncle's gaze, Nancy's words made what they had done seem a terrible crime. "We painted each other's fingernails a matching color." Nancy looked down and promptly clasped her hands behind her back.

"Have you been home?"

"No."

"You may want to wipe off some of that bright red lipstick before you go in the house, and uh, rearrange your outfit."

"Uncle Herb, we haven't done anything wrong." Sarah began to feel a sense of anger. What seemed a grand adventure, was now being ruined by her uncle's distrustful attitude.

Still looking troubled, Herb Mitchell stood. Sarah had not seen such a sad expression on her uncle's face since the death of his wife, Louise. "Sarah, I have no experience in giving a teenager advice. All I can say is, please be careful." Without answering, the girls turned, left the room and joined the others at the front of the store.

"Would you like a magazine or a fan? How about another cold drink," implored Kevin, determined to have the girls stay.

"Let's go, Marnie," said Sarah. The tone of Sarah's voice caused Marnie and Sylvia to hurry after the two. Sarah, remembering her manners, paused and thanked Mr. Case for the sodas.

"Will you be coming back?" implored Kevin, following them. The only answer was the screen door slamming behind the last girl. Kevin hurried to the door, his gaze following them down the sidewalk.

Mr. Case and Herb exchanged glances. "That poor boy has a lot to learn," said Mr. Case.

"Yeah, and so do the girls," added the uncle.

The little group continued window shopping, drawing attention and admiring glances from people they passed. Nancy linked her arm through Sarah's. "You know, your uncle is really good looking. His dark curly hair and tiny mustache are quiet dashing. I noticed him looking at me just now in a different way. He should forget Miriam and wait for me. I'll be eighteen in three years. That's not too long to wait for someone you truly love."

Sarah pulled her arm free. "Yes, and he'll be almost *forty years old*! He'll be too old to do the jitterbug and other dances we taught him." Sarah felt injured inside by her uncle's words. He had looked so strange, like he was disappointed in her. *Oh, so what,* she decided. *He's acting like an old fuddy-duddy who doesn't want me to have any fun.*

"There's an althea bush in that yard," observed Sylvia. "I want a flower behind my ear, like Sarah."

"Why do you want to be like Sarah?" asked Marnie, pouting. "You should want to look just like me." Marnie patted her hair with one hand in a characteristic gesture.

Sylvia shrank before Marnie's cruel gaze. "Oh, I do, Marnie. I want my hair just like yours."

The girls walked slowly past stores and continued walking until they reached the post office. Parked across the street was the familiar old truck. The boys were out on the government dock eating lunch. The first one to see them waved furiously, the others doing the same.

"Hello, ladies. Won't you join us?" the driver of the truck asked.

Marnie needed no more encouragement. She led the girls across the street, swaying her hips as she walked. As they approached, Sarah realized they were all about her age or maybe a year or two older. All eyes were on Marnie, but when she and the older boy walked to the end of the dock, the others began to pay attention to the three remaining girls.

"Where are you all from?" asked one of boys, opening the conversation. As they introduced themselves, Sarah noticed they talked rough, and even cursed occasionally. *This must be what my mother refers to as filling station talk.* Sarah decided. She knew her mother, stopping to get gasoline, never went inside the station. There were always men sitting around, and their conversations were not meant for a lady's ears.

"Uh, Nancy, let's go. I need to check in at home."

"You can't go," whispered Sylvia, poking Sarah in the ribs. "I don't want to stand here with these boys!"

"Go get Marnie and tell her we need to leave." Sylvia looked fearfully in her friend's direction.

Marnie was laughing and talking to the driver of the truck. He was leaning over, she looking up, their noses almost touching. They had forgotten there was anyone else on the planet. Finally, Bobby White, one of the boys wearing glasses, called, "Come on Terry, we're past our lunch break. Let's go." Bobby looked up reluctantly. As he moved toward the truck, Marnie followed, laughing and talking.

When the truck moved away, Marnie turned to the others, wearing a smug expression. "I don't know about you girls, but *I have a date tonight!*"

"A date!" the three chorused.

"Yes," she replied, smiling triumphantly.

"Does your mother let you go out on dates?" asked Nancy.

Marnie's satisfied expression turned to a scowl. "She wouldn't dare try to stop me."

"How about me, Marnie?" asked Sylvia. "I'm your company. What will I do all evening?"

"How should I know?" answered Marnie, tossing her blonde curls, blue eyes cold as steel. "I guess you can sit in the parlor and listen to the radio with the old folks." Brittle laughter followed her remark.

Sarah reached for Sylvia's hand. "You and Nancy can come down to my grandmother's house. I brought my movie star magazines with me. We can look at them and practice doing each other's hair."

Sylvia's expression brightened. "Thanks, Sarah. That would be fun."

The girls separated, Sylvia trying to keep up with Marnie who was taking large strides, forgetting to sway her hips.

When Sarah stepped up on the porch, Joshua and Papa Tom were enjoying a glass of iced tea. "Hi, darling. Won't you join us for a cool drink?"

"No, thanks Papa. I'm not thirsty."

When the screen door closed, Joshua turned to his grandfather, "Papa Tom, what's happened to Sarah? She looks different."

"I'm not sure, Joshua. Sip your cold drink and don't get in the middle of women stuff. If there is a problem, your mama will take care of it."

"She doesn't look like my sister, but she looks mighty pretty."

"Hmmm, that's what I'm afraid of Joshua," commented his grandfather.

As Sarah stepped inside, she heard her mother reading a story to Amy. They were sitting on Granny Jewel's prized sofa which was covered in flowered chinz. Hesitantly, she stepped into the room. "Hi, Mama. Hi Amy." She moved slowly around the sofa.

Amy pointed one chubby finger at her lips. "Sahwah, is hurt?"

"No, Amy," Sarah rushed to explain. "It's only lipstick."

Sarah watched the expression on her mother's face change. Moments before she had looked soft and motherly. "You say it's *only* lipstick!" she hissed, her expression harsh and accusing. "Where did you get such a garish shade, and what are you doing dressed like that, young lady?"

For a moment Sarah was frightened. Then her back stiffened. There was that hateful expression again, 'young lady'. She knew whenever she heard it, she was in trouble. "Marnie styled our hair, and showed us how to put on make-up," said Sarah, her voice rising.

"What have you done to your clothes?" asked Peggy, closing the story book with a loud smack, Amy forgotten. "Your father and I are not in favor of you dressing in such a skimpy outfit. I hope you came straight home from Marnie's. I wouldn't want you to parade downtown looking like that."

Sarah stood. "As a matter of fact, we did go downtown and lots of people gave us admiring looks."

"I hear raised voices," said Granny Jewel, coming down the stairs. "Is everything all right?"

Sarah turned toward her grandmother as she came into the room. "No, Granny Jewel, nothing's all right," declared Sarah, close to tears. She was hoping her grandmother would take her side, since she had enough bottles of perfume, powder and lotion on her vanity to start a drug store. Sarah also knew that her grandmother never *looked* like she was wearing a lot of make-up. Her skin and lips always looked natural and beautiful.

Sarah watched her grandmother's eyes widen, but never spoke of Sarah's unusual appearance.

"Go upstairs, wash your face and put on a decent outfit – something that doesn't expose your stomach! There is nail polish remover in the bathroom. Please clean that garish red paint off your nails!" commanded Peggy, pointing toward the stairs.

Sarah stood, giving no indication she had heard her mother's voice.

On the porch, Joshua turned to his grandfather and whispered, "Papa, should we go in and be on Sarah's side?"

"Oh, no, son. We must never volunteer to wade into a battle of this magnitude."

"What do you mean?"

"What I mean is, us menfolks have to lay low."

"Oh."

Suddenly, the screen door flew open. "Daddy," spoke Peggy. "Please come in here and explain to Sarah that decent young girls do NOT parade the streets looking like she does. Mama won't help me one bit."

"Peggy, honey, it would be hard for me to…."

"Daddy!"

"I'm coming, sweetheart." Peggy flew back into the house, again letting the front door slam.

"Come on, Joshua," said his grandfather, slowly getting to his feet.

"But Papa, you said we should lay low."

"That was five minutes ago."

"I think I'll stay out here."

"Not a chance. I'm not going to be the only man in there with three generations of women."

Joshua, pleased at being considered a man, hurried behind his grandfather. If Papa Tom needed reinforcements, he'd be right there to back him up.

The tension in the living room could almost be felt. It was as if sparks flew between mother and daughter.

"Papa, help me," wailed Sarah, close to tears.

"Tom. This is what I think…"

"Daddy, you have to do something!"

Tom Mitchell looked from one to the other. He instantly took command. "Joshua," he ordered, "Go sit with your mother and Amy. Jewel, sit by me. Sarah, take a seat across from your mother." He looked up to see if all were settled. He turned his head slowly and saw Clara standing in the kitchen door.

"Don't put that eye on me!" she called. "You're not going to tell me what to do. I'll get busy and fix everybody a glass of iced tea and see if that will cool off some tempers."

"Thank you, Clara. Now let's get to the bottom of this. Sarah, I want you to start, and there are to be no interruptions." He gave his daughter a stern look.

Sarah's lavender flower, which hours ago was an exotic blossom, now drooped sadly and hung over the girl's ear. At some point, Sarah had tried to wipe the bright lipstick from her lips, but only succeeded in smearing it.

"Papa Tom, Mama likes me to visit with Marnie, because we're cousins. So, I went down there this morning and then Nancy showed up. Marnie fixed our hair and made up our faces. Our outfits didn't look any different from Lana Turner's clothes in the movie magazines."

"Lana Turner is a grown woman and a …." Peggy's words died on her lips when she looked at her father's expression.

Sarah turned to her grandfather. "Papa, it was fun to walk downtown and have a lot of people stare at us. We felt SO pretty. Some boys were yelling at us, and Marnie has a date with one of them tonight."

Peggy never said a word, but fanned herself and Amy with the story book. Amy had given up on hearing any more of her story, and was napping in her mother's lap.

"Sarah, I hope no strange boys are going to show up on our doorstep tonight," stated Papa Tom.

"No, sir. None of them know where I live. Marnie's company is coming by tonight, because Marnie is going out on a date. I hope that's all right," Sarah said with a sneer, not unlike the one she had seen on her cousin's face earlier.

"Be careful, Sarah," warned her grandfather, his eyebrows knit together.

Sarah uncrossed her legs and stamped one foot, a tear meandering down her cheek. "You expect me to act like an adult when it suits you, like watching Joshua and Amy. I have chores at home I am expected to do. Yet, if I want to *act* like an adult, it's the end of the world! Besides, you all are too old to remember what it's like to be young." She leaned against the chair back, arms crossed, lower lip out, and stared at the intricate design in the hammered metal ceiling of her grandparents' home.

Peggy Bowers started to speak, hesitated, and looked at her father.

"Go ahead, honey. It's your turn."

Boy, thought Joshua. *My mama waited for Papa to give her permission to speak.* He looked at his grandfather through new eyes, impressed that one man could possess such awesome power.

"Sarah," said her mother in a more subdued tone, "it's true you are no longer a child, but neither are you an adult. No matter the age, if you are to have a good reputation, you must look and act like a lady." Peggy looked directly at her daughter. "Your behavior determines how people will think of you. You want to be treated with respect and what's important also is self-respect, how you feel about yourself."

Peggy was interrupted by Clara bringing tall glasses of iced tea with a lemon wedge. The glasses had already frosted, so coasters had to be used to protect the furniture. She put the tray down on the coffee table with a bang.

Clara put her hands on her hips. "Yeah, honey, you don't want to walk the streets of this town dressed like a floosie and have people wagging their tongues. The gossips will point and say, 'There goes Sarah Bowers from Raleigh. She must be fast and loose, judging from the way she dresses.'" Now she clasped her hands over her heart, and spoke in a high pitched voice, "I know it breaks her grandparents' hearts seeing her grow up like that. "And *real* old gossips will add, 'It's a blessing her great-grandmother Frances, isn't alive to see this.'"

"Clara, that will be all," spoke Papa Tom.

With a loud sniff, Clara put her hands on her hips and slowly walked back to the kitchen.

Fast and loose? wondered Joshua. *How could words like that upset the grownups? He remembered both words had been on his vocabulary list in school.*

"Peggy, is there anything else you would like to say?"

"Well, Daddy, I think Clara pretty much summed it up for me."

It was on the tip of Joshua's tongue to ask the meaning of the fascinating new word, but dared not interrupt. If he did, he knew he could be banished to his room way, way upstairs. This was a rare experience for a boy who was usually the one on the hot seat.

"OK, my sweet," said the grandfather, softening slightly when he looked at her grandmother.

Granny Jewel paused, looking from one to the other of her beloved family members. "A person's reputation cannot be bought with gold. If you ever lose it, you can't buy it back with a king's ransom. I'm sure living in the city is quite different from living in a small town where people know you and know your business. There may be a few gossips, but for the most part, everyone is genuinely concerned about the people they know. Therefore, if you dress like a street walker, you will be branded as one."

Wow! thought Joshua. *More words that upset grownups. A street walker is bound to be somebody who walks in the street, but it could be dangerous unless they look both ways.* Joshua sat quietly, his hands folded in his lap. *Tomorrow I will ask Mackie what these words mean,* he decided. *If he doesn't know, he'll beat the truth out of somebody who does.* Joshua sighed contentedly and smiled at his beloved grandfather.

Granny Jewel took a deep breath and looked at her daughter. "This is what I would like to propose. Sarah will remove the harsh red lipstick and nail polish. Her hair will come down and once more let the southwest wind toss it about. Her shirts and shorts will once more be cool, but modest."

"But Mama," interrupted Peggy.

"I'm not finished," Granny Jewel snapped. "Sarah holds an important place in this family. It's true she has the responsibility of her siblings a lot of the time. She helps Clara when needed and I know she would do anything for her grandparents that was in her ability to do."

There was not a sound in the entire house. Everyone sat without moving. There was no sound from the kitchen.

"Therefore," spoke Granny Jewel, looking cool and serene. "Since Sarah is fifteen years old and no longer a child, I think she should have permission to wear a soft, pale pink lipstick and a delicate rouge on her cheeks when she wants to. Some matching nail polish wouldn't hurt, either." She looked at her husband. "There, I've said my peace."

Papa Tom shuffled his feet and picked at a tiny piece of lint on his dark trousers. "I guess it's my turn." He took a deep breath and looked at his older granddaughter. "Sarah, if I could have my way, I'd like for you to be twelve years old for the next twenty years. I'd like for your hair to be pulled back in braids, and a jelly stain on your shirt. I'd like to be your hero, because I take fish off the hook for you. But, that is not to be. Every day you become a more beautiful young girl. You are soon to be a beautiful young woman. Growing up is a difficult passage in your life, and you must use wisdom when you make choices. Whether you use make-up or not will be your decision. Whatever you decide, you'll always be my precious girl."

Sarah was crying, making no attempt to hide her tears. "You *are* my hero, Papa Tom, and always will be." She went over to her grandfather, and sat in his lap, as she had done years before. Handing her a clean handkerchief, he patted Sarah's back while she cried.

"I'm sorry, Mama," she was finally able to say.

Peggy, unable to move with Amy in her lap, replied, "I'm sorry I fussed at you, Sarah. I hope you can forgive me, too. And, let me add, Marnie may be your cousin, but I do not approve of her behavior. I'll be glad to hear she has gone home."

"Then it's settled," declared Granny Jewel. "Tomorrow morning let's go to Bell's Drug and find a proper lipstick."

"I'll go, too," stated Peggy.

A tiny voice piped up and added, "Me, too."

Chapter 10

"Daddy's here! Daddy's here!" screamed Joshua. He was playing on the upstairs porch and saw his father arrive in his new, 1946 Ford truck. His bare feet slapped against the hardwood floors in the upstairs hall and down the steps. Family emerged from every direction, converging on the front porch. James Bowers stepped out of his red truck and swept Peggy up in his arms. He barely had time to kiss her cheek before the children surrounded him, each vying for attention.

James turned to his wife. "Peggy, darling, who do these lovely children belong to?" he asked, surrounded by his son and daughters. "They resemble ours, but these are two inches taller, two shades browner and more beautiful than I remember."

"Daddy," said Amy, caressing her father's face.

"Daddy, is it? Well, these must be *my* children!"

With one child in his arms, and one on each side, James Bowers entered the house. He hugged Granny Jewel and shook hands with Papa Tom. "Did I make it in time for lunch?" he asked, looking toward the kitchen.

"Clara insisted on holding lunch for you. She said we wouldn't starve if we didn't eat on the stroke of twelve," said his mother-in-law.

James sighed, "I wouldn't be here now, if it wasn't for a kind farmer on his way to Kinston. I love that truck, but Tom, I declare it is a lemon! When I go somewhere, I never know who is going to push me home. It's embarrassing to be towed by a truck ten years older than yours. The trucks built before the war are tough. The vehicles now are made of cardboard it seems."

"Industry still isn't on its feet from the war, James," added Papa Tom, putting his arm around his son-in-law. "Come in the living room and rest a minute."

"I can't rest until I've seen my favorite girl," called James, grinning. "I hope you're not trying to hide from me, Clara. I won't stop until I've found you." James continued walking toward the rear of the house. "Um-um, there are some mighty good smells coming from the kitchen." James stuck his head around the door. Seeing Clara, he stepped in and gave her a hug. Clara gave the man one of the rare smiles she reserved for him.

"You carry on something awful, Mr. James," Clara said, grinning. "Anybody would think you haven't had a mouthful to eat since you were here last time."

Putting his arm around her shoulders, he raised a finger to his lips, "Shhh, Clara, I wouldn't want anybody else to hear this, but you're just about right."

"Oh, go on! You don't look like you've missed any meals," she said, patting his stomach. "Now get yourself in the dining room and let me get this food on the table. "Did you wash your hands?"

"Yes, Ma'am."

"Oh, Clara," observed Papa Tom, when everyone was seated, "I see you put on the new tablecloth. If you did it for me, you didn't need to go to so much trouble." He winked at his grandchildren as he spoke.

Clara, serving steaming bowls of thick, creamy clam chowder, glared at her employer. "I'll put it on in your honor when it's old and raggedy, just like its owner."

"Ah, I feel right at home," sighed James, unfolding his napkin. "Do these two ever declare a truce?"

Putting her spoon in the bowl, Sarah grinned at her father. "No, Daddy. It goes on all the time, some times are worse than others."

"An emergency will bring them close in less time than it takes to wink an eye," observed her grandmother.

"Daddy, are you going to stay all summer?" asked Joshua, biting the end off a cornbread hush puppy.

"No, son, but I can stay for at least one week." James looked at his wife and in-laws. "It's a lot easier to get away now that Malcolm Vane is working for us."

"Who is Malcolm Vane?" asked Papa Tom.

James smiled. "We met under unusual circumstances. It was summer before last when I was bringing Peggy and the kids to spend the summer in Beaufort. He helped me change a tire during a rain storm. Just home from the war, he had enrolled at NC State College, majoring in chemical engineering. He's going to school on the GI Bill and works part-time. I hope he'll join us full time when he graduates. This week he is between semesters and is working full time at the plant."

James paused, "We can't let me do all the talking. What have my children been doing this summer?"

"I have a pet chicken named Little Chick," Joshua began. "We had to help him out of his shell 'cause he was too weak to get himself out. Mr. Owens said he'd never live, but he did. Papa Tom got stuck in the mud when he was helping rescue a horse. Some men were going to leave him there, but I made them haul him out. Frisky went courtin' but the girl dog, Buff, wouldn't have anything to do with him and it about broke his heart." Joshua paused. "Sarah got in a lot of trouble 'cause she got all dressed up and went downtown in red lipstick and red fingernails." Joshua paused for breath, wondering if he dared try out the new high powered words. Suddenly, he felt a stabbing pain in his right ankle and opened his mouth to yell. Seeing the look on his sister's face he quickly pressed his lips together.

"I'm thinking of getting a new car next year, James," said Papa Tom, quickly changing the subject. "Do you have any suggestions? What are the people in the city driving?" The next few minutes were spent discussing the types of automobiles and the advantages of each.

While the men were talking, Sarah leaned over to her brother and whispered, "You forgot to tell daddy about smoking cigarettes."

"Oh, Sarah," Joshua said quietly, eyes big and round, "Daddy already knows about that. Mama called him long distance and told on me so he won't want to hear about it again. He would be bored."

"I'll wait until Sarah gets here next summer and let her pick out the new car," said Papa Tom proudly. "After all, she'll be the one driving it since she'll have a license."

"Do they have pink cars? Papa Tom, you know pink is my favorite color," she added, smiling.

"I'll be on the lookout for one, but I've never seen one of Mr. Paul's dodge cars painted pink."

"I'm not going to ride in a pink car," announced Joshua. He looked at his sister, and seeing her expression, quickly tucked his feet up in the chair. He knew that one more kick like before, and he'd be walking like Little Chick.

"That's all right, silly boy. You can stay home."

"Papa Tom, you wouldn't leave me home, would you?" he wailed.

"Ah," sighed James, rolling his eyes, "how I have missed my children's gentle voices."

"Me too, go bye-bye," added Amy, mashing a potato wedge on the high chair tray.

"Thank you for that delicious lunch, Clara," said James when the dishes were being cleared away.

"It's a pleasure to cook for you, Mr. James."

"How about me, Clara?" asked Papa Tom, winking at her. A loud sniff was her reply.

"Why don't the menfolks go out and sit on the porch where it's cool. We'll clean up and join you in a few minutes."

Joshua followed his father and grandfather. "Mama, why does Joshua think he is one of the 'menfolks'? Why isn't he in here helping, too?"

Peggy paused, hands on hips. "Hmmm, you can't consider him one of the women folks, and, if he was in here helping, it would take us twice as long to finish."

"You're right, Mama. At least he's not under foot. Why don't I clean Amy up, and get her down for a nap. Four women in the kitchen may get Clara 'riled up.'"

Granny Jewel stepped out on the porch. "I called Herb and asked if he and Miriam could eat supper with us tonight. We have some fresh butterbeans and tomatoes from the garden. I'll run down to the store and get anything else we may need. Clara wants to cook one of her famous 'shore dinners,' for James, of course. She doesn't think he gets enough seafood, living in Raleigh."

"Honey, do you want me to go to the fish house and get some fresh fish?"

"No, Clara doesn't even trust me to do that. She's planning to go herself in a few minutes."

"Papa, we could go fishing and catch our supper," suggested Joshua.

"I would hate for eight hungry people to have to depend on our luck for their supper," said Papa Tom. "Maybe we'd better let the boats fishing off shore catch our supper."

Once again Clara set the table extra nice. She put on a special tablecloth, one reserved for Sunday dinner when the preacher was invited. There was also a bouquet of colorful zinnias for the centerpiece.

While the family greeted Miriam and Herb, the uncle looked about for Sarah. "Were you looking for me, Uncle Herb?" someone beside him whispered. He turned suddenly and was relieved to see his niece was wearing a simple dress, hair soft and flowing, and just a hint of pale pink lipstick. "I'll bet you were worried I would look like I did the other day."

"Truthfully, Sarah, it did cross my mind. You look far more beautiful tonight although, I'll have to admit, you were a knockout!"

"Thanks, Uncle Herb," she said, as he smothered her in a hug.

On their way in to dinner, Herb cornered his father. "Daddy, I thought you were going to have some trouble with Sarah when she came out in her 'new look.'"

Papa Tom placed his arm around his son. "Herb, that's all been taken care of."

Herb Mitchell looked admiringly at this father. "Wow, Dad, someday, when I have teenagers, I hope you'll be able to help me keep them straight."

"Your mother and I kept *you* straight, didn't we?"

"Oh, yes! I remember those trips to the wood shed as if it were yesterday."

With Peggy's help, Clara served plates of steamed shrimp, fresh fried sea mullet, and clam strips for dinner. After Papa Tom returned the blessing and all plates were full, James began teasing Herb. "You don't look too nervous for a man about to walk down the aisle," he said, smiling at his brother-in-law across the table. "I thought all men had wedding jitters this close to the big day."

Herb glanced at Miriam. "Everything is going smoothly, James. Miriam and I are a team. She tells me what to do, and I do it."

Shaking her head, the bride-to-be said, "It doesn't seem fair that the bride has to make so many decisions. She has to decide on style and color for the bridesmaid's dresses, music, flowers, write thank you notes for gifts, attend parties, order invitations and a million other things. It's easy for a man. He gets up that morning, gets dressed in a dark suit and shows up at the church. It doesn't seem fair!"

"Yes, but those are all things that women *love* to do. Men are supposed to fish, hunt and listen to ball games on the radio," answered Herb.

"Why, I wouldn't have a dress to wear if it weren't for Granny Jewel and Clara. She had to practically remake my sister's dress so it would fit. I can never thank you enough," said Miriam, looking at the lady who would soon be her mother-in-law.

"It was my pleasure, and if I may say so, you will be the most beautiful bride ever married at St. Paul's Episcopal Church."

"I beg to differ," interrupted Papa Tom. "My wife was the most beautiful bride ever married at St. Paul's."

"No, no, Peggy was the most gorgeous bride, ever in any church!" declared James indignantly.

Clara stepped to the door of the kitchen. "If you rowdy men don't behave yourselves, there will be no dessert for you. I can throw your portion in the yard for the neighborhood cats."

Joshua, fearful he may be linked with the men in the family, quickly announced, "I haven't said a word, Clara. I'm being real good."

Sarah leaned close to her brother. "I thought you liked being one of the 'menfolks.'"

"Not when it comes to dessert," he replied with conviction. The rest of the main course was eaten in silence. Only Amy, examining her bowl of steamed shrimp, was unmindful of the peril of speaking aloud.

At breakfast, the following morning, Peggy announced she and Granny Jewel would be going to the parish house to help decorate for the annual church picnic that was always held on the Fourth of July weekend. "Sarah, I want you to look out for your brother and sister while I'm gone. If I take Amy I won't get a thing done."

"I would like to take a walk on the waterfront with my children," announced their father." At home it's rush, rush, rush. While I'm here, I want to enjoy my kids."

After breakfast, Joshua hurried to get Amy's stroller off the back porch, while Sarah packed a diaper bag in case of an emergency. As the little group moved slowly down the sidewalk, Peggy turned to her mother. "Phew, suddenly the house is silent as a tomb. Don't you and Daddy love the peace and quiet when we're gone?"

"Yes, it's nice and quiet while we sit and mark off the days until you're back."

"Ah, the famous south breeze blowing off the ocean, clear skies, sandy beaches and an ocean for swimming. What a paradise!" exclaimed James. "I wish I could move Bowers' Chemical Co. to Beaufort. How about you, Sissie? Are you sad when it's time to go back to Raleigh?"

Sarah thought a moment. "Well, yes, I'm sad, but it's exciting to start a new school year and see my friends again. I really miss Lindsey during the summer. Someday, when I finish college, I plan to move to Beaufort for good. Granny Jewel and Papa Tom will be old then and I'll take care of them."

"That's very kind of you, Sarah. I'm glad you love your grandparents that much." James smiled at his lovely daughter. "Suppose you meet a handsome young man who wants to carry you away to another part of the country?"

Sarah thought a minute. "If he wants me, he'll have to carry me away to Beaufort."

"Let's go down to Capt. Jake's dock," suggested Joshua. "We could rent a row boat and row across the channel."

"That sounds like a good plan," agreed the father. When they reached Capt. Jake's dock, Sarah called. There was no answer, so they walked to the end of the dock where a small building stood. Sarah called again.

"Come aboard," someone answered. They stepped inside the small room and were pleasantly surprised at the cool interior. With the front and back doors open, a breeze sailed through.

"Hi, Capt. Jake," greeted Sarah. While their eyes were growing accustomed to the dark interior, Sarah introduced her family. "This is my father, James Bowers, my brother, Joshua, and my sister, Amy."

Capt. Jake rose slowly, put his unlit pipe in his shirt pocket and extended a rough, work scarred hand. His grip was surprisingly strong for an older man. "You folks have a seat and tell me what you're up to."

"Daddy's here for a few days, and we thought it might be fun to rent a skiff and go for a boat ride." Sarah's suggestion was met with silence. Capt. Jake, unhurried, tapped tobacco residue from his pipe, slowly repacked and struggled to light it. All sat silently and watched.

"You want to rent a skiff, you say," replied Capt. Jake, between puffs.

"Yes, sir, Capt. Jake. It will be a nice experience for the children," said their father.

Capt. Jake made no move to get up. He squinted at the father and grinned. "I remember you, now. You were a Duke student a few years back. It appears you've put on a little weight," observed the captain.

"Yes, sir."

"Don't have much opportunity to row a boat in Raleigh, I guess."

"No, sir."

"It appears the little one can get about pretty good. You planning to tie her to the seat? If she goes over the side, she'll be gone in an instant." Capt. Jake had been observing Amy's constant motion in the dock house.

"I'll admit my rowing skills are not what they could be," mumbled James.

Capt. Jake was relentless. "What if you get caught in an outgoing tide? If an oar pops out of the oarlock, you could fall backwards and hit your head. You won't be much help to these young'uns if you're unconscious." The old man's gaze never left the younger man.

"Uh, perhaps you're right. I'd better have some lessons, first."

"That's a wise choice, Mr. Bowers. No wonder you've got a prosperous business in the big city. You've got common sense."

The father rose to go. "Leland," called out the captain. A young man stuck his head inside the door. "Yes, sir, Capt?"

"Take these nice folks for a turn around Piver's Island and under the bridge. They're upstaters and want to go for a boat ride."

Leland Davis turned his attention to the visitors. "Sarah? Is that you, Sarah? Boy, am I glad to see you! I heard you were here." Leland barely acknowledged the others, as Sarah made introductions. He hurried to the first boat tied to the dock. After helping the others aboard, he untied the bow and stern lines and shoved off. With an ability born from years of experience, Leland effortlessly guided the boat out into the channel. The wooden boat glided along with the incoming tide as the young man steered and maneuvered the boat with a pair of oars.

"Does your granddaddy still have that stern kicker on the back of his boat?" asked Leland grinning.

"He still has it, Leland, but it doesn't work so good. Ramie, Clara's nephew, tries to keep it repaired, but Papa Tom *never* goes out in the boat without his oars and oarlocks."

"Smart man," said Leland, turning in the seat to see where he was going. Sarah hoped to see Katie Higgins as they rowed around Piver's Island. Sarah still remembered the night she and Porter Mason nearly drowned while they were floundering. *I owe my life to Katie Higgins and her daddy,* thought Sarah.

In order to clear her mind of that terrible night, Sarah asked, "Leland, have you been taking pictures? You are such a good photographer."

Leland beamed under Sarah's honest praise. "I sure have. I've been off to school and learned a lot. My parents gave me a really nice camera for my birthday." He looked at the girl shyly. "Would you like to see some of my pictures?"

"I sure would. Do you have them at the boat house?"

Leland nodded enthusiastically. "Yeah. I keep them in a scrap book so they won't get torn or wrinkled."

After they had been under the bridge and let cars drive 'over' them, they returned to Capt. Jake's dock. James, still holding Amy in a firm grip, paid for the use of the boat, and gave Leland a handsome tip.

The young man took a leather bound scrap book from a drawer in an old dresser. All gathered around as Leland proudly showed his pictures. James was mildly interested at first, thinking there would mostly be pictures of boats and cars. Instead, there were pictures of people whose expressions Leland had captured. There was one of a small boy holding a dead bird. He was wearing a curious expression, as if he couldn't understand why the bird was so still. In another picture, he had photographed a young mother hanging out diapers. The wind was strong, the diapers standing straight out as she tried to anchor them to the line while holding clothes pins in her mouth.

"I know just how he feels," murmured the father, looking at a picture of an elderly man struggling to change a flat tire. His clothes were muddy and he wore an angry expression. Leland had so artfully captured the gentleman's emotions, James could immediately identify with him. Near the back of the book, James picked up a photo of a familiar face. It was a girl, chin tilted, laughing as she held a lock of hair that was threatening to blow across her face.

"Why, Sarah, it's a picture of you," said James, awe in his voice. He studied the picture for several minutes. "You're beautiful, honey. Of course, you're always beautiful," he added quickly, "but there's something about this picture…." His voice trailed off.

"Sawah, my Sawah," chanted Amy.

"Leland, I must have three copies of this picture. Can you make them?"

Leland nodded. "I got more pictures of Sarah. Do you want copies of them, too?"

"Yes."

"But you haven't seen them."

"I see your work, Leland. I want three copies of any pictures of Sarah."

Back on the sidewalk, James remarked, "I'm not used to life in a small town. Everybody knows everybody. How did Capt. Jake know we own a chemical plant in Raleigh?"

"That's just the way it is, Daddy. That's just the way it is – and I hope it never changes," replied his older daughter.

Chapter 11

"Daddy," asked Joshua, thrusting his suntanned toes into a pair of white socks and Sunday shoes, "if we are going to a picnic, why can't we wear old clothes and go barefoot?"

Patiently, his father explained. "The picnic is *after* Sunday school and Church, so, you can't wear play clothes. This is one picnic where you have to be careful not to mess up your good clothes." His answer was met with a loud groan. James Bowers stopped wrestling with his tie, and sat down on the edge of the bed. "Joshua, you are nine years old, too old to whine and complain. Mackie Fuller is your guest today, so you must set a good example, because I don't think he spends a lot of time in church. I want to see your sunny smile, and a right attitude." He patted his son's head. "Consider this your first and only warning."

"Yes, sir."

For a special treat, Clara substituted thick, fluffy pancakes, covered in melted butter and golden syrup, instead of the usual Sunday morning bowl of dry cereal. "Mmmm, Clara," crooned Joshua, "these flapjacks are melting in my mouth!"

"Where did you hear them called flapjacks?" she inquired.

"In the movies, cowboys always say 'flapjacks.' They wash them down with a cup of strong coffee," he added.

"Well, you ain't gonna' have a cup of coffee, cause it's not good for growing boys."

Joshua looked at the clock on the dining room mantle. It was past time for Mackie to make his appearance. "Mama, do you think Mackie forgot?"

"I don't know, honey. If he doesn't come in the next few minutes, we'll have to leave without him."

"Maybe he overslept," suggested Sarah.

As Joshua sopped the last of the maple syrup with a morsel of pancake, they heard a loud banging on the front door. Joshua sprang from his chair. "I'll bet that's him," he said happily. When he opened the door, he was greeted by a new Mackie. His hair was parted and plastered against his head with grease that shone in the morning sun. His skin was several shades lighter than Joshua had ever seen, and he was wearing new clothes from head to toe. He wore a scowl Joshua remembered from the summer before.

"You laugh, and I'll shove you against the wall," he announced, clenching and unclenching his fists.

"I wouldn't laugh, Mackie. I have to wear Sunday clothes, too. It isn't so bad after you get used to them."

"I don't plan to get used to them. I'm not doing this again until there's another picnic."

"Good morning, Mackie," said Papa Tom, holding out his hand. Mackie held out his hand while staring at the floor.

The boys walked behind the rest of the family. After a few minutes, Mackie asked, "Why do you go to church, anyway? What good does it do? I can see going today, because of the food, but what about all the other times?"

"I go because I've been going all my life, and because my parents make me."

"Those ain't good enough reasons to have to get all dressed up in these painful clothes," added Mackie.

"There's another reason that's deep down inside."

"What's that?"

"I want to go because I love God, and He loves me, and it would hurt His feelings if I didn't go to church."

"What's He ever done for you?"

"He sees that I have everything I need," explained Joshua.

Mackie grinned, "No, kid, your daddy does that."

"He gave me my daddy."

"Hmmm, I gotta think about that. My daddy has a job now and we have a new house. Do you think God did that?" asked Mackie.

"Yeah, and He made you big and strong so you can take care of yourself."

"I can take care of other people, too," he grinned slyly, pounding a fist into the palm of his hand.

"I don't mean like that, Mackie. I mean you are healthy."

"Yeah, kid, and I'll take care of anybody that messes with you, too. Maybe God wants me to be your bodyguard."

"Thanks, Mackie," answered Joshua, inching away. "I'll try to think of that as a blessing."

William Davis, the boys' Sunday school teacher, welcomed Mackie with enthusiasm. "I'm just here for the food," was the boy's reply. The teacher, unable to think of a suitable reply, launched into the day's lesson.

Church was even more painful for Mackie. He had already been still for one hour, and another hour loomed before him. The ancient pews, torturously uncomfortable, made the hour seem unending. The church was stifling, no breeze able to find its way past the lovely old stained glass windows, which were shoved open at an angle.

"Joshua," he whispered loudly, "if you ever try to talk me into coming to church again, I'm going to give you one of these blessings – right between the eyes." Mackie balled up his fist and brought it dangerously close to Joshua's nose.

"I promise, Mackie."

"Shhh," Joshua's mother cautioned.

After the benediction, the boys escaped before the congregation could gather their belongings and block the aisles. "This is what I've been waiting for all morning," declared Mackie, rubbing his hands together. I can't wait to get at that food. Are you sure there's going to be fried chicken *and* chocolate cake?"

"Sure. My mother and grandmother and even Clara spent yesterday cooking a lot of stuff."

"You're lucky to have somebody to cook all that food. Mama feels bad most of the time, and daddy has to come home and fix supper."

"Is your mother sick?"

"Yeah, She's got something, but I can't remember the name. They don't say much around me, but I hear them talking after they think I've gone to sleep."

"Maybe she'll feel better soon," consoled Joshua.

"Nah. I don't think she's ever going to get well."

The horror of Mackie's words caused Joshua's breath to come in small gasps. *What if it was his mother? What would he do if his mama was too sick to laugh and play with him and his sisters?* It was too horrible to think about.

"Wait, Mackie. We can't go in the parish house and start filling our plates yet."

"What's the problem now?"

"The preacher has to bless the food."

"He's been blessing stuff all morning. Doesn't that count?"

"Uh, no, that was part of the service. This is different. If we start loading our plates before everybody gets here, it would be bad manners, and I'd catch it when I got home."

Mercifully, the congregation, a few at a time, joined the boys at the head of the line. "Boy, am I hungry!" said one man in a loud voice. "I hope the preacher doesn't take all day."

"Why is it all right for grown people to talk like that, but it's bad manners if little kids say it?" whispered Mackie.

"I don't know, but it's always been that way. At least when we get old, we can say whatever we want to and not worry about being reminded of our manners."

With their plates loaded, the boys started to sit down in the cool parish hall. "Let's sit under the tree in the courtyard, Mackie. Some of the other kids are out there. Save us a seat, and I'll get two glasses of lemonade."

Joshua hurried, unsure of the fate of any child who unknowingly sat in the chairs Mackie was saving.

A boy, sitting across the table spoke, "Hey, I know you. I've seen you at school."

"So what," asked Mackie, struggling to talk with a mouthful of fried chicken.

The boy shrugged his shoulders. "No reason. I just thought if you're going to start coming to church, we'd like to have you on our baseball team."

Mackie nodded enthusiastically, "Yeah, that would be great! I don't get to play at school, because I always get bad grades on conduct."

"We don't care about that. We want you to help us win the championship in our diocese. Besides, Mr. Davis gets all excited when we get a new member in our Sunday school class."

"Does that mean I have to suffer through his class just so I can play baseball?"

"Afraid so."

With things going well at their table, Joshua took the empty glasses inside for refills. While he was waiting in line, Katie Higgins walked up behind him.

"Hello, Joshua," she said in her solemn voice. "Are you having a good time?"

Joshua turned briefly. "Yeah," he said and again faced front.

"You're welcome to sit with my parents and me," Katie offered.

"No, thanks. I'm sitting with my friends," said Joshua, continuing to face forward.

"I thought I was one of your friends," Katie persisted. "Why don't you come over to Pivers Island and play anymore? There's a lot of fun things to do."

Joshua turned and hissed at the blonde, brown-eyed girl. "Because, you think you can do everything better than me."

"That's not true!"

"Oh, yes it is!" Joshua moved closer, a sneer on his lips. "You laugh at the way I swim, and how long it takes me to climb a tree, and you can run faster." Remembering Mackie's hurtful words the summer before, he used them on the girl. "Get lost, Katie." When he saw her terrible reaction to his harsh words, Joshua was immediately sorry he had spoken. He watched his playmate of the summer before turn and hurry away. *So what*, he thought. *Only sissies play with girls.*. He returned to the table of boys with two full glasses of iced cold lemonade. He forgot about Katie until he saw her leaving with her parents. He could tell she had been crying because of red splotches around her eyes. Neither parent looked his way. *I better think up some good excuse for hurting her feelings, just in case her mother tells my mother.* The whole incident ruined Joshua's appetite for a slice of rich, chocolate cake.

His thoughts were interrupted by his guest. "Hey, ain't you gonna eat that cake? If you're not, I am!" Mackie expertly slid Joshua's portion onto his plate and ate it.

Inside, the family was joined by Herb and Miriam. Their lunch was interrupted several times by so many well-wishers stopping by the table. Men teased Herb about losing his freedom, and women asked for an update on wedding plans. "Jewel, are you going to need these two chairs?" asked a strident voice.

Granny Jewel looked up into the face of Gladys Hill, the town's worst, or best, gossip. She and her husband, David were standing across from them, plate and drink in hand.

"Oh, no, Gladys, please, sit down," she said without enthusiasm. For awhile all were occupied with fried chicken, fresh cooked vegetables and homemade bread. Later, Gladys, one elbow resting on the table, leaned forward.

"Jewel," she began, "isn't that the Fuller boy with your grandchild?" Eyes riveted on Granny Jewel, she waited motionless for an answer.

"Uh, yes, Gladys, Mackie is our guest."

Leaning closer, the woman asked again, "Aren't you afraid he'll be a bad influence on your grandson?" Before Granny Jewel could answer, she continued. "He is the neighborhood bully on our street, and if you say anything to him, he talks back, and I've even heard him curse!" Gladys Hill straightened in her chair, wearing a satisfied smirk. She looked at her husband for verification.

"Yes, dear," he replied attacking a slice of thick, moist chocolate cake. It was obvious to Joshua's grandmother that David Hill had perfected the ability to agree with his wife without being fully aware of the subject.

Granny Jewel could feel anger seeping around the edges of her good mood. "Gladys, God expects us to love each other. Nowhere in the scriptures does it say, 'love only the clean, well-mannered people.' He expects us to love the ones who may not be easy to love."

The woman squinted one eye, dipped her head, and pointed a bony finger in Granny Jewel's direction. "Well, it would take a heap of effort to love that boy. He's in trouble all the time and I've even seen the police car parked in front of his house." Gladys Hill warmed to her subject. "Why, I'll bet he's in jail before he's twenty-one. Mark my words, Jewel Mitchell, before the summer's out you may change your tune."

"Thank you, Gladys, I'll try to remember that." She turned to her family and joined in their merry conversation.

Late in the afternoon, when the air began to cool, the family moved to the front porch to enjoy the breeze. Joshua was busy lining up his tin soldiers on the railing. "How did Mackie enjoy going to Sunday school and church, Joshua?"

The boy paused for a moment. "I thought he was going to get up any minute and walk out of Sunday school, and especially in church. It was only the thought of all that good food that kept him in the pew. He may start coming more, because some of the boys in our class asked him to join the baseball team."

"Whatever it takes," replied his uncle.

By Friday, the words of Gladys Hill returned to haunt the Mitchell household. After lunch on that day Mackie called. "Come on over. Me and Billy are going to have some fun."

"I'll be right there," was the boy's reply. Joshua put down the phone and ran upstairs to find his mother. "Mama, can I go to Mackie's?"

"Come and sit on the bed while I fold clothes," his mother replied. Joshua sat reluctantly, anxious to be gone.

"Son, I'm uneasy when you're with Mackie. I know you like to play with him but he has a bad reputation with people in Beaufort. He got you in trouble once this summer. If it happens again your father and I will not be as lenient. Promise me you won't do anything foolish."

"Yes, Mama," he agreed easing toward the door.

"One more thing."

"Yes, Mama?" voice tinged with impatience.

"Mrs. Hill was telling us at the picnic that Mackie and Billy sneak rides on the train. That's very dangerous. Promise me you'll stay away from the train."

"Yes, Ma'am, I promise." When his mother once more turned her attention to the mound of clean clothes, Joshua plunged down the steps, leaped across the bottom two, burst through the front door and ran down the driveway. He wiggled through the broken fence paling, stopping only when he reached Mackie's back porch. He rapped on the screen door frame, and waited impatiently for Mackie to come through the kitchen.

"We were about to leave without you," was Mackie's gruff greeting.

"Where are we going?"

Billy appeared at the kitchen door, a finger on his lips. "Not so loud," he whispered. Joshua, accustomed to having a baby in the house, lowered his voice.

"Why are we whispering?" He knew there was no baby, and if there were, its chances of survival would be slim.

"Mama's asleep. She always sleeps after she takes her medicine." The three stepped out on the back porch.

"So," he asked in a normal voice, "what are we going to do?"

Mackie shot Joshua a sly grin.

"We could go down to your grandfather's store and steal some more candy and cigarettes."

"Not a chance," Joshua answered quickly. "My uncle will give us some candy. We don't have to steal it." The boy suddenly remembered the day they smoked cigarettes in the old shed. Even now, the memory of that day made his knees weak.

"Or," said Mackie, slapping at a mosquito. "we could hop the train and ride over to the fish factory."

"Count me out," Joshua mumbled reluctantly. "My parents told me not to mess around the train. It's dangerous."

"Oh," mimicked Mackie. "Our 'city boy' can't ride the train. He has to stay home and mind his mama." He strutted up and down the porch, swaying his hips and fanning with one hand. Joshua looked at Billy for support. The other boy, so relieved Mackie's wrath was not being directed at him, nodded with every comment. "I didn't think you were going to be a 'sissy pants' anymore," the boy said, stopping in front of Joshua, noses almost touching. Mackie coiled his hands in tight fists. With tremendous effort, Joshua returned his stare without blinking. Sensing this approach wasn't going to work, Mackie put an arm around Joshua's shoulder. "Look, it's more fun than a circus ride and lasts a lot longer. Me and Billy do it all the time."

Joshua remained silent, studying an ant crawling across the ground.

"Come on, Billy, we're wasting time."

The larger boy stomped off, not looking back. Billy hurried to keep up. Joshua watched them leave, their bare feet padding on the sidewalk. More than anything else, at that moment, Joshua wanted to be with them. He heard his own voice call out, "Wait, wait for me." As he ran to catch up, a voice hammered inside his head. '*This is wrong. Turn back.*' The boys waited, smiled and beckoned. It felt *so* good to be included.

Before the boys reached the end of Broad Street, they could hear the steam engine chuffing. Today there was a huge boiler to be delivered to the fish factory. It was secured to a flat-bed car by massive chains. Joshua noticed the boiler was a shiny silver color held together by rivets and bands of steel. His eyes wandered down the track and stopped. He wanted to move closer to the shiny green engine trimmed in gold with a coal car painted to match.

"This is our lucky day," declared Mackie, as they crouched under the flat bed car. "When she pulls out, we can jump on and hide behind the machinery. Nobody will ever know we're back here."

Suddenly there was a burst of steam from the engine, as the great iron wheels began turning. The boys grabbed a bar on the end and pulled themselves up, being very careful to not stand up, since there was always the chance of being discovered by the engineer. Each sat, legs dangling from the end of the train car. Below was the coupling which would connect another car if needed.

Joshua leaned over and watched the cross ties fly by beneath his feet. The sound of the wheels hitting the track ties gave a rhythmic staccato. Now the boy understood the cadence in music class when they sang about trains. He glanced at his two friends. "This is great. It's even better than a ride at the state fair," he shouted.

"I ain't never been to the state fair," offered Billy.

"Hey, you two, pipe down! Do you want us to get caught? We could end up in the jailhouse, and our parents would have to come and bail us out." Mackie gave a wicked laugh and thumped Joshua on the back.

A feeling not unlike being sick at your stomach washed over Joshua. Suppose he did end up at the police station. Would they call his parents and ask them to come and get him? Maybe they'd be so angry, they would leave him there. In the movies, convicts wore striped suits and were fed bread and water. They had to sleep on narrow cots, too. He liked wearing shorts and going barefoot. He loved his bed and soft pillow that always smelled fresh and clean. He would miss out on Clara's cooking. Worst of all would be the expression of disappointment on his parents' faces.

"I'm jumping off when the train slows down to cross the highway," Joshua announced.

"What's the matter 'fraidy cat,' scared of getting caught?"

"Maybe he's seasick," offered Billy, grinning at Joshua.

"Maybe he's train sick," laughed Mackie.

Moments later the train began to slow. Joshua braced himself, looking for a soft spot where he could land. Suddenly, the air was split with a thunderous blast from the whistle, warning traffic on the highway to stop. The wailing, ear splitting sound was like nothing Joshua had ever heard before. Sure, he heard train whistles in Raleigh, but they were a long way off, and sounded so lonesome. This was different! He wanted to stand and answer with a war whoop that would rival the steam engine's powerful voice. The train crossed the highway, flashing lights and bells warning cars to stop. *I know what I'm going to be when I grow up*, he decided, waving at people in waiting cars. *I'm going to be an engineer on the train, and I'm going to let all the boys in Beaufort ride every day..*

Waiting patiently at the railroad crossing was Gladys Hill, on her way to Miss Carraway's farm to pick up fresh milk. She stared at the train as it passed, her mind miles away. Suddenly, her eyes flew wide open. Young'uns had no business hitching a ride on the train! They'll probably all three grow up to be hobos, she decided, taking one last look before putting her car in first gear. Why, that one in the bright red shirt looked for all the world like Jewel Mitchell's grandson! "Ah ha!" she cried to the empty car. "Just give me enough time to get my milk, and I'll be making a phone call." Gladys thought a moment, then turned her car around. "To heck with the milk. I'll get some tomorrow. It won't kill David to drink water with his meals."

The ringing of the telephone interrupted Peggy Bowers while she was reading the morning newspaper. "Yes, she's here, just a minute." She called upstairs, "Mama, telephone." Unclipping an earring, Granny Jewel put the receiver to her ear.

"Hello? Oh, hello, Gladys." The grandmother rolled her eyes heavenward.

Peggy returned to her chair in the living room. After a few moments, she looked up, slowly lowering the paper as her mother's conversation continued.

"I'm sure you're mistaken, Gladys. My grandson promised us he wouldn't go near the train." Again, there was a long pause. "No, Gladys, I don't think my grandson is better than anyone else's, and living on Ann Street has nothing to do with it."

Peggy quietly folded the newspaper and laid it on the coffee table. She knew by her mother's voice that somebody on the other end of the line was close to getting their ear adjusted.

"I can assure you Gladys, we will tend to the matter. No, I'm not going to call and tell you anything. It's not *really* any of your...,any of your... uh, uh, concern. Goodbye, Gladys." The receiver hit the cradle with a loud whack. "Peggy," called her mother.

"Yes, Mama!"

"Where is Joshua?"

"He's over at Mackie's house."

The older woman sat down heavily on the edge of a nearby chair. "That was Gladys Hill. She's sure she saw Joshua and two other boys riding on the train today. "Peggy," she asked hesitantly, "what shirt was Joshua wearing?"

"He has on the new red one we bought at Upton's last week. Why?"

"Gladys said the boy who looked like Joshua was wearing a bright red shirt."

Before Peggy could reply, they were interrupted by voices on the porch. Papa Tom, James and Herb came in laughing. "Ah, here are our lovely wives, waiting patiently for our return," said James. "Are we in time for lunch? At breakfast Clara promised to fix brunswick stew and cornbread with gallons of strong iced tea." He listened for a moment. "Where are the kids? It's mighty quiet in here."

"Sarah has gone to see Nancy, Amy's in her playpen, and Joshua..."

"Joshua, what?" asked James. "Where is he? Is anything wrong?"

"He went to Mackie's house to play, and uh, we got a phone call telling us he was seen riding on the back of the train."

Granny Jewel offered, "One of the ladies from the church saw him as the train was going toward the fish factory."

"He'll be sorry he ever saw a train," his father said angrily.

"James," said Papa Tom, "you don't know if the boy on the train was Joshua. When he comes in, give him a chance to tell you where he's been. Boys can be under a lot of pressure if others dare them. Peer pressure for boys his age knows no bounds."

A troubled group gathered for lunch. Clara placed the soup tureen on the table. She returned to the kitchen, mumbling, "I knew that boy would be trouble." Later, she reappeared, the long wooden stirring spoon in hand. Using it to point toward Mackie's house, she announced, "If HE has caused my baby to get hurt, there's going to be *big* trouble."

"Thank you, Clara. Peggy and I will wash the dishes so you can get home early and enjoy your afternoon off."

"Uh-huh. You all want old Clara out of the house so you can punish that innocent lamb." Clara crossed her arms over her chest, the long, wooden spoon firmly clenched in her right hand. I may decide I don't WANT the afternoon off."

"William is waiting for you," Granny Jewel said smoothly.

"Humph," huffed Clara, returning to the kitchen. A moment later the back door slammed.

"Clara can get the last word without ever speaking," said Papa Tom, trying to be amusing.

"No matter the circumstances Tom, if Joshua was on that train, he must be punished. If someone dares you to do something dangerous, you have to learn to walk away."

Herb quickly finished his lunch, rose from the table, and kissed his mother on the cheek. Amy, smeared with gravy, received a pat on the head. Giving his sister a hug, he said, "Good luck, or God bless, or whatever you say at a time like this." He waved at the men and was gone.

When Joshua returned an hour later, he was surprised to see his parents and grandparents sitting in the living room, neither smiling nor talking.

It reminded him of the years during the war when all grown up people sat by the radio and listened to the news.

"Hey," he said in greeting.

"Joshua, you're late," began his father. "Have you had lunch?"

"Yes, sir."

"Where?"

Joshua began to feel as sense of fear in the pit of his stomach.

"Uh, I ate with Mackie." The boy suddenly felt compelled to study a tiny crack in the ceiling overhead.

"What did you have?" asked his mother.

"Hmmm, biscuits and butterbeans."

"I thought his mother was too weak to prepare meals," she added.

"Uh, you're right, Mama. I forgot. We had jelly sandwiches." He looked imploringly at his grandparents. "I think I'll go upstairs now because I need to do some reading." He began to back toward the door.

"Stay, Joshua," came his father's deep voice. Slowly the boy inched around the sofa and sat down beside his grandfather, his hand on the man's knee.

"What did you do today?" asked his father.

Joshua brightened. "Oh, we played army. Billy and I were the good guys, and we pretended to…"

His father interrupted. "Did you boys go anywhere near the train?"

"No, sir." Joshua stared straight at his father but it was obvious he was having trouble swallowing.

Silence filled the room. The boy nervously picked at his fingernails until Papa Tom gently closed his hand over his grandson's smaller one.

"I'm going to give you a chance to tell the truth, son. Were you riding on the train today, and let me add, a boy fitting your description was seen by someone your grandmother knows."

The boy sighed deeply. After several minutes he spoke. "It was me, Daddy." Joshua's voice rose. "Mackie made me do it! He forced me to get on the train! I didn't want to!"

"Are you telling the truth?"

"Yes, sir," he whispered, looking at his toes.

"I think I'll call Mackie over to see if your stories are the same."

"No, no," he begged. Tears rolled down his face, mingling with a film of coal dust. "I told him I couldn't go, so he made fun of me and called me a sissy. I had to show them I wasn't afraid to disobey."

"I understand, son, and most people would do just as you did."

Joshua hastily wiped away his tears with the back of his hand and looked hopefully at his father.

"However, because you lied, you will be punished. Go to your room and wait for me." Joshua stood and moved slowly toward the door.

"Jewel," asked Papa Tom, "why don't we take Amy for a walk?"

"Oh, let's, dear! We can take her to the library and check out picture books." Quickly the grandmother went into the next room, scooped Amy up in her arms and followed the grandfather through the house and out the back door. Papa Tom banged the stroller down the steps and unceremoniously stuffed his granddaughter inside.

"This is fun, Ganny Jool," announced Amy, clapping her hands.

A block from the house, they slowed their pace. "Tom, you put your belt on Herb more than once, and he grew to be a fine man."

"Yes, and Joshua will, too." Papa Tom smiled down at his wife. "You know, I'm very proud of our grandson."

"What?"

"Yes, I'm proud he's such a terrible liar."

Long after slivers of sunlight had disappeared from the edges of his window shades, Joshua lay, staring at the ceiling. When a soft knock came on his door, he sat up slowly. "Come in," he called.

The door opened, revealing his sister with a bowl of soup, soda crackers and a glass of milk on a tray. "I thought the condemned man was supposed to eat a hearty meal *before* his execution," Sarah whispered. Joshua never smiled. "Sorry, bad joke," she said quietly. "Do you mind if I sit down?"

Joshua slid over and patted the bed.

"Do you want to talk about it?"

He swung his feet over the side of the bed, taking the tray on his lap. "Sarah," he said, between spoonfuls of soup, "riding the train was like nothing else in the whole world. The speed makes you feel like you're flying, the sound of the train whistle and hearing the clickity-clack of the iron wheels is more wonderful than anything I've ever known." He paused and looked at his sister. "Has everybody gone to bed?"

"No, why?"

"Because, when they do, I'm running away. Nobody loves me anymore."

"You've got it all wrong, little brother. Daddy punished you *because* he loves you, and don't you forget it."

"I'm sorry," he said, brushing cracker crumbs from the sheets.

"Are you sorry it happened, or are you sorry you got caught."

"I'll have to think about that."

Sarah, taking the empty tray, got up to leave.

"Goodbye, Sarah. I'll never see you again."

Sarah stopped at the door and looked back. "I wish you wouldn't go. Tomorrow morning Clara is making fluffy, golden pancakes with melted butter, drowning in maple syrup. She'll be disappointed if you're not here."

"I suppose I could put off leaving one day."

"That's a wise idea. By the way, what are your plans?"

"I'm going to join the army."

"Army life is pretty tough."

Joshua eased back on the bed, careful to lay on his stomach. "It can't be as tough as getting caught in a lie in this family."

Chapter 12

Sarah could hear voices in the front hall. She opened one eye, stretched, and quickly pulled the sheet up to her chin. It was much too early to be concerned. She had already been awakened once by Mr. Peavy. Even with a pillow over her head, she could hear her grandmother and Clara talking excitedly. She tossed the pillow aside when she heard a gentle knocking on her door.

"Sarah, are you awake, dear?" came her mother's voice.

"Yes, Mama, I'm awake," she answered wearily.

"Miriam is here. Your bridesmaids' dress came in the mail, and she thought you might like to see it."

Like a bullet from a gun, Sarah leapt from her bed. Her nightgown floated through the air, landing softly on the unmade bed. "I'm coming, Mama! I'm coming!" In a moment, Sarah was dressed in clean shorts and shirt, hair combed. As she left, she slammed the door so no one would see the condition of her bedroom.

She was stopped suddenly by Clara, standing in the middle of the kitchen, hands on hips. "Good morning, Clara," mumbled Sarah, trying to ease past.

"Now where are you off to in such a hurry?"

"I can't stop now, Clara. Miriam is here with my dress for the wedding."

"I know all that," she replied, still blocking Sarah's path. "You're not going anywhere on an empty stomach. You stand around half the day in the heat while the dress is being fitted, and pretty soon you'll get the vapors, and pass out in the floor. You could fall and break your nose! Now wouldn't that be a pretty sight, sashaying down the aisle in your new dress, and a big, white plaster cast on your nose."

Sarah sighed, rolled her eyes and reached for two slices of cold hard toast, left from breakfast. They were sitting on the counter, soon to be crumbs for the birds. Sarah stuffed the tasteless slices in her mouth, and washed them down with a few gulps of orange juice. "Is this good enough?" she asked, when she could speak. "May I go *now*?"

"Humph! Don't go getting sassy with old Clara. I'm just trying to look out for you."

Sarah lowered her eyes. "I'm sorry, Clara. I guess I'm too excited to eat."

Clara stood aside and watched Sarah's retreating form. "This wedding gonna' cause everybody in this house to lose their mind. Looks like it's up to me to hold the family together," she mumbled, while mercilessly scrubbing breakfast dishes in hot soapy water.

Sarah brushed bread crumbs from her blouse before she stepped into the living room. Her mother, grandmother, and Miriam were discussing wedding plans.

"Ah, there you are, Sarah," said Miriam, smiling. "Your dress came this morning, so I hurried over. You must be anxious to see it."

"Yes, ma'am. I can hardly wait to try it on."

"Why don't we go upstairs," suggested Granny Jewel. "The dress may need to be altered, and Miriam, your gown needs a final fitting."

The bride-to-be reached down beside her chair, picked up a large box wrapped in brown paper and tied with heavy twine. She handed it to Sarah. "It hasn't been opened," said Sarah, surprised.

"I thought it would be nice if we opened it together." Sarah looked into the soft, blue eyes of her almost aunt. At that moment she felt that through the years Miriam would not only be her relative, but a dear friend.

Sarah hurried to the kitchen. "Clara, I need a knife so we can open the box. Come upstairs so you can see it."

Clara hurriedly dried her hands, and selected a sharp paring knife. "I don't have time for this foolishness. There's hungry men coming home in a little while, and they'll be expecting a hot meal."

"Clara, can't you *please* forget the kitchen long enough to see my dress?" pleaded Sarah.

"Oh, all right. I suppose I have time to take one little peek," the woman said, hurrying behind Sarah.

Peggy Bowers sat holding Amy firmly in her arms. When Miriam reached for the knife, Clara refused to give it to her. "You might let it slip and cut yourself. Now, wouldn't that be pretty, going up the aisle, holding a bouquet of flowers and a big white bandage on your finger. Or worse, suppose you cut your ring finger. There you are holding out your dainty hand and my precious boy trying to shove a ring over gauze and adhesive tape."

"I don't want you to get hurt, either, Clara," said Miriam.

"Honey," the older woman replied, "when you've cut up as many chickens as I have you won't have any trouble opening a package."

Twine and brown paper aside, there was a shiny, white box with the name of the store embossed on top. "Oh, Sarah, let's see what's inside," whispered Miriam.

Slowly, the girl lifted the lid. All leaned forward, saying not a word. Inside was layer after layer of white tissue paper. Reaching under, her hand felt smooth, soft fabric. Pushing the tissue aside, the girl slowly drew the gown from the box. Only soft 'ooh's' and 'ah's' were spoken. The dress Sarah held was lavender organdy, lined with matching taffeta. The skirt was three tiers of deep ruffles, the same delicate color.

"A fairy dress," squealed Amy, clapping her hands. "Mine, mine!"

"No, honey," corrected her mother. "That's Sarah's dress. Maybe someday she'll let you wear it when you are a little older."

"Try it on," said Granny Jewel. "I'm anxious to see how it fits." Sarah, many hands helping, slid the dress over her head. "Hold your hair up so it won't get caught in the zipper, honey."

When her grandmother finished, Sarah moved into the middle of the room. When she took a step, the dress rustled and whispered. She couldn't resist the temptation to spin around. The dress answered by fanning out in a wide circle. She grabbed handfuls of the organdy overskirt and held it out as far as she could reach.

"It's more beautiful than I remembered," said Miriam.

"It doesn't need to be altered," added Granny Jewel, relieved.

"The neckline is too daring," said Peggy, nervously.

Without taking her eyes off the dress, Granny Jewel answered. "The dress is supposed to be off the shoulders, but it has two narrow straps to hold it up. It looks just fine."

"I'll press it," declared Clara. "I can't take a chance on somebody in this house burning a hole in the front of *that* frock."

Sarah spun around once more, the skirt billowing. Seeing her reflection in the mirror over the fireplace, she exclaimed, "My hair! I can't wear it drooping around my face! It looks awful with this dress."

"We'll think of something, dear," comforted her mother.

"I am taking charge of Sarah's hair and make up for the wedding," declared Granny Jewel, winking broadly at Sarah. She was rewarded with a look of gratitude. "After all, the mother of the groom hasn't much to do but dress up and show up."

"What am I supposed to do?" asked Peggy.

"Honey, think about it. You have a husband *and* a son who bear close watching. They would gladly go to the wedding in a pair of old sneakers, hair uncombed."

"How about daddy? He's not to be trusted in polite company, either."

"You'll have to keep an eye on him, too."

"Thanks, Mama. I should be exhausted by the time they're man and wife."

Miriam's final fitting was also a success. The dress, once too large, now fit perfectly on the bride's thin girlish figure. The sleeves that had been long and heavy, fit over her slender arms, coming to a point on top of her hand. A dozen satin-covered buttons on each sleeve matched the ones on the back of the dress. Miriam turned, tears threatening to spill. "Thank you, Mrs. Mitchell. It is the most beautiful bridal gown I have ever seen."

The older woman embraced her soon-to-be daughter. "You are what makes it so beautiful, Miriam. When it's in a box or on a hanger, it's just another dress."

"Did you have a bridal veil?" asked Peggy, still struggling to keep Amy in her lap.

"I brought the lace mantilla my grandmother wore for her wedding. It will be perfect, since the dress is rather plain."

"And your hair? How will you wear it?"

Miriam studied her reflection. "My hair has grown this summer. I'm thinking about wearing it in a bun on the nape of my neck."

All were silent as they pictured this lovely woman on her wedding day.

The ringing of the telephone interrupted their thoughts. "I'll answer it," said Clara. I need to work on lunch, anyway. The menu has changed to roast beef sandwiches."

"That sounds fine, Clara. It's too hot to cook," added Granny Jewel.

The phone continued ringing as Clara made her way downstairs.

"Don't you think I hear you? Old Clara is coming as fast as she can. Telephones are nothing but a nuisance, interrupting people's lives," she mumbled.

"Granny Jewel, do you think Clara will ever quit making her speech to the telephone before she answers it?"

"No dear, Clara hopes to live long enough to see them go out of style. She feels people talk too much already."

"It's the jewelry store," called Clara. "Miss Mattie wants to talk with you or the bride." The Grandmother hurried downstairs while Peggy helped the girls struggle out of their dresses and carefully hang them.

"That sounds fine to me, Mattie, but I'd better ask Miriam and Herb before I can say for sure. Thanks for calling."

Jewel Mitchell replaced the receiver and turned to Miriam. "Miss Mattie said people are coming in every day buying gifts for you and Herb. She wants to know where they are to be delivered."

Miriam thought for a moment. "Our apartments are too small to properly display gifts. Would it be imposing if they came here?"

"Heavens, no! We can set up tables in the front room where everybody can come and see the presents."

"I'm glad that's decided," laughed Miriam. She looked at her watch. "If I don't hurry, I'm going to be late for a lunch date with my fiancé."

When Miriam was gone, Granny Jewel, spun around and headed for the kitchen. "Peggy, Sarah, follow me!"

Clara had finished making a stack of roast beef sandwiches. A tray of lettuce and fresh tomatoes was covered with wax paper, waiting in the refrigerator. A pitcher of iced tea,frosted, sat at the ready.

"Clara, stop what you're doing and help us, please."

"What about lunch?"

"We can eat later."

"How about the menfolks?"

Granny Jewel was beginning to sound exasperated. "Clara, they can fend for themselves just this once."

"Lunch is all fixed. All they gotta' do is eat it."

"Clara, you are a genius," said Peggy, hugging the older woman.

"Do you think for one minute I would let those men loose in my kitchen? There'd be mayonnaise dripping from the ceiling and mustard on my clean floor. Now, what kind of a bee have you got in your bonnet?"

"Clara, the wedding gifts are coming here to be displayed. We have to prepare the front room."

Clara dried her hands on her apron and followed the others to the front hall. Together, they moved the furniture against the wall. "We can make tables from saw horses and boards. White sheets can be draped over the dressers for extra space. "

"Granny Jewel, are we going to wait for Papa Tom and Uncle Herb to help us?"

"No, sweetheart, this is a job we can handle."

Peggy and Clara hurried to the shed, bringing saw horses and wide boards. When all was ready, Clara and the grandmother hurried upstairs to the linen closet. Sarah followed close behind. When the door was opened, Sarah's nostrils were filled with the delicate, lilac and lavender scent that reminded her of her grandmother.

"Hmmm, the sheets and towels smell so good!" said Sarah.

"That's because of sachet, honey. You buy it in little bags and put it among your linens, and they always smell good."

"May I hang a big bag around my brother's neck? Sometimes he smells mighty strong."

"Sorry, Sarah, little boys need soap and water, and plenty of it. Here, take this stack of white sheets."

All three carried sheets to the downstairs room, and spread them over the furniture in preparation for the gifts. As they finished, a knock was heard. "Come in," called Granny Jewel. When the door remained shut, she stepped into the hall. On the porch stood a young man with stacks of beautifully wrapped gifts in his hands.

"I'm sorry, Ma'am, I didn't have a free hand to open the door."

"Here, let me help you with those boxes." All stepped on the porch and relieved the young man of his burdens.

"Miss Mattie says be careful with this stuff, because some of it is mighty breakable."

"We promise to be *very* careful." Once inside the house, the boxes were placed on the sheet-covered shelves. "Miriam and Herb can open gifts tonight after supper."

"Wow," rang a voice behind them. "It looks like a birthday party in here."

"Joshua," asked his mother, "did you catch any fish?"

"No, Mama," he answered, sounding disappointed. "The tide was low and the fish weren't biting." He moved closer. "I've never seen so many presents, not even at Christmas. Can we open them?"

"No, Joshua. They belong to your Uncle Herb and Miriam," explained his mother.

"Getting married might be fun, if you get a lot of presents," decided Joshua.

"Nobody is going to marry you, brother."

"Why not?" he demanded.

"You sweat all the time, and you're too noisy."

"MAMA! Is it true nobody will ever marry me?" asked Joshua loudly.

"Why no, son," said his mother, giving him a hug. "If nobody else will marry you, I will."

"See there, Sarah," he said, sticking his tongue out at his tormentor.

The conversation was interrupted by a light tap on the screen door.

"Yoo-hoo, is anyone home?"

Sarah moved swiftly toward the front door. "Miss Nettie, please come in." Sarah held the door for their guest.

"I heard voices, so I thought you all might be home."

"You probably heard my children having one of their lively conversations," said Peggy, giving Miss Nettie a warm embrace. The older woman held out a package, wrapped in white tissue and tied with satin ribbon.

"This is a little something I've been working on ever since I heard Herb was courting. I might say, he certainly made a good choice. All of the teachers think highly of her."

"Just like you, my dear friend," said Granny Jewel, stepping into the hall. "Come back to the dining room and we'll have a Coca-Cola and I'll catch you up on the wedding plans."

When all were seated, enjoying soda and cookies, Granny Jewel described the dresses to her friend. "I'm especially proud of the way Miriam's dress turned out after it was altered. The dress has a train which...."

"A *train* did you say, Granny Jewel? I don't want to hear any talk about a *train*." Joshua grabbed his soda, an extra cookie, and went in search of his grandfather.

"Jewel, dear, what was that all about?" asked Miss Nettie, mystified.

"My grandson had an unfortunate experience involving the train, Nettie, and I think the very mention of the word upsets him."

"Oh, my, the poor dear! I hope he'll soon get over it."

"It may be a very long time before he gets over it," said Sarah.

"Yoo hoo," came a voice from the hall.

"Come in, come in," called Granny Jewel. "We're back here talking about the wedding." She rose to greet her new guest.

Mary Stewart stepped into the room, holding a box wrapped in white paper and a silver bow. "Hello, everyone. Nettie, I haven't seen you since the church picnic."

"Mary, you can have Joshua's seat. I'm sure he's not coming back." Granny Jewel hurried to get her friend a soda.

"I have a little something for the bride and groom," Mary said. "It's a set of pillow cases I embroidered." She added shyly.

"Thank you, Mary. If you made them, I know they're beautiful. Now tell us all about your adoption plans. The whole town is anxious to meet your baby. Do you have any news?"

Mary Stewart looked around the table, smiling. "We got our final papers this week. We have to be in Washington, DC. on August 20th, to meet our daughter, and bring her home. "At first," Mary added, "we thought our child would be a boy, but the authorities are sending us a girl." Mary smiled. "We don't care if it is a boy or girl. We're so anxious to meet our child."

"Oh, Mary, that's wonderful news!" All were talking and congratulating her at once. The back door slammed and Papa Tom appeared in the doorway in time to hear the good news.

"I was beginning to worry," he whispered to Clara, while opening a bottle of Coca-Cola. "They painted, redecorated and waited over a year. I know they're excited." He wrapped a napkin around the bottle and turned to Clara. "Say, why don't you adopt a baby, Clara?"

Clara, peeling boiled eggs, shot her employer a hard look. "I don't have time for no baby. All my time is spent tending to you!"

When their company left, Sarah turned to her mother. "Mama, I have a problem."

"What is it, dear? I'll help if I can. Come sit by me, and we'll see if we can work it out." Peggy Bowers patted the cushion beside her on the living room sofa.

With a lowered voice, Sarah said, "Everybody is bringing gifts for the wedding. Even Nancy has embroidered a set of tea towels for their kitchen. I don't know how to do stuff like that. If I sewed something for Miriam, she'd think I didn't like her." Sarah was practically in tears.

"Now, Sarah, let's put our heads together, and I'm sure we'll think of something. Hmmm, how about a pretty vase for flowers, or a tea pot? Miriam loves to drink tea."

"I've been to her apartment, and she has a lot of things like that."

"Why don't you call Nancy, and the two of you can go downtown and look around. Maybe you'll see the very thing."

"Nancy is lucky, because she can make pretty things. All my extra time has been spent diapering and chasing Amy, or checking on my brother."

"That's the very thing, Sarah! You have a very wonderful talent any mother with small children would appreciate."

"What do you mean?" asked Sarah, with interest.

"I mean, you could make a book of coupons, entitling the bearer to two or four hours of baby sitting."

"Mama, they're not even married!"

"No," said the mother, in a practical tone, "but, they will be, and they are not going to wait long to start a family. Herb's in his late thirties, and Miriam isn't many years behind him."

"I'd be embarrassed to give it to them."

"Believe me, honey, it's the finest gift you could give a young mother with small children. The times you have helped me with Amy have been priceless. I could actually sit a minute and think, without being interrupted."

"The more I think about it, the better I like the idea. It will be different from any other gift. If they are offended, I'll tell them it was my mother's idea."

"I'll gladly take the blame."

"It sounds like Amy is up from her nap. I think we'll go for a long walk, if Clara doesn't need me to help with supper."

On the sidewalk, Sarah chose streets with the most shade. The sidewalks on Ann Street were shaded by giant elms, whose branches met, creating a cool green passage.

"Well, sweetheart, where would you like to go?"

"Go swimming, go swimming," demanded Amy.

"OK, we'll go down to the shore where Papa Tom keeps his boat. You can play on the shore and I'll build you a big sandcastle. If you get wet and muddy, it won't hurt you."

Sarah painstakingly built her sister a castle in the sand, decorated with sea shells. When Sarah stood back to admire her work, Amy quickly planted a tiny foot in the middle. When she saw what she had done, she began crying. "Fix it, Sawah, fix it!"

"If I fix it, do you promise not to step on it?" Amy nodded, a tear forming in the corner of one eye.

Sarah carefully repaired the damage, noticing how pleasant it was to sit on the shore with the warm sun overhead, the sea breeze and the sound of water lapping against the shore. "Amy, when we grow up, let's live in a castle by the sea. The shore birds can wake us in the morning, and the cry of the black skimmer can sing us to sleep at night."

"Oh, boy," crooned Amy, once more planting a chubby foot in the middle of the reconstructed castle.

"That's it, Amy! I'm not going to build you another thing!"

"What's going on down there?" asked a voice from the boardwalk. "Are you girls having problems?" Sarah looked up into the kind face of Leland Davis. He was wearing a broad grin and shaking his head.

"Yes, Leland. We're having construction problems. My sister thinks it's great sport to stomp my lovely castles."

"You have to be patient, Sarah."

"Leland, do you have a two year old at your house?"

"No."

"Then, you have no idea what life is like with a toddler."

Afraid she had hurt his feelings, Sarah changed the subject. "What do you have in the envelope, Leland?" She noticed he carefully held the envelope so the breeze would not bend it.

"These are pictures I had developed at Eubanks studio." Shyly he added, "Do you want to see them?"

Sarah smiled at her friend. "Sure. I love to look at your photographs."

"Come over to my house so you can see them better. The glare is too strong out here." The three crossed the street and stepped up on the front porch.

"Mama," the boy called, "we got company."

Mrs. Davis hurried to the door. She was just as Sarah remembered her the day in court two summers ago, only today she was wearing a cotton 'house dress.' "Why, what a nice surprise! Sarah isn't it, and who is this young lady?"

"This is my muddy little sister, Mrs. Davis. I tried to clean her up, but I'm not sure it helped."

"Come in the bathroom. I think a warm wash cloth will work wonders." While they were scrubbing Amy, Mrs. Davis turned to Sarah. "It's kind of you to stop in, Sarah. Leland has so few friends."

"I think I'm lucky to have Leland for a friend."

"Leland is a wonderful son, but he's uh, slow," Mrs. Davis whispered She hastened to add, "You know what I mean." Nervously, the woman scrubbed Amy until her pale skin turned a rosy pink.

Sarah looked into the mother's pale blue eyes. "Yes, Ma'am, I know Leland is slow. He's slow to judge others. He's slow to anger. He is *not* slow when it comes to loyalty, gentleness, and kindness to others. In those ways he is far ahead of many people."

Mrs. Davis's eyes never left Sarah's face. Neither were aware that Amy was happily chewing on the wash cloth. Sarah took a deep breath and continued, "I guess you could say I'm slow. I cannot grasp algebra, although I have tried. All I can hope is that I will never need it. I'm slow when it comes to needlework. I cannot sew two stitches that look the same. Once, I took some pictures with my father's camera. I cut off the top of people's heads and feet." Sarah picked up her little sister, started toward the door, and stopped. "Leland is a genius when it comes to taking pictures. Somehow he captures people's feelings in a way no other photographer can."

Mrs. Davis took Sarah's arm. "Thank you, Sarah. Everything you said is true. Sometimes other people just don't see it." She embraced Sarah and Amy. "You are truly the most exceptional child I have ever met. You are a blessing to your family, and others whose lives you have touched."

"Sarah, come here," called Leland. "I want you to see my pictures."

The dining room table was covered with photos of different scenes in town. On closer inspection, Sarah saw they were not just pictures of things, but of everyday life. There were several photos of fishermen on the end of a small dock, patiently waiting for a bite, their lunch beside them in a lard tin. One was sound asleep, his mouth dropped open. Another was a picture of a small child happily licking an ice cream cone, unworried that it covered her hands and face. "Tell me about this picture, Leland," she said.

Leland gave her a lazy smile. "That's about my favorite picture of all. The light was just right that morning, so I went down on the dock with my camera. There was a school of minnows in the channel, and the gulls were diving and squawking. They all wanted breakfast at the same time."

Sarah picked up the picture and studied it. There were probably a dozen birds in that one scene. Some had beaks open, some with fish clamped firmly to avoid having their breakfast stolen. The morning sun sparkled on the water as the sun sent shafts of light across the sky.

"Leland, can you make this picture bigger?"

"Sure, I can have it enlarged. Do you want one?"

"You bet I do. It's going to be the best wedding present anybody ever got."

Sarah was fighting to keep Amy from grabbing the picture. "Mine, mine," Amy chanted. "That's right, Amy. It's going to be from you and me. We'll buy a frame and wrap it up."

"Sarah, are you sure anybody would want a picture of sea gulls?" Leland looked unsure.

Sarah patted him on the arm. "Leland, you know what my aunt Miriam told me when I met her? She said what made her fall in love with Beaufort were shore birds, pelicans and gulls. This picture will make the perfect gift."

Leland shook his head. "Your poor uncle."

"Huh?"

"He'll always know his wife fell in love with a sea gull first."

Chapter 13

During the evening meal, Joshua's eyes kept returning to the gifts that had now been moved to the living room. The suspense of what each box held was almost overwhelming. The family, however, was enjoying a lively conversation, ignoring the stack of tissue wrapped mysteries in the next room. Guns, tools and fishing equipment were his first thoughts. Finally, when dessert had been served, and everyone had scraped the last drop of ice cream from their bowl, Joshua could wait no longer. "Uncle Herb," he implored, "can't we *please* open the presents now?"

"Joshua," answered Miriam, smiling "let's wait a few more minutes. We need to clear the table and wash the dishes. Then, we can open gifts. I am as excited as you, so we'll hurry."

Later, when the kitchen was sparkling, the family sat in the living room and watched while Herb and Miriam opened the mysterious boxes. Joshua sat on the floor beside the coffee table, carefully watching their every move.

"Oh, look, Herb," exclaimed Miriam when the first box was opened. "It's a goblet in our chosen crystal."

"It looks like a glass to me," said Joshua, disappointed. He cast a doubtful eye at the stack of gifts still to be opened. Surely there would be something better in the next box.

"Look, dear," said Uncle Herb, when the tissue had been removed from the next box, "it's a dinner plate in our china pattern." He proudly held the plate for the family to admire. It was the first time Joshua had ever pitied his uncle. His hopes rose when Miriam selected a small, narrow box. Surely this would hold fishing lures, thought Joshua. You couldn't stuff a plate or glass in a box that size. When the ribbon and paper fell away, the boy was crushed that the box revealed nothing more than a fork.

"Oh, Herb, this is our first piece of sterling silver." Miriam proudly passed around the flatware by Gorham. "The pattern is English Gadroon."

"It's a *fork*!" declared the frustrated boy. "Granny's kitchen has a drawer full of forks. We got lots of them in Raleigh, too. What's so special about a fork?"

Papa Tom, secretly tired of exclaiming over each gift, leaned over and whispered, "Joshua, why don't we step out on the porch for some cool air. The gifts are open, so they won't need us."

Twilight had passed, and the street lights were softly burning when the boy and his grandfather selected the first two rocking chairs. For a few minutes, neither spoke. The crickets chirped, joined by the bass voice of a frog.

"Old Mr. Frog is calling for water, Joshua. We haven't had a good shower in two weeks or more, and he's getting mighty impatient."

"Papa Tom," asked the grandson, his face barely visible, "how come you know *so* many things?"

"Ah, Joshua, I've been around a long time," said his grandfather, gently rocking. "When you're my age, and you have young'uns and grand young'uns of your own, then you'll know what frogs and beetles and critters like that are thinking."

"When I'm that old, where will you be, Papa?" he asked fearfully.

"Oh, I'll be in Heaven, looking down listening to you tell your grandchildren what frogs are thinking."

"Will you be asleep in the sweet bosom of Jesus?"

"I will."

"Papa, there's something else I don't know besides what frogs are thinking."

"Oh, what can that be?"

"I don't understand why everybody is all excited about plates and glasses."

"Now you've gotten in an area more complicated than frogs." The grandfather rubbed his chin. "Let me see, womenfolk put a lot of store in stuff like fancy glasses, plates and shiny silverware."

"Why?"

"Uh, that's hard to say."

"Is this going to be like when I ask how babies get in their mama's stomach?"

"What do you mean?"

"Oh, when I want to know where babies come from, suddenly everybody is REAL busy. Mama says Daddy will tell me when I get older. Daddy says, 'Go ask your mother.'"

"Let's get back to talking about glasses and plates." Papa Tom settled lower in the chair, picked up a fan and began to move it lazily back and forth. "When a couple falls in love and plan to marry, there are things they need to set up housekeeping, like furniture and cooking pots. Sometimes the husband invites the boss and his wife for dinner. So, they want the table to look very beautiful, and the food very good. Special glasses made of crystal are used instead of jelly glasses. Plates have to be made of fine china, and the silverware must be real silver. It's all very grand. Your mama and your grandmother have china cabinets where they store all these valuable things. Silver is kept in a special chest so it won't tarnish. There are white cloth napkins, white tablecloths and lots of candles. These things are only used on special occasions."

"I know what you mean," said Joshua brightly. "Once, in Raleigh, Daddy invited some important men to dinner. Sarah was helping, but Mama was real nervous setting the table and cooking special food."

"Who were they?"

"I don't know. Before they got there, Granny Bowers came and snatched Amy and me up and out of the house faster than you can imagine. Mama was so grateful. She kept saying, "Thank you, Mother Bowers, thank you, thank you!"

"Were you disappointed you couldn't stay and meet the guests?"

"Heck, no. When something like that happens, you have to put on company manners you didn't know you had. I'm scared to take a deep breath, for fear I'll do something wrong."

"Let's go inside, son. The mosquitoes have discovered us, and I think we're on their menu for the evening meal."

The next morning, a familiar voice called through the screen door. "Is Miss Sarah Bowers in residence? There is a letter for her in a pink envelope with tiny rosebuds around the edge. I would guess this is not from a handsome prince."

"Good morning, Graham," said Granny Jewel to the postman. "How's your family?"

"All are well, thank you."

The grandmother placed the rest of the mail on the hall table, taking Sarah's to her room. "Knock, knock, sleepyhead," she called through the door. "You have a letter." The sound of bare feet could be heard on the other side of the door.

The door opened slowly, an arm reached out, took the envelope and disappeared. "Thank you," came a voice, thick with sleep.

Returning to her bed, Sarah tore the envelope open. Quickly she read the letter, bounced off the bed, and went in search of her mother. "Guess what!" she began when she found her mother upstairs making beds. Before she could ask, Sarah continued, "Lindsey is coming for the wedding! She's going to come with daddy."

"He's coming a week before the wedding, you know."

" Lindsey, Nancy and I will help. We can run errands and polish silver and do lots of other things." Sarah remembered how busy everyone was the week before her cousin Julia's wedding three years before.

Peggy sat on the bed and stared at Amy who was happily playing in her playpen. "Come sit by me, honey." She patted the smoothly made bed. "Miriam's family is coming a week before the wedding, too. They want to spend some time with their daughter before she's married. Her parents will be staying at the Inlet Inn, but the two sisters are going to stay with Miriam. I guess this is the last time they will be together before Miriam is married. Her older sister is her maid of honor, and, as you know, the other will be a bridesmaid like yourself."

"I know, Mama. I'm so happy to be in the wedding and wear that beautiful dress." The ringing of the phone downstairs interrupted.

"Granny Jewel has gone to the grocery store," whispered Sarah. "There's no one downstairs, so Clara will have to answer the phone. Listen to Clara's speech before she picks up the receiver."

"I'm coming, I'm coming, you aggravating, no-account instrument. The world was better off before these blasted things were invented." She put the receiver to her ear, and said sweetly, "Mitchell's residence." After a pause, Clara called upstairs, "Oh, Miss Sarah, you are wanted on the telephone."

Sarah, hurrying to the top of the stairs, said, "Thank you, Clara. I'll be right there."

"Humph," puffed Clara, placing the receiver on the table, none too gently. "I got more to do in this house than answer that sorry telephone."

Sarah quickly picked up the receiver. "Ow, Sarah, I think my ear's broken."

"I know. Clara doesn't like telephones."

"What are you doing?"

"Nothing. Mama and I were just talking about the wedding. Nancy, it's going to be a wild and wonderful time. I'm so excited!"

"I have Miss Thompson's wedding present ready. May I bring it over?"

"Sure, I want you to see the presents. There is already a room full, and more arriving every day."

By the time Sarah dressed and ate breakfast, she heard Nancy's light tap on the front door. "Yoo hoo," she called.

Sarah hurried to the door. "Come in, Nancy."

Nancy Russert stood in the hall, a tissue wrapped package in her hand.

"Nancy, come and see." Sarah guided her friend into the room where wedding gifts were displayed.

"Oh, Sarah," breathed her friend. "I have never seen so many lovely things!" The early morning sun in the east window reflected off the smooth surface of the china, and shiny kitchen appliances. A crystal vase sent myriads of tiny rainbows across the ceiling. Woolen blankets and snow white sheets and towels were arranged on the bed. Nancy looked down at her small, carefully wrapped gift. "Oh, Sarah, my gift is so small beside all the others. I feel awful!"

Sarah put her hand on Nancy's shoulder and gave her a light shake. "Nancy, how can you say such a thing! Every stitch was done with love. Miriam will treasure gifts like yours, Miss Nettie's and Mary Stewart's above all the rest. Most people go in a store, choose something, have it gift wrapped and send it to the bride and groom. Their heart is not involved."

Nancy stared at the fine stitches in the pillow cases, and the intricate design of the quilt carefully displayed on the bed. "Let's go to my room and talk about the wedding. Lindsey is coming next week with Daddy, and the three of us are going to be busy."

"I can't stay. I am practicing twice as much this week, so I'll be able to help every day next week. It seemed like the wedding was so far away, and now, it's almost here."

"You're not leaving without seeing my bridesmaid's dress." Both hurried upstairs to the grandparent's bedroom. Hanging on the closet door was the cloud of lavender taffeta and organdy.

Nancy clasped her hands over her heart. "Oh, Sarah! It is the most beautiful dress I have ever seen!"

"There's one dress prettier. Remember the one my granny made for Julia's wedding when I was twelve? It is the most beautiful dress ever."

"Do you still have it?"

"I'll keep it always. It hangs in my closet and someday, my daughter can wear it when she is twelve."

"That is a lovely thought, and now, I must go!" Nancy hurried downstairs and was gone. Sarah remained, staring at the dress she would soon wear standing in front of a church filled with people. Her thoughts were interrupted by her brother's strident voice.

"Please, Mama. I promise not to go near the train! We want to go in the old burying ground and see the grave with the cannon on top. There's nothing else to do!"

Sarah heard the familiar whine in her brother's voice. *What does he want now?* she wondered. The girl crossed the hall and stopped in the door of her mother's bedroom. "What are you whining about today, little brother?" she asked impatiently.

"Me and my friends…" A look from his mother helped him correct the poor grammar.

"My friends and I want to go in the cemetery behind the Methodist church, but Mama won't let me." Joshua's lower lip protruded.

"If Sarah went along to keep you all out of trouble, it would be all right."

"Mama!" Sarah was horrified at the very thought of spending her morning in the graveyard with three little boys.

"Sarah, the wedding is now less than two weeks away. It's not too soon to start cooperating in every way, even to entertaining your brother."

"Yes, Ma"am." Joshua flashed his sister a triumphant smile. "I'll get Billy and Mackie, and meet you on the porch."

"Oh, brother," muttered Sarah, starting down the stairs. While waiting on the porch, she decided it could be worse. I could be in algebra class, or I could be with Nancy's sewing circle, embroidering a whole bed sheet. Maybe a walk among the tombstones isn't such a bad thing after all.

The boys hurried, Sarah following slowly. *I'm not anxious for anyone to see me escorted through the cemetery by three rowdy boys..*

"Come on, Sarah," urged her brother. "I want you to see Otway Burns' tomb. It has a cannon on it."

"I've seen it before, Joshua," she replied, bored.

"How about the grave where a soldier from the Revolutionary War was buried standing up?"

"I've seen that one, too." Sarah found a shady spot on top of the low stone wall surrounding the cemetery. While the boys wandered, her mind went back two summers. She and Porter Mason had found an oak tree in the Episcopal cemetery they could climb and sit among the branches. *Will I ever see him again?* she wondered. Presently, someone shook her arm. Slowly she opened her eyes.

"Hey, Sarah," spoke Billy. She was surprised to see he seemed nervous.

"What's the matter, Billy?" she asked impatiently.

"We been hearing a strange noise up near the church. Can you come over and see if you hear it?"

Sarah followed, more to humor the boy than to identify a strange sound. They wound around tombstones and bushes filled with briars, following a narrow path. Billy and Mackie were standing near a corner of the church. Neither spoke.

"Billy says you all heard a ghost," said Sarah, smiling. The boys did not return her smile.

"Listen, and you can hear it," Joshua whispered, eyes round.

Sarah stood motionless, looking up through sturdy branches of ancient oaks. She heard car horns in the distance, people walking by, the lonesome wail of the bridge siren, but no moaning laments by a resident ghost.

She looked at the three boys, sweaty, dirty and frightened. "Your ghost has gone to lunch, and it's time for us to go, too. You can come back next summer and see if he's still here."

As she turned to leave, a high, thin sound was heard. Eyes wide, she looked back at the boys, but before she could speak, Mackie put his finger on his lips. No one spoke. Joshua grabbed his sister's hand and whispered, "What is it, Sarah? Do you think it's a ghost? Are we scared?"

"No, *we* are not scared," she said unconvincingly.

"Shhh," commanded Mackie. "There it is again! This time the sound seemed to be coming from the direction of the church.

"It must be the ghost of a little girl," offered Joshua.

"Yeah, maybe it's the one buried in a barrel of rum," added Billy, nervously.

"Wouldn't it sound like it's underwater," asked Mackie, laughing nervously at his poor attempt at humor.

"You better not get that ghost mad at you, Mackie," whispered Billy.

"Ah heck, a ghost can't hurt you," scoffed Mackie, wiping perspiration from his forehead with the sleeve of his shirt.

"If she scares you to death, I'd call that being hurt," returned Billy.

"Hush, all of you," ordered Sarah, listening intently. When the soft, crooning sound came again, Sarah smiled. "Boys, it sounds like a kitten. We'd better find it." Sarah walked toward the back wall of the church.

"It could be a ghost kitten," suggested Billy, unwilling to abandon the idea of it being something from the spirit realm.

"Here, kitty, kitty," each called softly. Still, there was no sign of a kitten anywhere. Ready to give up the search, they again heard the soft cry, now sounding much closer.

"It IS a kitten and it's close," declared Sarah, perspiration dripping from her nose. Turning a corner of the old building, she saw a metal grate in the crumbling foundation. On her hands and knees, she looked through the iron work, but could see nothing, only smell the dank, stale air of a place too long closed up. As she started to stand up, the small head of a kitten suddenly appeared. On seeing Sarah, it mewed louder. "Well, hello there." She put her finger through the grate and touched the kitten's nose. It had white fur, and big, blue eyes.

"Hey, boys, I think I found your ghost!" The boys hurried over.

"It's a kitten!" they exclaimed. All stared at the tiny face, peering at them through the grate. A tiny white paw reached through.

"What do we do now," asked Joshua quietly.

"He got in there, let him figure how to get out," grumbled Mackie, disappointed.

"Suppose he was born in there, and doesn't know the way out," added Billy.

"There must be a door somewhere, so workmen can get under the church," reasoned Sarah. The four slowly walked the perimeter of the building. On the second try, Mackie pulled aside the branches of an over-grown bush.

"I found it," he yelled. "Help me hold this bush." While Sarah held the branches the boys struggled to open the half-rotten door. When they loosened the latch and began pulling, the hinges squealed in protest, and resisted from disuse. When the door finally gave way, Mackie shoved the smaller boys aside and stuck his head in the dark hole. Straining, he whispered "It's as dark as the inside of a pocket."

"It smells bad," said Billy, poking his head around Mackie.

"I'll bet there's monsters under there," added Joshua. No one moved.

"Slide over and let me call," said Sarah. The boys gladly moved aside.

"Here, kitty, kitty," she called several times. There was no answering 'meow' from the depths of the building. "This isn't working, boys," she said backing away from the opening and brushing dirt from her hands and knees. "This opening is on the opposite side of the building. He probably can't even hear me. Besides, if he was born under there, he doesn't know he's a 'kitty.'"

"What do we do now, Sarah?" asked her brother.

The four sat in a circle trying to decide what they should do. "Somebody has to go in and get him," announced Sarah.

"Why don't we tell our parents?" suggested Joshua.

"My mama's sick and my daddy is working," said Mackie.

"Both my parents are working," added Billy.

"Our mama would panic and call the fire department," said Joshua.

Billy brightened. "Yeah, let's call the fire department! They're right around the corner, and could be here in two shakes of a lamb's tail."

"A what?" questioned Mackie, giving his friend a funny look.

"Uh, never mind."

"No," said Sarah, a fireman wouldn't fit in that little space. I can see it now – the fire truck is parked on the street, red lights flashing, other firemen waiting while one man rescues a pint-size white kitten.

"It's going to be up to us, ain't it?" questioned Billy.

"I'm afraid so. I'm going in and get the kitten. You all yell, so I'll be able to find my way out." The boys didn't argue.

Kneeling in front of the opening, Sarah peered into the darkness, and almost changed her mind. "I can do all things through Christ, who strengthens me," she chanted, and crawled into the face of utter darkness.

With the pin point of light, and the boy's voices behind her, Sarah crawled forward, unafraid of ghosts and restless spirits, but of tiny six and eight legged monsters lurking in the crawl space. *I think you're supposed to whistle at a time like this, but I'm kicking up so much dust, I dare not wet my lips.*

The young heroine almost cried with relief when she saw a gray square of light ahead. As she crawled forward, she saw the white form of a kitten. "Come here, kitty, kitty," she crooned softly. She knew if she frightened the kitten and it disappeared in the darkness, there was no way of ever saving it. Luckily, the kitten hurried over and began rubbing against Sarah's arms, purring loudly.

"OK, Snowball, this isn't going to be easy for either of us." Knotting the hem of her blouse tightly against her waist, Sarah tucked the kitten down the front of her blouse, turned and started back, listening intently for the boys' voices.

At that moment, thunder was heard overhead. Sarah recognized the sound of the pipe organ in the church. The deep, bass notes vibrated the very foundation of the old church, drowning all other sounds. In a crouched position, surrounded by smothering darkness, Sarah lost her sense of direction. "Oh, God, be not far from me," she prayed fervently. The kitten snuggled contentedly against Sarah's stomach, happy to no longer be alone.

Inside the church, the organist finished practicing the first hymn for Sunday. As she reached to turn the page of the hymnal, her hand knocked the book to the floor. In that brief moment, Sarah heard the welcomed sound of the boys' high pitched voices. Soon, a glimmer of light guided her to the opening as the sound of the organ began once more. She plunged through the opening, filling her lungs with fresh air. When she stood, the boys backed away, staring. Finally Joshua mumbled, "Sarah, you don't look too good."

"That may be true," she said, grinning, but look what I got for my trouble." The girl reached inside her blouse and produced the white kitten. "He's nothing but a bag of bones, but we can fix that."

For years Joshua would recall the day his sister emerged from the crawl space of the old church, her thick, dark brown hair gray with cobwebs, dirt and scratches on her face, elbows and knees, proudly holding the kitten she had rescued from certain death.

"What are you going to do with him?" asked Billy on the way home.

"Are you going to find him a good home?" asked Joshua.

"He already has a home, boys," she announced, holding the kitten tightly against her chest. "I'm keeping him. He's going to be *my* pet."

"Can he be *our* pet?"

"No, brother, while I was crawling through the dirt, banging my head, and getting lost in the smelly darkness, I decided I would keep him for myself."

"What are our parents going to say?"

"What can they say? You have Frisky and a crippled chicken. Surely I can have the most beautiful kitten in the whole town. Besides," Sarah gave her brother a smug look, "I found out that Clara *loves* cats!"

"What are you going to name him?" asked Mackie as they started up the grandparents' sidewalk.

"I'm not sure," she replied, continuing to hold the kitten.

"How about 'Ghost'?" suggested her brother.

"Hmmm, that sounds good, but I think his name will be 'Spooky.'"

Chapter 14

"Mama, Mama, guess what!"

"Joshua, please don't come in the house yelling - and, you know better than to slam the door! Your sister might be asleep."

"This is important, Mama. Look at what Sarah has." His sister stepped in the living room, whispy cobwebs floating around her face, dirt and scratches on her hands and knees.

"Sarah Bowers," her mother exclaimed, "Have you been in an accident? Were you hit by a car?"

"No, Mama, I….."

"She saved a kitten, Mama.," interrupted Joshua. "He was trapped under the church, and Sarah crawled under and got him. We were in the graveyard and thought we heard a ghost, but…"

"That's enough, Joshua. Sarah, you need to get cleaned up. You have company."

Sarah's eyes traveled in the direction her mother was looking. Emerging gracefully from her grandmother's wing-back chair was her cousin Marnie. Her eyes slowly traveled Sarah's length, wearing a look somewhere between pity and triumph. Sarah saw with dismay she was wearing a creamy white sun back dress, trimmed with gold braid, matching gold sandals and earrings. Her blonde hair smoothed back with ivory combs. Before Sarah could speak, Clara appeared. "What's that I see in your arms, Missy? Is it what I think it is?"

Sarah, relieved to take her eyes from her beautiful cousin, answered, "Clara, it's a kitten we rescued, and he's nothing but skin and bones."

"Skin and bones," repeated Clara. "Nothing around here gonna stay skin and bones if old Clara has anything to say about it. Bring him back in the kitchen and let's see if we can interest him in a bowl of milk."

Sarah, relieved, excused herself and followed Clara's retreating form. In the kitchen, she poured a saucer of thick cream, fresh from one of Mrs. Carraway's cows, and placed it on the floor. At first, Spooky had no idea what to do, so Sarah dipped his chin in the rich liquid. He needed no more prompting. They stood over him and watched as he eagerly lapped the saucer's contents. Sarah and Clara exchanged looks. "Of all the times for her to show up," whispered Sarah, frowning.

"The little hussy's been here for almost an hour, asking all about the wedding. She told your mama in a real pitiful voice that no body has asked her to be in the wedding, and her feelings are hurt, and can't dear cousin Peggy do something about it."

"What did Mama tell her?"

"Your mama stuck by her guns. She told Miss Marnie her brother and his bride made all the decisions about the wedding, and that she didn't have anything to do with it. So, then she started getting all pouty, and was about to leave when you came strolling in, looking like you been crawling around under somebody's house." Clara leaned closer and squinted one eye, "Where have you been?"

"I wasn't crawling around under somebody's house, Clara."

"Thank the blessed Lord for that!"

"I was crawling around under an old church."

Clara grabbed the girl's arm. "Those scratches need tending to, or they're going to get infected. You skedaddle up those steps and take a hot shower. Scrub those places that are bleeding with plenty of soap."

"Oooo, Clara, that's going to hurt!"

"If you don't scrub them, I will."

Sarah took a step backward, fear in her voice. "No, no, I promise I'll do it!"

"You go on now, and I'll bring you some clean clothes."

Sarah hurried through the hall, pausing at the foot of the stairs. "Excuse me for a few minutes, will you? I have to freshen up a bit." She remembered the line from a movie and thought it sounded dramatic.

- Spooky was still lapping cream when Clara hurried upstairs with clean clothes on her arm. "Your clothes are out here on the banister rail," she said through the bathroom door. As she turned to go downstairs, she was startled to see Marnie behind her.

The girl shook her head. "My poor cousin," she crooned. "She can't possibly be in the wedding with all those *awful* scratches." Words, soft and sympathetic were contrasted by eyes cold as steel.

Clara took a step closer, eyes narrow. "Let me tell you something, Missy. Sarah Bowers is going to be in her uncle's wedding if I have to tote her down the aisle on my back."

Minutes later Sarah, wrapped in a towel, opened the bathroom door and reached for her clean clothes. She was surprised to see Marnie holding them.

"Please hand them to me, Marnie," she said nicely.

"I'll be glad to as soon as you show me the dress you're wearing in the wedding."

"Sure, my dress is no secret. Nancy Russert has seen it, and she thinks it's beautiful." Marnie's face twisted into an ugly scowl. Sarah brushed past her cousin, tucking the bath towel more firmly around her. "It's hanging in my grandparents' bedroom." Sarah watched Marnie's expression change from admiration to envy when she saw the frothy, lavender dress. The angry girl threw Sarah's clothes on the bed and hissed, "I should be the one wearing that dress, not you! Look at those *ugly* scratches on your arms! You'll ruin the whole wedding." Marnie put her hands on her hips. "*I* have the perfect figure for that dress, and *I* should be the one to wear it!"

"Marnie," said Sarah quietly, "you'll look gorgeous in any dress you wear to the wedding, and I know your daddy will buy any dress you want, but here's one dress you *won't* be wearing, because *I'll* be in it." Sarah, hands on her hips, didn't move as Marnie stormed from the room and down the steps, letting the front door slam behind her.

All thoughts of Marnie vanished by early afternoon when a strange car stopped in front of the house. "Jewel," announced Papa Tom, peering through lace curtains, "I think the folks from New York are here."

"Well, honey, let's invite them in and show some southern hospitality."

Four hot, tired people gladly accepted the invitation to come in, relax and enjoy refreshments. Their conversation mostly centered around the long trip. Soon, footsteps were heard. "Yoo hoo," came Miriam's lovely voice.

"We're in here, Miriam," called Granny Jewel, as the young woman appeared in the doorway.

"Mother, Daddy," she exclaimed happily, giving each a hug. Harriet and Esther waited patiently for their chance to greet their sister. When her older sister hugged Miriam, she whispered, "Yoo hoo? What does that mean?"

"You'll find out Esther, if you stay down South long enough." She turned to her parents, "Herb is getting off early, so we can help get you settled." Moments later the groom appeared, anxious to see his future in-laws. After more greetings, Miriam took her mother's hand, "Come across the hall. I want you to see all the lovely gifts." While the women exclaimed over the many presents, Papa Tom tapped Ralph Thompson on the arm. "Why don't we go out on the porch? It may be cooler out there."

The father-of-the-bride gladly left the women while they were admiring the presents. "Phew," he said, "that's all I hear, day and night. I've never seen women so worked up over a wedding. My oldest daughter, Gloria, had a real nice wedding so I guess I'll survive."

"Why don't we go fishing tomorrow morning," suggested Papa Tom. "The women may be glad to have us out from under foot. What do you say, Herb? Think you'd like a fishing trip before you tie the knot?"

"Thanks, Dad, but Miriam wants me to run errands with her. Maybe next time."

Soon the parents were on their way to a room waiting at the Inlet Inn. The girls were dropped off at Miriam's apartment where they were staying. "I invited them for supper tomorrow night," said Granny Jewel, joining her husband on the porch.

"I'm taking Ralph fishing in the morning. Herb had to beg off because Miriam already has plans for him. Lordy, Jewel, that boy isn't married yet, and already he's taking orders."

"He's not lonely anymore, Honey, and he's in love. That's what counts."

The smell of ham baking filled the house the following day. "Sarah," said her mother when she came into the dining room. "You have a choice, snap beans and peel potatoes, or watch Amy."

"Where's the knife?"

With a paper bag for peelings and a large pot, Sarah stepped out on the back porch where the air was a little cooler. As she worked, being careful not to cut away too much of the potato, Sarah thought of the day in the distant future when she would be a bride. *It doesn't seem possible that this could be me in seven years. I don't even know what I want to be someday.*

"Hello, there," came a deep voice from the driveway. Sarah looked up from her task and saw Ramie coming toward the porch.

"Hi, Ramie. Are you looking for your Aunt Clara?"

"Yes, she told me you all were going to need some help this weekend setting up tables for the reception."

"You best call through the screen before you step inside. Clara is turning round and round in the kitchen making supper for five extra people tonight. There will be thirteen in all. If you accidently let the door slam, and her three layer chocolate cake falls, you might not be able to help this weekend. You may be in the hospital."

"Sarah, you've got me scared. I think I'll come back tomorrow when things have calmed down a little."

"I'll tell Clara you stopped by."

Tuesday afternoon, James Bowers and Lindsey arrived. Wednesday morning before the sun came up,, there was a knock on Sarah's bedroom door. It was Clara. "Get up you sleepy heads," she commanded. "Get that kitten off your pillow and outdoors so she can tend to her business."

"Clara, what if Spooky is a boy cat? You always say 'her."

"I've never seen a boy cat that smart."

"Do you think she's smarter than other cats?"

"You see where she sleeps every night. I'd call that being smart." Clara smiled at the snow white kitten as it stretched and jumped off the bed.

Sarah, Lindsey and Nancy washed and dried cups and glass plates to use at the reception. "We mustn't forget to put a paper doily on every plate," said Nancy, who paid attention to every detail.

"Now," said the girl," I must go home and get ready for the afternoon tea we'll be attending."

At four o'clock Nancy returned, wearing a dress, and hat, matching purse and shoes. Sarah was wearing a new dress she bought in Raleigh before summer vacation. "Mama knew there would be parties and I would need more than one Sunday dress this summer."

Lindsey chose one of the three dresses she brought. The five walked two blocks to Ma Baylor's house, all in white dress shoes, white straw hats and flowered dresses. Before they left, Miriam and her sisters arrived, out of breath. They wore more tailored looking dresses with hats and high heels.

"That's a pretty sight, Tom," commented James when they left. "You'll get to go next time," he comforted Amy, who was threatening to cry. "This summer you could do a lot of damage at an afternoon tea."

As they stepped on the porch, the screen door flew open. "Oh, you all look so pretty," exclaimed Cousin Helen. "Come in, and let's get acquainted before the guests arrive."

Sarah noticed the house was banked in lovely summer flowers. Every surface had been polished to a high shine. The long dining room table held a huge silver punch bowl, cups, plates and napkins. The rest of the table held silver trays of tiny cakes with buttery icing, bite size sandwiches, nuts, mints and sliced fruit.

"I wonder where my dear cousin is," whispered Sarah. She didn't have to wonder long. The front door banged and Marnie appeared from her grandmother's house next door. Sarah braced herself, but was relieved when the girl gave her a sunny smile and a warm embrace. She welcomed Miriam, her mother and each of the girls, asking questions about their trip and making them feel at ease in a house full of strangers. Sarah watched fascinated, as Marnie moved among the guests, laughing and talking, giving some a hug, others a pat on the back. All responded to her sparkling smile and seeming sincere affection.

In the early evening, when the oppressive heat of the day had subsided, Miriam and her sisters came over with their dresses and accessories for the wedding.

"There's no reason why you should try to dress in the apartment. We'll chase all the men away, and you can have the whole upstairs," reasoned Granny Jewel.

Sarah marveled at the pale lavender dress like hers, eyes lingering on the dress to be worn by the maid-of-honor. It was exactly like the others, but the color was a soft pink.

During dinner Peggy and her mother entertained the family with talk of the afternoon tea. "Jean Baylor has declared she will be directing the rehearsal Friday night and the wedding on Saturday." explained Granny Jewel. "So, all changes, or plans have to be cleared through her. I thought I was doing a fine job, overseeing the reception, but with the wave of a hand, I was relieved of that job. Helen is in charge."

"What did Helen say?"

"Absolutely nothing. She only nodded. Jean has spoken, and none of them, including me, would dare oppose her. She said I have enough to do without fretting over food. She's right, of course."

"What did Miriam's family from up north think about the way Southern women do things," asked Papa Tom, smiling.

"Bless their hearts! They mostly stood, eyes wide, fascinated by Jean. Miriam's mother whispered she should have been a general during the war. Julia is here with her little boy. She's expecting again. Her parents hope this baby will be a little girl. Mary Stewart was there, telling everyone about the baby they are expecting next week. They are due to pick the child up from the airport in Raleigh the week after the wedding. I believe she is more excited than our bride."

Granny Jewel continued talking through dinner. Her eyes were bright with excitement. *My granny must have been the most beautiful girl in Beaufort when she was young,* thought Sarah, staring at her grandmother. *Papa Tom says she was often enough.*

"Sarah, Sarah," whispered Lindsey, tugging at Sarah's sleeve. "You were a million miles away. Do you think we can sneak away for a little while and walk downtown? I love looking in shop windows."

When they returned from their walk, the girls heard Joshua's voice before they stepped inside the house. "Only sissies and babies wear short pants! I'm nine years old and I want to wear long pants or, I'm not going!" His father looked over the top of the newspaper, his steady gaze resting on his only son. "Or, at least, I'm going to think about not going," whispered Joshua, amending his declaration.

"If it's all right with your parents, you and I will go to Upton's tomorrow and find a fine pair of dark pants any man would be proud to wear," declared his grandfather.

The Duchess beauty parlor reserved Friday afternoon for the wedding party. Seven women and three teenage girls needed their hair done for the wedding on the following day. "My mama said I wasn't in the wedding, so I didn't need a special hairdo," declared Nancy.

"Nancy, you and Lindsey have worked hard all week tending to details. You are just as much a part of this wedding as the bride and groom!"

"Sarah, you have such a wonderful way of making a person feel welcome," answered Nancy, giving her friend a hug.

Sarah slowly shook her head. *You wouldn't say that if you know how harshly I talked to my cousin.*

"Emily!" exclaimed Sarah when she stepped in the Duchess Beauty Parlor. "I thought you had, uh, moved away."

The hairdresser smiled a sad smile and nodded. "Yes, Sarah, I was gone for a while, a very short while. But," she said, her smile widening, "I'm here and luckily I got my old job back."

"Oh, Granny Jewel, do you think Emily could fix my hair?"

"If it's Emily you want, it's Emily you shall have."

Sarah gladly claimed the chair the beautician offered, and studied the woman in the mirror. Past summers Emily seemed glamorous and carefree.

Now she was quieter, her hair was no longer piled on top of her head, and was decidedly darker. There was no bright, silk scarf around her neck. "I'm so glad you're here, Emily. You always work wonders with my hair."

Emily picked up a handful of Sarah's long, thick, hair. "I hope you're not planning to cut this gorgeous hair."

"I don't know, Emily...."

"I know," said a voice behind them. Granny Jewel had stepped up behind Sarah's chair. "Emily, honey, this must be your finest 'do' ever. My granddaughter is a bridesmaid in her uncle's wedding tomorrow. Long hair is beautiful, but not for the dress she's wearing."

"Mrs. Mitchell, you can count on me. I know just what to do."

While Emily was shampooing Sarah's hair, the girl thought back to the summer before, when she was so anxious for Uncle Herb to meet and fall in love with Emily. Now she couldn't imagine anyone but Miriam becoming her aunt.

When Sarah's hair was dry, Emily turned the chair so she could see the other members of the family. Each person seemed transformed as their hair was combed out and styled. She was aware of Emily pulling and pinning her hair, but she could not see her reflection. When finally the beautician turned the chair around, Sarah could not believe her eyes. Her hair had been swept back in a deep wave on either side, up to the crown of her head. Held in place with a wide silver barrette, a mass of long, dark curls cascaded to her shoulders. "Oh, Emily, I can't believe it's me!" Behind Emily the grandmother nodded her approval.

That evening the wedding rehearsal went smoothly. Everyone, including the minister, did exactly as Jean Baylor instructed. "I don't know why people think a wedding rehearsal can be confusing. This one went smoothly enough," the commander declared.

No one replied. All exchanged glances.

Before going to bed, Sarah announced she was going to sleep in a chair, so her hair would not be ruined. "No, no," disagreed Granny Jewel. "We're all going to bed early and get a good night's sleep. Tomorrow is an important day in all our lives, a day none of us will ever forget. We must be rested, and in a cheerful mood."

"With all those fancy dresses in our bedroom, I feel like I'm sleeping in a flower pot," announced Papa Tom.

"Thomas Mitchell, you can start behaving yourself right now."

"Yes, Ma'am."

Heavy hair nets, pinned firmly in place, preserved the hair styles.

Granny Jewel handed Sarah a tiny, flowered box. "This is rouge, to make your cheeks look rosy. You girls use it *sparingly*, just like the lipstick."

"Thanks, Granny Jewel. You are the best!"

Seconds later, someone knocked on the front door. Sarah and Lindsey hurried down the hall. A delivery man stood with a tower of white boxes. "Flowers from Beaufort Florist," he announced. The girls hurriedly took the boxes and rushed them to the kitchen.

"Clara, aren't these flowers supposed to be kept cold so they will stay fresh?" asked Sarah. "The refrigerator will never hold all these boxes."

"Do you think old Clara was born yesterday? There was a time, young ladies before electricity, when people had to use ice boxes to keep food cold. That big old wooden chest on the back porch was your grandparents' ice box. Every morning the ice man would deliver a huge block of ice in a horse drawn wagon, and put it in this box on the back porch. Ramie brought a block over early this morning and it should be cold enough now for the flowers to keep till this afternoon." The girls, amazed, held the lid as Clara deftly arranged the boxes and quickly closed the lid.

"Clara, how is it you think of everything?"

"This ain't nothin'. Wait till you see me strut my stuff at the reception in my black silk dress, white lace apron and cap. You're going to be so proud."

"A silk dress? I thought uniforms were made of cotton," wondered Lindsey.

"There's no rule book says a uniform got to be cotton. When I said I wanted a silk one, your granny ordered three yards of the finest silk in the Sears and Roebuck catalog and I made myself a dress fit for a queen."

The wedding breakfast was held at the Inlet Inn on Front Street. Clara stayed with Amy and together they guarded the wedding presents. The front room looked like a king's treasure with packages coming from up north most every day."

At breakfast, Herb and Miriam sat at the head table. Miriam looked different with her hair arranged in a bun on the nape of her neck. Sarah noticed they couldn't take their eyes from each other. Sarah leaned toward her mother, "Mama, Uncle Herb used to love Aunt Louise. Now he loves Miriam. Suppose Aunt Louise hadn't died. Would he still love her? Then who would Miriam fall in love with?"

"Sarah you're asking questions no wise man can answer. Your uncle lived through a terrible tragedy, but has found happiness. I guess you can look at life as chapters in a book. Today, my brother begins a brand new chapter of his life. It is a time of celebration and joy. I pray God will bless their life together. Who knows," Peggy smiled at he daughter, "you may have to do some babysitting one summer. Wouldn't that be wonderful?"

"You're right, Mama. The other chapters are finished, and today they can start a new chapter together."

"God blessed you with beauty and intellect. I hope He will bless all the chapters of your life."

"Thank you, Mama. He's already blessed me with the best parents a person could ever have." For a moment Sarah remembered a wedding breakfast much like this one, three years before. Porter Mason had attended because he was acolyte for Julia's wedding. *I wonder if there is a chapter in my life that includes Porter Mason.*

"We're going to the Parish House for one last check," announced Granny Jewel on the walk home. "Peggy and I have to make sure everything has been done." In a few minutes they were back.

"That was quick," said Papa Tom.

"Jean is there, waiting for the wedding cake. She wants it in the middle of the center table so ivy can be placed around it. She told us to get on home and rest. It sounded like a good idea."

No one wanted lunch, since they had a late breakfast. For three hours there was nothing to do but wait. "This feels so strange," commented their grandmother. "For weeks we have been so busy getting ready for the wedding. Now it's here, and there's nothing else to do, but do it!"

During the lull, Clara disappeared to dress for the wedding.

At two o'clock the family dressed, so the upstairs and the bathroom would be free for the girls. It seemed no different from getting ready for Sunday school and church. Later, when the bride and her sisters arrived, the house filled with an air of excitement. Upstairs, there were squeals of laughter as each helped the other with her dress, make up and hair. Miriam's parents arrived, the mother going immediately upstairs, the father joining the men in the living room. All sat looking grand, listening to the sound of high heels clicking on the wooden floor overhead. "Is that what machine guns sound like in the war?" asked Joshua.

"Pretty much, son."

A loud banging on the front door startled the men. "Hi, Roy," the others heard Papa Tom say. "Come in." He went to the dining room and called, "Honey, the photographer is here." Before the man could unload his equipment and get ready, another, more timid knock was heard. "Hello, Leland, please come in." Granny Jewel held the door open.

"The girls will be coming down in just a moment." Turning to Roy Eubanks, she said, "I hope you won't mine if Leland takes pictures, too. The bride loves his work."

"He does have a lot of talent, Mrs. Mitchell." Turning to Leland he whispered, "Take all the pictures you want, kid, just don't get in my way."

The clicking overhead stopped, laughter and talking ceased. All downstairs exchanged glances.

"The bride is ready," whispered Granny Jewel. Only the rustle of dresses was heard as the bride appeared at the head of the stairs. The photographer positioned himself at the foot of the stairs as Miriam, in her white satin gown and lace mantilla covering her head, paused for a moment. Flashbulbs fired as quickly as Roy Eubanks could replace them. All stared at the bride while Miriam's eyes, searching, rested on her father. The instant their eyes met, Leland, from a corner of the hall, snapped a picture of the father, capturing the expression of love and tenderness etched on the father's face, knowing that today he would give his daughter's hand to another.

Clara and Lindsey appeared with boxes of flowers. Each bridesmaid chose a bouquet of pink roses and baby's breath, the bride's being white roses against dark green fern.

Group pictures were taken of the families against the fireplace in the living room. Leland, staying out of the way, was able to capture Papa Tom, dressed so handsomely, as he leaned down and straightened his grandson's tie. Another time, Granny Jewel, dressed in gray silk, was photographed giving Sarah an opal ring worn by her grandmother on her wedding day. Sarah's tearful expression was silhouetted against soft lace curtains, as she placed it on her ring finger.

"It's almost four o'clock, people," announced Papa Tom. "We have to get this show on the road, or, the sidewalk. Miriam, you don't want people to say you were late to your own wedding." Nervous laughter followed, as the group lined up for the short walk to the church.

"Miriam and I will be last," declared Ralph Thompson. "They can't start without us."

"Oh, Daddy, I can't walk even one block with the train dragging the ground. She turned, and seeing Joshua, looked down. "Joshua, will you please carry my train? I know you won't let it get dirty."

"Yes, Ma'am, I'll do it." He looked up at his father. "It may be the closest I'll ever get to a train again."

The photographer hurried ahead, taking pictures of the wedding party as they walked to the church. Leland, staying behind, was able to capture Joshua, holding the train high.

The cool interior of the church was welcomed after the hot sidewalk. Last minute guests were still arriving as the organist played. Jean Baylor met the bridesmaids at the door, arranging them in the proper order. Four of Herb's classmates served as ushers, seating the mothers. At the appointed time, Herb and his father, the best man, appeared. The organist, Mrs. Holmes, played the wedding march and the first bridesmaid began the procession. Guests smiled at the lovely girl slowly walking down the aisle. Suddenly, with a nudge from Jean, Sarah found herself moving slowly forward, followed by the maid-of-honor. Familiar faces and warm smiles were a blur as Sarah rounded the front pew. Now she could see her family. Her parents were smiling proudly, her grandmother smiling and gently wiping tears. Sarah took her place near her grandfather, and let her eyes sweep across the congregation. There were ladies in fine hats, and white gloves, men in dark suits and a surprising number of young people. *They must be students from Aunt Miriam's English classes*, she decided.

With the maid-of-honor in place, all attention was focused on the back of the church. The music slowed, faded, then swelled, filling the church. All strained to see the exquisite bride, on her father's arm, walk the aisle. Her gown was a perfect contrast to the full, ruffled dresses worn by the bridesmaids. Herb Mitchell had eyes for no one but his bride.

Sarah was surprised at how quickly the sacred ceremony was over. The bride and groom, now man and wife, turned and faced the congregation. Once again, joyful music filled the church as they left.

After taking pictures, the bridal party joined others in the parish house next door for fellowship and refreshments. Sarah saw Nancy introducing Lindsey to some of her high school friends, then hurried to the punch bowl where she was to pour punch for the guests. A large group of teen boys captured Sarah's curiosity. As she drew near, she could see her cousin Marnie in the center, flirting. She was tossing her curls, and batting her eyelashes. Her merry laughter could be heard above the hum of the crowd. She slowly moved toward Nancy who was industriously filling crystal cups with icy, refreshing punch.

"I didn't realize I was thirsty," she told her friend. Wedding guests, some she knew, complimented her dress and told her she looked beautiful. Marnie probably hears this every day, she decided, thanking each for their compliments.

Even with the help of fans, the Parish House gradually became warmer, until the heat was uncomfortable. Joshua, armed with a cup of punch and a plate of goodies, ducked through the kitchen and out on the back porch. "Ramie," he exclaimed. "I didn't know you were out here. Would you like some food or punch?"

"I'm fine, Joshua," he said, blowing a perfect smoke ring. "Aunt Clara keeps me supplied so I'll hang around and help clean up."

"Ramie," asked Joshua, "why aren't you married?"

The young man thought for a minute. "It's like this, I haven't found the right girl. Not every young lady wants a man with only one good leg."

"How about you, Joshua," he asked, smiling a lazy smile. "Surely a handsome fellow like yourself has plenty of chances to court the girls."

Joshua thought for a moment about Katie Higgins. He had seen her at the wedding in a fluffy dress, her blonde hair hanging in bouncy curls. He was having trouble getting her image out of his mind. "I can't get married, Ramie. I'm going to join the army. Army men are too tough to kiss girls."

"It takes a lot of courage to kiss a pretty girl. You have to be brave, too."

"What's going on out here, you two?" Sarah stepped out on the back porch of the parish house and sat down, her dress ballooning around her.

"We were talking about getting married someday," replied Ramie.

Hmmm, thought Sarah, looking up into the ancient oak tree where she and Porter Mason had spent hours sharing ideas. "*Someday. Yes, maybe someday.*"

Chapter 15

"*Please,* Sarah! If you'll help me this time, I promise I'll never ask you again."

"Probably not for the rest of the day."

"It's all right if you won't help," he replied, "Maybe Katie will call me."

"She won't call, Joshua. It isn't proper for girls to call boys. Boys have to do the calling."

"How come you know so much? There sure haven't been any boys calling here to talk to *you.*"

"That's what you think, Mr. Smarty Pants. Why, I..."

"Hark, are those perhaps the tender voices of my first born daughter and my only son?" asked their mother lowering the day's newspaper.

"Mama, Sarah won't help me call Katie."

"Why should you need any help calling that dear girl?"

"That dear girl is a big tom boy," he replied.

"Son, I thought you and Katie were friends"

Joshua sank into a chair, looking sorrowful. "I hurt her feelings at the church picnic."

"Why, Joshua!" responded his mother. "Why would you do such a thing?"

Peggy Bowers laid aside the newspaper, its contents forgotten.

Joshua slumped in a large overstuffed chair in his grandmother's living room and stared at the floor.

"Well, Mackie and I were sitting at a table outside with the boys in my Sunday school class. When I went inside to get some lemonade, Katie asked me to sit with her."

Suddenly, Joshua sat straight and stared at his mother. "Can you imagine how awful it would be if I was seen sitting with a *girl* at the picnic? I would be teased until I was an old man with a long, gray beard."

Joshua glanced at his mother, hoping she would understand. Somehow, from her expression, Joshua wasn't sure if he was in trouble.

"What else could I do?" he implored, his arms extended.

His mother's eyes narrowed. "What did you say to Katie?"

A feeling of getting in water over his head crept into Joshua's thoughts. "I told her to get lost," he mumbled. "I heard Mackie say it to somebody and I liked the way it sounded. So, I guess it's really Mackie's fault I hurt her feelings." He looked hopefully at his mother.

"The picnic was several weeks ago. It's time for you to mend your fences."

"What do you mean, Mama?"

"You should make things right between you two. Call and apologize for being rude." Joshua didn't move.

"Well," said his sister, hands on hips, "are you going to call her?"

"I can't call her with you all standing around. I need some privacy!"

"Sarah," said her mother, struggling to maintain a serious expression, "let's go in the kitchen and see if Clara needs any help with lunch. She may want us to peel shrimp for the salad."

Peggy put her hands on her daughter's shoulders and guided her gently from the hall. "Mama," she whispered, "let's hide and listen to the conversation."

"Do you want him to listen when you're on the phone?"

"No, Ma'am. Sorry."

The numbers 3-4-9-6 swam before his eyes, as Joshua, with trembling hand, dialed Katie's number.

"Hello," came a voice over the phone.

"Can I talk to Katie? This is Joshua." He struggled to talk with a mouth suddenly gone dry.

"Hello, Joshua. Katie is outdoors. Wait while I get her."

"Yes, Ma'am." *She's probably outside wrestling a grizzly bear*, he thought.

An eternity later, he heard Katie's voice. "Katie, this is Joshua. I'm sorry I hurt your feelings at the church picnic, and you looked pretty at the wedding." There was a long pause as Katie assimilated this information.

Finally, "Would you like to come over to the island and play?"

"*Yeah*! That would be great! When can I come?"

"How about tomorrow, and bring your bathing suit and wear sneakers." There was a pause, "Uh, I'm glad you called."

"Me too!"

Joshua hung up feeling as if a tremendous weight had been lifted from his shoulders. With wings on his feet, he flew through the house, yelling.

Sarah whispered to her mother, "Katie must have invited him over to her house." *Hmmm*, thought Sarah, *Katie is six years younger than I, and already getting phone calls from a boy.*

"Mama, can I go to see Katie? She invited me to come spend the day tomorrow."

"I'll drive you over first thing in the morning," she replied, going upstairs to check on Amy.

Before Sarah finished peeling the shrimp, Granny Jewel rushed in. "Sarah, Mary and Morgan are leaving for Raleigh. They're backing out of the driveway right now. Let's go out on the front porch to wave goodbye. We must pray that nothing happens to keep them from getting their baby. I don't think they could survive the disappointment."

"Let's go sit in the swing, and pray together," suggested Sarah.

"You're right. Jesus says when two or more are gathered together, He will be there also."

Sarah smiled at her grandmother. "Should we pour a glass of lemonade for Him, too?"

Granny Jewel smiled. "Maybe not, but you can tell your mother we're in the backyard and to join us when she can."

With hands clasped, the grandmother prayed, "Father God, we pray for the safety of your servants, Morgan and Mary. We pray also for the child you chose to be a part of their lives. Please bring them back in our midst so we may open our hearts to another. This we pray in Your Holy name."

"Would this be a bad time for us to talk about something that's bothering me?" asked Sarah, watching her mother hurrying across the yard.

Granny Jewel sipped her lemonade. "Sarah, there is never a bad time for us to talk."

"Wel-l-l," the girl said, digging the heel of her sneaker in the dirt. "I'll soon be a sophomore in high school, and no boy has asked me for a *real* date, or even called me."

"What about other girls your age?"

Sarah slapped at a mosquito on her arm. "Lindsey told me she had a few dates this summer, mostly going to the picture show. Some of the other girls in our crowd have been on dates."

"How about Nancy Russert?" asked her mother.

"Oh, Mama, Nancy probably won't go out on a date until she's forty years old. She's in love with her piano."

"Did you have a chance to meet some of the Beaufort boys at the wedding reception? I noticed a lot of Miriam's English students were there."

"Ha!" laughed Sarah without mirth. "They were too busy stepping all over each other to get a glimpse of Marnie. She was pouring on the charm and they were lapping it up."

Granny Jewel tapped her chin with one finger. "Honey, you don't want a fellow who can be so easily taken in by a pretty flirt."

"Yes I do!" Sarah stamped dirt back in the shallow hole.

"Sarah, someday you will meet a fine young man who appreciates your quiet beauty, and the wonderful person you are. Why, every time I go downtown, someone comes up to me and raves about what a sweet girl you are, and tells of some kind deed you have done."

"If he's out there, Granny Jewel, I wish he'd hurry, before I'm too old to care." Sarah didn't see her grandmother try in vain to hide a smile.

"While you're still young, why don't you come to the Parish House and help the church women decorate for Baby Stewart's reception."

"I might as well. It's not too soon to practice someday being an old maid aunt to my brother's and sister's children."

"You'll feel better, Sarah, I promise," said her mother.

Crepe paper streamers, balloons and flowers decorated the hall. A large punch bowl sat ready at one end of a long table covered with a linen cloth reaching to the floor. As she helped the ladies decorate and listen to their laughter, Sarah could feel her spirits lift. One way to get over a bad mood is to do something nice for someone else, she decided.

"The reception isn't until tomorrow night, but we want to be ready in case they get home early," Florence Brooks told Sarah.

"Do they know about the reception?"

"Oh, yes," Mrs. Brooks answered. "They're going to stop here before they go home."

Supper was early the following evening. Joshua entertained the family with adventures he and Katie had shared on Piver's Island. "Katie told me I shouldn't be upset because I can't run or climb as fast as she can. She said, 'Joshua, my daddy says a person can't help being the way they are, but, they can help staying the way they are.' She thinks I do pretty good for a city boy," he said proudly.

"I can swim as fast as she can now, because she showed me how to cup my hands under the water." Demonstrating, he promptly turned over a glass of water, flooding the table. When the water was mopped up, he continued. "She also showed me how to climb a tree real fast!"

"Joshua," interrupted his grandfather, "why don't you wait to demonstrate when we are outdoors?"

At eight o'clock, the Stewarts still had not arrived. Friends, neighbors and the congregation of St. Paul' parish sat quietly, waiting and listening.

Ice cold punch and trays of refreshments were in danger of being ruined when someone near the front door announced. "They're here, and they have their little one!"

A chorus of happy voices greeted the weary couple. As they stepped into the Parish Hall, the voices slowly died.

"Where's the baby, Mary? We thought you were getting an arm baby, not a toddler."

Mary Stewart, weary from the long ride, hugged the young child even closer. When she spoke, a hush fell over the crowd. Some in the back of the room strained to hear.

"Love doesn't come in sizes, like a pair of shoes," explained Mary. "When we saw Elaina with an officer of the court, I didn't say, 'Oh, she's too big. Do you have someone in a smaller size?" Nervous laughter followed her remark.

"Isn't Elaina a French name? Is she from France," someone asked.

Again, there was silence.

Morgan took a deep breath and spoke firmly. "No, she was rescued from a bombed-out building in Berlin when she was an infant. She was the only survivor."

"*Berlin?*" Voices, like waves rippling across water, echoed through the room. "Berlin? She's *German!*"

Silence enveloped the once merry group. That word, hated and feared by all for years, was now centered on the thin, fair skinned child.

"I just remembered I have to get home early," remarked someone in the crowd. Several others, unable to meet Mary's gaze, started moving toward the door.

"Wait," begged Morgan, hands raised. "Please don't leave. Don't turn your back on us. The war is over. It's time for our nations to heal. What better way than through an innocent child? Haven't we all suffered enough? Look at the price Elaina has paid."

Mary stepped forward clutching the young child. "The Bible says, 'A little child shall lead them.' Perhaps this child can help lead us into a deeper sense of healing between the nations."

Morgan put his arm around Mary and the child, whose head rested on her mother's shoulder. Morgan continued, "From the moment we saw our daughter, the years of disappointment and longing disappeared. She was born to us in that moment, as much as any child is born to its parents." He looked around the crowded room. "I am looking at the faces of people I have known and loved my whole life. But, if you cannot accept our daughter, we will leave Beaufort."

When Morgan finished speaking, silence again filled the room. As the weary couple turned to leave, the voice of Graham Duncan, the postman was heard by all. "Aw, heck! We forgave Herb for marrying a beautiful Yankee, surely we can forget 'Laney's previous address."

Whistles and cheers echoed through the room, filling it with a spirit of peace and happiness. Laney, still fearful of sudden noises, scrambled from her mother's arms and dove under the table filled with refreshments.

"Amy," spoke Granny Jewel, holding up one corner of the white table cloth. "Please take a cookie and a cup of punch down to Laney. Oh, and be sure to have some yourself."

"Clara, pour yourself a cup of tea and let's talk. I have to tell you about last night." Often, while the rest of the family was sleeping, Clara and Jewel Mitchell enjoyed a cup of coffee or tea, and talked.

"It was like nothing I have ever seen, Clara." Taking a sip of the steaming tea, she described the evening. "When Graham Duncan made his remark, the tension vanished, and Laney was accepted. You could almost feel love encircling her."

"It's a whole new generation coming along, Jewel. Amy and Laney will grow up playing together every summer."

"Yes, Clara. Their generation will grow up with no prejudice toward the German people."

"Yes, sighed Clara. "There's too much of that already."

Their conversation was interrupted by the sound of feet on bare floors above. "Time for me to get in the kitchen. There's gonna be some hungry folks appearing in a few minutes, wanting to know where their breakfast is."

"I'll set the table," answered Granny Jewel.

Before the family could finish their meal, a timid knock was heard at the front door. "Come in," called Papa Tom, unwilling for anyone to leave their plate of steaming scrambled eggs and bacon. They heard the screen door squeak, and a small voice call out, "Yoo -hoo." A moment later, Marie Wallace stood in the doorway.

"Well, hello Marie," welcomed Granny Jewel. "Won't you join us for breakfast?"

"No, Ma'am, but thanks. I came to tell Joshua his dog is a daddy." Joshua, fork poised half way to his mouth, could only stare.

"Marie," asked Sarah, "how do you know Frisky is the father?"

"That's easy. Three of the puppies look like their beautiful mama, but the other one looks just like *him*!" Marie pointed a tiny, accusing finger at the back door where Frisky sat, patiently waiting for his breakfast. His tail thumped expectantly as he pressed his black nose against the screen.

"Your dog stayed inside the fence, Marie," reminded Sarah. "Frisky couldn't climb over."

"I don't know how, but I know who, and he's the one."

Clara, filling coffee cups, remarked, "Sounds like that old dog is living up to his name."

"Mama, can I go see the puppies?"

"Is that all right with you, Marie? Do you think your mother would mind?"

"Oh, no, Mrs. Bowers. My mama thinks your children are wonderful, especially since she and Joshua had a talk one day."

'I'd like to see the puppies, too," said Sarah.

"Me too, me too," added a tiny voice.

"Can Frisky come? He might want to meet his children."

"I don't see what it will hurt," said Clara, helping the boy get the stroller off the back porch. "The damage is already done."

It was too hot to stroll along the sidewalk, so the little group hurried before the sun was high overhead. All was quiet when they passed Marnie's grandmother's house. Sarah felt a sense of relief, knowing she had returned to Greenville. *I suppose she has to have a whole new wardrobe for the opening of school,* thought Sarah.

"Oh, they are *so* cute," whispered Sarah when they peeped in the box where mother and babies were resting. Buff wagged her short tail when Marie gently lifted out a puppy and placed it in Sarah's waiting hands. The big sister let Amy pat the top of the sleeping puppy's head.

"Joshua, would you like to hold one," she asked hopefully.

"Sure! I'd love to hold one," thinking she would choose the one who looked like his father. Again Marie scooped up a puppy and placed it in Joshua's waiting hands. With only two left in the box, Marie chose one. "I love to smell a puppy's breath," she said, laughing. Joshua glanced in the box. Only one puppy remained. It was the one that resembled his father. All the others were copies of their beautiful mother. Mrs. Wallace was busy in the kitchen making a pitcher of iced tea. When it was ready she appeared in the doorway of the wash room. "You need to put the puppies back, now. We don't want their mother getting nervous."

Gently each puppy was placed in the box with the others. Joshua felt sorry for the one like Frisky, because no one held him. *At least he slept through the whole thing, and didn't know he wasn't chosen*, thought Joshua.

"Let's see if Miss Nettie's home," he suggested as they walked past her house. "We really should stop in and visit, so she won't be lonesome."

"That's very nice, Joshua. I'm glad to see you are beginning to think more about others as you get older."

"Yeah, and besides, she has homemade cookies and Coca-Cola."

"Oh, brother," mumbled his big sister.

Sarah lifted Amy from the stroller. "We can't stay long, because Amy will try to tear her house apart. It's not baby-safe like our grandparents' home."

"Yoo-hoo," called Sarah through the screen door.

"Let me do the 'yoo-hoo', Sarah," demanded her brother.

"No, Joshua! Who ever heard of a boy doing 'yoo-hoo?'"

"Why not? I can do it real loud."

"Because you don't 'yoo-hoo' real loud, or real deep. It's something women do, and they learn how to do it when they are little girls. Did you hear Marie this morning? She did the 'yoo-hoo' just right for a little girl."

"Oh, I guess you go to 'yoo-hoo' school if you are a girl. Is Amy too young to go? She can't even talk good, but I'll bet she can 'yoo-hoo.'" The brother brought his face close to his baby sister's. "Say 'yoo-hoo, Amy'. Say 'yoo-hoo.'"

Amy, enjoying a new game, said, "oo-oo, oo-oo."

"Sorry, Amy," Joshua said, pretending disappointment. "You flunked."

"Merry voices! I hear merry voices, and they're music to an old teacher's ears." Nettie Blackwell held the screen door wide for her visitors.

"Frisky, you stay on the porch," Joshua ordered.

"Do you think he'd like to come in?"

"No, Ma'am, Miss Nettie, he has fleas."

"My dear Muffin had fleas too, but I kept her dusted with flea powder. It didn't help much, though. The best thing for fleas is January."

When all were seated at the round table in the cozy kitchen, eating warm chocolate chip cookies and drinking a glass of iced cold Coca-Cola, the hostess asked, "What brings you all to the neighborhood?"

"Marie's dog, Buff, had puppies, and we think Frisky is the father," explained Sarah.

"We're going home next week, and I'm real worried about one of the puppies," said Joshua, looking sorrowful. He tilted his head to one side and slowly let his eyes roll toward the lady of the house.

"What on earth is wrong with him," asked Miss Nettie, giving Joshua her full attention.

"There's nothing wrong, he just looks like his father."

"Oh, my, I can see why you're concerned."

"Suppose all the puppies get good homes, and nobody wants him," said Joshua, sadly. "He'll be a stray just like his daddy was. I'll be in Raleigh, and I won't know if he's cold or hungry, or dead." He paused between bites of a homemade oatmeal cookie and let out a deep sigh. "I won't know a moment's peace."

Miss Nettie cleared her throat, and took a long sip of soda. "You know, Joshua, I'm not looking forward to another winter with long, lonely nights. It would be so nice to have someone to talk to, and share my fire. I think Frisky is an uncommonly grand dog in many ways, and I suppose his son will be the same. If it's all right with you, I'll step over to the Wallace's tomorrow and put in my order for Frisky's son."

Joshua, fighting back tears of relief, hugged Miss Nettie, whispering, "Thank you, thank you!"

When the children turned the corner of Moore and Ann Street, Sarah remarked, "Miss Nettie is one of the sweetest people I have ever met."

Joshua nodded, "Yes, she is an uncommonly grand lady in many ways."

Chapter 16

"Oh, look, Joshua, Uncle Herb and Aunt Miriam are back from their honeymoon." exclaimed Sarah, seeing a familiar car parked in front of her grandparents' home. She grabbed Amy up in her arms and rushed inside, eager to see the couple.

"Sarah, there you are! Who are these lovely children?" joked their uncle.

"Aunt Miriam," questioned Joshua, "would you like a nice puppy? I know where there are some that are real pretty."

Miriam, in slacks and an old shirt, looked lovelier than ever. "Joshua, Herb is away from home all day, and when school starts next week, I won't be home either. A puppy would die of loneliness. Besides, I'm going to have my hands full taking care of your uncle."

"That's right, Joshua, I'm her baby until another one comes along." He gave his wife a broad wink. Herb Mitchell was standing in the middle of the gift room, surrounded by cardboard boxes and newspaper. "Mama," he said, "I don't know where we're going to put all this stuff. My apartment isn't much larger than Miriam's."

"You'll find a place for everything eventually. If not, you can store a few things in the closet of your old bedroom."

"We'll probably start looking for a bigger place."

Granny Jewel looked alarmed. "You're not thinking of moving very far, are you?"

Herb Mitchell put an arm around his mother. "Now, Mama, you know we're not going to move away. Who knows, we may need grandparents to babysit someday."

"Oh," said Granny Jewel, smiling at her son. "Maybe I'd better start making baby clothes."

"Herb, don't tease your mother! We've been married a week, and we need some time together before we start a family." Turning to Sarah, she said, "We have the wedding pictures. They turned out really well." Here her voice dropped. "Leland's pictures looked natural, because none of them were posed." They went in the living room, where the photographer's pictures were spread out across the coffee table. Each pose showed different members of the wedding party standing before the altar after the ceremony. Sarah marveled at ones she was in, since she looked as mature as the bride and her sisters.

"You look so beautiful, Aunt Miriam," she remarked.

"You look lovely, too, Sarah." Miriam carefully gathered the pictures and laid them aside. From another stack, she laid out different pictures. No one appeared stiff or far away.

"Oh, look, he took a picture of Granny Jewel giving me her mother's opal ring," said Sarah. "When she put it on my finger I thought about my great grandmother being my age long ago, and it made me want to cry. He captured the sadness I felt."

They were joined by others, who marveled at the photos taken by Leland. "The best one by far is the one of Joshua carrying Miriam's train. He had hoisted it so high, you can see her satin slippers," laughed the grandmother.

"How about this one of Clara," said Herb. "She was bringing in a tray of food, and saw some little kid with his finger in the wedding cake. The look she gave him could stop a freight train."

"Our favorite," said Miriam, looking at Herb, "is a picture of us on the Parish House steps. He's wiping a drop of perspiration off my nose, and we are looking deeply in each other's eyes. I think it's the first time we realized we were man and wife."

"You folks are gonna have to stop admiring yourselves long enough to eat lunch," announced Clara.

"Where is Thomas?" asked Granny Jewel. "I just realized he wasn't here. Is he at the store, Herb?"

"He left the store a long time before I did. He said he was going on a secret mission, and not to wait lunch."

"If he's not here soon," threatened Clara, "that worthless dog on the porch is gonna have one fine meal."

"Clara, you wouldn't give this delicious beef stew and hot biscuits to Frisky, would you?" asked Miriam, alarmed.

"I'll save him a piece of gristle. He can chew on that."

"Am I late?" sang a voice from the porch. The back door slammed, as Papa Tom appeared in the doorway. He grinned at Clara, who was filling iced tea glasses. "Ah, Clara, I knew you'd put aside the best for me. You really shouldn't, you know. We wouldn't want the rest of the family to know I'm your favorite."

"Humph," snorted Clara. "One more minute, and you'd have to arm wrestle that dog for your food. I'll be the one cheering for the dog."

"Honey, where have you been? I was beginning to worry."

"Sweetheart, I have been on a secret mission, and I can't talk about it." When Joshua finished his ice cream and asked permission to be excused, his grandfather called him aside. "Go ask Billy and Mackie to come over here."

"Why, Papa?"

"I cannot tell."

"Yes, sir."

Moments later, three boys stood before Papa Tom as he read the Beaufort News. Others were helping Miriam and Herb with the last of their packing. After waiting several minutes, Joshua whispered, "We're here, Papa Tom."

The paper was slowly lowered until piercing, dark eyes stared at the three. "Sit, while I finish reading the paper."

Not making a sound, the boys sat on the sofa's edge, poised for flight. Each time he turned a page, the grandfather could see three sets of eyes staring. He was careful not to lower the paper enough to reveal a broad smile. Finally, satisfied that he had read the most important news of the day, he folded the paper and brought it crashing down on the coffee table.

The boys were startled, but remained in their frozen state. Only their round eyes betrayed their feelings of apprehension.

Joshua's grandfather stood. The boys' stare followed him until heads rested on the back of their neck.

"All right, men, let's load up!"

"Huh? Where are we going?" asked Mackie, the bravest of the three.

"You'll find out soon enough," Papa Tom replied gruffly.

He held the car door open as three reluctant boys climbed in the back seat. Slamming the door, he opened the front door, slid under the wheel and started the engine.

"Are we going to jail, Mr. Mitchell?" asked Billy, his voice quavering. "Cause, if we are, I have to tell my mama."

"You'll see," was the only answer.

"It wasn't us that done it, sir."

"It wasn't you that did what?"

"Whatever you're thinking about."

"I haven't accused you of anything."

Mackie leaned forward. "We did take candy and cigarettes from your store, Mr. Mitchell, and we're sorry."

"WE?" questioned Billy. Mackie elbowed him into silence.

"We're not going to the police station."

"We're not?" asked Joshua, relief in his voice.

"We're going to the train station." The boys, bewildered, exchanged glances. Papa Tom stopped near the engine at the train station.

"Good afternoon, Mr. Lee," called Papa Tom over the chuffing and hissing of the great steam engine. The engineer was seated in the cab, waving. "Come aboard, gents, we've got a full head of steam, and this baby's raring to go!"

Billy and Mackie needed no more encouragement. They grabbed the brass handles and joined Mr. Lee. Joshua, still on the ground, turned to his grandfather. "Does my daddy know about this? Will he be mad?"

"I talked it over with him before he went back to Raleigh. We're in the clear." Both scrambled aboard as the engineer pulled the lanyard. From the heart of the iron beast, there came a blast, sending a shock through the boys and Papa Tom.

"You fellows can hang out the other window, just don't fall out."

Slowly, the metal mammoth began moving. Iron wheels on iron tracks spun and squealed. The engine moved down the track, gathering speed. Papa Tom stood with the engineer and looked at the happy boys, his eyes resting on his grandson. *He's going home the day after tomorrow*, he thought as the train rumbled through town. *I don't know how I'm going to stand telling them goodbye.*

Joshua turned, sensing his grandfather's eyes on him. "Thank you, Papa! You're the best!"

That's not going to help, he decided.

When the train had finished at the sawmill, the next stop was the fish factory. While workmen loaded barrels of menhaden fish oil onto train cars, the boys sat in the cab and waited. "It's a lot cooler up here," observed Mackie. They marveled at the gauges and instruments the engineer read.

"Do you fellows want to be train engineers when you grow up?" All nodded. "Well, I'll you what you need to do." Mr. Lee pushed his cap on the back of his head. All three waited, giving him their full attention. "You have to quit hitching rides on the train when you think the engineer is not looking. It's dangerous and you could get hurt so badly, you might never get to be an engineer." All nodded solemnly.

"We promise," they replied in unison.

With the fish oil loaded, Mr. Lee turned toward Radio Island, where it would be stored in huge tanks. As they steamed across the trestle, he pointed at the lanyard, and nodded at Joshua. The boy eagerly grabbed the rope and pulled. Once again the steam whistle bellowed a warning to all in its way.

Late afternoon, the train returned to the station. Everyone shook hands with Mr. Lee, and thanked him for their trip. In the car, on the way home, each thanked Papa Tom for such an exciting experience. Mackie got out last, extending his hand. "Thanks Mr. Mitchell. I never rode in the cab before."

"Mackie, that's where I want you to ride from now on. Maybe you can be a help to Mr. Lee. Oh, and Mackie, if your sweet tooth is hurting, and you don't have a nickel, stop by the store. I told the men your candy bar is 'on the house,' so you won't be tempted."

Mackie gave the man a sly grin. "Mr. Mitchell, you just took all the fun out of stealing."

"Thomas, are you awake?" whispered Granny Jewel. The silver gray light of early morning sifted through lace curtains hanging motionless.

"Yes, honey, I'm awake." He sighed deeply. "It's their last day. By noon tomorrow, this home will echo like an empty warehouse."

"I know, but they have to get ready for school. We're fortunate they spend their summers with us." She patted him on the arm. "All winter, we can remember the fun we had. The secret is to keep busy. In October we'll be going up for the state fair...."

"That's one of the many reasons I love you, old girl, you can always make me feel better."

"That's a nice compliment, dear, except for the 'old girl.'"

"I hear our grandson stirring," he said, quickly changing the subject.

"He and Sarah are going fishing this morning. We're going out to the bar and troll for blues and mackerel, and hope to bring home supper."

"I'll have Clara cook a roast, just in case the fish aren't biting. If you bring home a boat load, we'll have roast beef sandwiches the rest of the week."

"I'm ready," came a voice from the hall. Framed in the doorway was the grandson, wearing a floppy hat, shorts, shirt and sneakers. In his hand was a large paper bag.

Granny Jewel sat up and turned on the bedside lamp. "Come here and give me an early morning hug, my darling." He closed his eyes and breathed in the delicate scent that was always his grandmother. "Now tell me, what do you have in that big paper bag? It must be something very important."

Joshua held the bag up proudly. "This is our breakfast."

"Oh. May I ask what it is?"

"Yes, Ma'am. It's jelly sandwiches. Clara let me make them after supper last night when she was washing dishes. They're going to be a surprise." He held open the bag and let his grandmother peek. Her eyes rested on wads of bread, already soaked through with grape jelly.

"Oh, yes. Your sister and grandfather will surely be surprised."

"If you're ready, how about going down and check on Sarah. There's a remote possibility she may have overslept."

"Aye-aye, Papa."

They walked briskly to Front Street, pulling the wagon holding the outboard motor. "Can we *please* slow down," implored Sarah, trying to keep up. She was wearing her oldest clothes, sneakers and a sailor hat with the brim turned down. Fearful she would meet someone she knew, she kept her head lowered.

"Sarah, the fish aren't going to wait around for you. They feed on first light, and we have to be there."

"Yes, Mr. Fish Expert. Maybe we should use you for bait."

With the motor clamped firmly to the stern of Papa's skiff, Joshua cast off the bow line. The motor sputtered and caught. The bow lifted as the wooden boat planed across the clear, sea-green water. Joshua dropped the lunch bag in Sarah's lap and hurried to the bow. Throwing his legs over the side, he quickly unbuttoned his shirt and held out his arms. "I'm flying," he yelled to the entire waterfront.

Sarah turned to her grandfather. "Does he do this every time you go out?"

"Every time."

With a top speed of six miles an hour, they headed for Beaufort Inlet, and hopefully schools of sleek, silver fish.

The sun was still low on the horizon as the tiny boat rounded the end of Bird Shoal. The eastern sky was turning from rose, to pink, to gold. Out at sea, on the far horizon, pillows of cumulus clouds sat watching the new day unfold. A dim outline of the outer banks was visible in the distance.

Sarah turned to her grandfather. "Papa, this is almost too beautiful to be true. If I saw a painting like this, I would think the artist was exaggerating."

"God does have a way with color," said Papa Tom. "I think it pleases Him when we show an appreciation for His world."

Suddenly the grandfather cut the engine to idle. Now they could hear the cry of hundreds of shore birds feeding on schools of silver minnows. Across the inlet flocks of birds were diving on the tiny fish. "We have to follow the birds, kids. The fish we want are feeding on the schools of minnows from below. We'll troll through a school and see if we have any luck."

Papa Tom began unreeling twine that was wrapped on a narrow board. "Papa, where's the bait? Fish won't bite without bait."

"We're using a lure for this kind of fishing, so we won't need live bait. When this loon bone flashes through the water, they think it's a fish, and grab it. They'll bite the hook on the end of the bone, and we'll have fish for supper!"

"You sure don't know much about fishing, Sarah."

"Hush, brother. This is a great spot to dump you overboard."

"Now don't start fussing or you'll scare all the fish away," said Papa Tom. "This is serious business." He let the twine out gradually off each side of the boat. "Now, when you feel something tugging on your line, give it a jerk, and pull it in. Make sure you don't tangle the line." With both lines trailing in the water, their grandfather pointed the boat toward a nearby flock of birds circling a school of minnows.

Presently, Joshua yelled, "I've got one, Papa! I can feel him jerking on the line!" Hand over hand the line was brought in. At the end a large blue fish struggled to escape the hook caught in his lip.

"Stay away from his mouth, son. Bluefish have sharp teeth." With the fish safely in a bucket of water, Joshua was ready to try again.

What's so great about trolling for fish? wondered Sarah. *It's fun, but there's no reason to get all excited.* Before she could continue her thought, there came a mighty tug on her line. "Oh, Papa," she squealed, "I think I have one!"

"Reel him in, sister," and we'll fry him in a pan tonight," answered her grandfather.

Hmmm, thought Sarah, looking down at the silver mackerel, *I could do this all day.* But by nine o'clock, the fish stopped biting. "What happened, Papa? Where did all the fish go?"

"The tide is turning, and the sun is overhead. Just before dark, they'll feed again, but we'll be home. I don't like the idea of being out here in a boat this small, with night coming on."

"We have enough fish for two suppers," bragged Joshua.

"Yep. Maybe we should go home and start cleaning fish. Clara's roast will go a-begging tonight."

"I would help you clean fish, Papa, but Nancy and I are going to take our last walk downtown. We do it every summer."

"Cleaning fish is men's work, Sarah."

"Are you going to help?"

"Of course," her brother answered indignantly.

"Then it must be boy's work."

Sarah showered, and wearing a fresh outfit, met Nancy at the post office corner. "Sarah," she said sadly, "it seems like you just got here. Remember how we went to Miss Thompson's – oh, I mean Mrs. Mitchell's apartment, and saw her dress? It seems like yesterday."

"It's been a wonderful summer, Nancy, but just think - we're sophomores in high school, no longer lowly freshmen. This year we'll get a driver's license and have dates. It will be a good year. Why don't you come to Raleigh with my grandparents, and we'll go to the state fair together. It's great fun."

"I'm sure my parents will let me. Now I have something wonderful to look forward to."

After gazing in the store front windows, Nancy said, "Mama gave me two quarters. Let's go in Bell's Drug store and have an orangeade." They were sitting in a booth, sipping on the cold sweet drink when a tall, nice looking boy came in. Sarah nudged her friend. "Who is he, Nancy?"

Nancy turned, and recognizing the young man, called, "Hi, Bruce." He turned, and seeing the girls, smiled and walked over.

"Hello, yourself, Nancy. Are you taking a break before we have to go back to jail?"

The girls laughed. "Bruce, I'd like you to meet my friend from Raleigh, Sarah Bowers. Why don't you join us?" Nancy quickly slid across the seat, making room.

Bruce stared at Sarah. "I saw you at your uncle's wedding. It must be exciting to have an English teacher in the family. She can tutor you if you get in trouble."

"It would be better for me if she was a math teacher," laughed Sarah.

As they started to leave, Bruce turned to Sarah. "We're having a youth revival at the Baptist church tonight. Do you think you could come?" He included Nancy in his invitation, but his eyes never left Sarah.

"Thanks, Bruce," Nancy said, steering her friend away. "We'll try."

"Well," said Nancy as they continued window shopping, "I might just as well be invisible. Bruce never took his eyes off you!"

"Nancy, I want to go to the revival tonight. Will your mother let you go?"

"Have you ever been to a Baptist church?"

"I don't think so."

"It's not like the Episcopal church. It's much more informal. They don't have all the ritual we have, and the sermons are *real* long."

"I still want to go."

"Are you interested in religion, or a tall, good-looking boy?"

"Maybe both."

After supper, Sarah took special pains getting ready for church. She tried on three dresses before one suited her. "Mama!" She called from her bedroom, "I'm so tired of these dresses! As soon as we get home, I want to go shopping and get some new fall clothes."

Peggy stuck her head in the tiny room. "Honey, how can you be tired of your dresses? They have hung in the closet all summer except for Sundays and parties before the wedding."

Before Nancy arrived, Joshua stomped downstairs, looking for his grandparents. "Granny Jewel," he said when he saw his grandmother, "Sarah won't come out of the bathroom! She's been in there so long, I think she moved in."

The grandmother went to the foot of the stairs. "Sarah, are you nearly finished? We have someone who needs to…"

Sarah stepped out on the landing. "Oh, my," said her grandmother, "you look very nice tonight."

Sarah floated down the steps, and into the living room where she sat waiting for her friend. "How did you and Nancy find out about a youth revival at the Baptist church?" asked Papa Tom.

Sarah, sounding vague, answered, "Oh, someone Nancy knows at school invited us."

"Who is she?" asked her grandmother, wondering why Sarah was not talkative. "Maybe I know her parents."

"Well, it's not a *she*."

Silence filled the room. Papa Tom, listening to the news, lowered the volume on the radio. All waited for Sarah to continue. At that moment, a light tap was heard on the front door. Sarah sprang from the chair, glanced in the mirror over the mantle and patted her already perfect hair in place once more. "I have to go. It isn't polite to be late. Oh, Mama," she remembered, "I'm not sure I'll be home the minute church is out. Is that OK?"

"Have a lovely evening, dear, and don't be too late."

"Phew, Nancy! I'm glad you got here when you did," sighed Sarah, relieved. "I think my granny wanted to ask more questions."

"You look nice, Sarah, and you smell good, too. You wouldn't be all fixed up for Bruce, would you?"

"Of course not! Who ever thought of such a thing!" The girls walked quickly along the sidewalk, their Sunday shoes tapping a lively rhythm. The pews in the back of the church were taken, so they sat near the front. Before the service started, a senior boy who was to deliver the message, walked down front. He was accompanied by a girl who would lead the singing. When the youth choir filed in, Sarah was pleasantly surprised to see Bruce McCoy on the back row, in the bass section. She looked down quickly, when she saw him staring at her.

When the service was over, the girls lingered, talking to others. Presently, Bruce came over and joined them. "Hello, Sarah. I'm so glad you came."

"Uh, Bruce, I came too, don't forget."

"You, too, Nancy," he said, grinning. Someone in the group suggested they walk downtown for a cool drink. Sarah and Bruce hung back, so they could walk together.

"When are you going back to Raleigh, Sarah?"

"We're leaving tomorrow morning."

"No," protested Bruce, catching her hand in his "You can't leave now. We just met. That's not fair!"

"I feel the same way, Bruce, but it can't be helped."

After walking Nancy home, Bruce and Sarah turned toward the grandparents' home. Again, Bruce took Sarah's hand. "Do you mind?" he asked.

"No, it feels natural."

Papa Tom was sitting on the front porch when they walked up. Sarah introduced Bruce to her grandfather. "Won't you have a seat, Bruce?"

"No sir, I need to be getting home. I don't want my parents to worry."

Sarah joined her grandfather when Bruce said goodnight. For a few minutes neither spoke, but listened to the music from a chorus of crickets.

"Papa the singing was wonderful. The congregation sang like they enjoyed it, and the words were so meaningful. The high school boy who gave the sermon seemed so dedicated to the Lord. He was as interesting as a real preacher."

"I'm glad you had a chance to go, and Bruce seems a nice fellow, but we best be getting to bed. You've got a big day tomorrow." Sarah had never heard her grandfather sound so sad. He held the door open. "Honey, you've got a job waiting for you next summer, if you want it. Everybody at the store wants you to come back."

"Thanks, Papa. I stopped by today and told them goodbye, and Uncle Herb offered me a job. He said I was good for business."

"If you get any prettier, we'll have so many customers, we won't be able to keep the shelves stocked."

"I love you, Papa."

"I know. I love you, too."

Sarah awakened to the sound of her brother's voice. "Why can't Little Chick come to Raleigh? I'll die of a broken heart if I can't see him till next summer." This outburst was followed by her mother's quiet voice, although Sarah couldn't quite make out what she was saying.

"It's time for big sister to step in," sighed Sarah. Putting on the dress she had laid out for traveling, she stepped into the kitchen. "Clara, what is my brother going on about this time?"

Clara, stirring a pot of grits, shook her head. "That boy wants to take his chicken home to Raleigh, but your mother wants him left here. Arguing with a young'un gets you nowhere."

Sarah stepped into the dining room. "Joshua, come here a minute."

Sensing reinforcements, he hurried to the kitchen. "Yes, Sarah?"

"Are you all packed and ready to go?"

"Yep."

Sarah, buttering toast, "I sure hope Little Chick survives the trip." She hurried on. "He has to stay in a tiny box with air holes in the floor of the car for four hours. He can't move and he'll be so scared. He won't be able to hear Mr. Peavy greet the morning. He'll have to live in a pen the rest of his life, cause city folks don't want a chicken strolling up and down the sidewalk. You'll be in school all day and he'll be lonely."

"Joshua, I'll look out for your chicken," announced Clara. "I promise not to fry him, or boil him or bake him. Your granny can write to you every week and let you know how he's doing. Why, by next summer, maybe he'll tune up with Mr. Peavy for a duet."

"Oh, brother," breathed Sarah. "That's all the neighborhood needs."

Joshua was still not convinced. "Honey," Clara said more softly, "Ramie loves that chicken. He says they have something in common. He'd be mighty hurt if Little Chick went away."

"I don't want Ramie to be hurt, Clara. He's my friend. Little Chick can stay."

As the suitcases were being loaded in the car, the phone rang. "I'll get it," said Sarah. She recognized Bruce's voice immediately.

"Sarah, I couldn't let you leave without saying goodbye. May I have your address, so I can write to you?"

Sarah thought for a minute about Porter Mason and how she was disappointed he never wrote.

"Sure, Bruce, and I'll write to you. If you come to Raleigh, maybe you can come see me."

"I'd like to do that."

"Bruce, I have to go, now. My mother is blowing the horn and my grandparents are standing in the yard, crying."

"Will you come back next summer, Sarah?"

"I'll try, Bruce. I'll really try." Sarah hung up the telephone and scooped up her cat. She glanced back as she stepped out on the porch. *Next summer,* she thought *I'll be sixteen years old. What could possibly be better than being in Beaufort your sixteenth summer?*

"If you enjoyed reading Fifteenth Summer, in Sixteenth Summer the family returns to Beaufort. Sarah works at her grandfather's grocery store to earn money for her new Fall clothes. She is fascinated in 1948 with the wonderful products that are now on the grocery shelves. Sarah and a boy her age become sweethearts. Occassionaly, Sarah is haunted by the memory of Porter Mason, her special friend she knew her during her Twelfth and Thirteenth Summers. Reputation and proper behavior for a young lady is addressed in this book as Sarah starts "stepping out" with a young man.

CPSIA information can be obtained at www.ICGtesting.com
Printed in the USA
BVOW010159131011

273535BV00003B/7/P

9 781456 763817